Geocache.

Errol Dadet

Gullion Media Limited

All rights reserved
Published by Gullion Media Limited 2009

This paperback edition published in 2009 by
Gullion Media Limited, c/o 11 Slieve Crescent, Dromintee,
Newry, Co. Down, BT35 8UF, Northern Ireland.

Copyright © 2007 Errol Bader

Errol Bader has asserted his right under
Copyright, Design and Patents Act, 1988 to be identified
as the author of this work.

First published in USA by Errol Bader through Booksurge, 2007.
Second Edition pulished in UK by Gullion Media Limited, 2009.

Editor of this Second Edition: George J. Kingsnorth
Final Proof Reader: Barbara van Heerden

A CIP catalogue record for this book is
available from the British Library

ISBN 978-0-9560403-2-9

Printed and bound by Lightning Source

This paperback second edition is sold subject to the condition that it shall not, by way of trade of otherwise, be lent, resold, hired out, or otherwise circulated in any form or binding or cover other that that in which it is published and without similar condition including this condition imposed on the subsequent purchaser.

Geocache

ACKNOWLEDGEMENTS

As legend has it, the great American author Stephen King wrote the novel The Shining while occupying room 217 of the haunted Stanley Hotel in Estes Park Colorado. It was a cool June night in 2006 when I was vacationing at the lodge in a suite just next to room 217. My wife Judith, daughter Heather Belmont, and granddaughter Alyssa Jade were discussing Mr. King's novel and its association with the old hotel. Heather reminded me that the character that the renowned actor Jack Nicholson played in the movie The Shining accepted the job of caretaker of the old hotel in the dead of winter. His character intended to finish writing his novel during that long winter's visit. Of course; he never finished his book because, as the story goes, he became possessed by ghosts from the hotels past.

Heather came up with an unusual idea. "Dad, why don't you finish that poor fellow's novel for him?" I responded that she was elevating the term "ghost writer" to a new level. But, what would I write a novel about? It was then that she suggested the plot for Geocache. We were Geocaching Estes Park the following day. So Heather and possibly some Stanley Hotel ghost hatched the plot of *Geocache*.

Apart from the hotel's ghost, several of my living friends and associates deserve a debt of gratitude for humoring me and for giving me very constructive advice. Thanks to George John Kingsnorth for editing this second edition and to Barbara van Heerden for additional proof reading. Ray Anderson provided practical suggestions and fed my ego. Don Wolcott contributed his considerable knowledge of Russian politics and the history of Russia's vast oil industry. Bob and Jeff Puckett gave me an education on the Colorado oil and gas history. Jon Strom lent his literary prowess to the project.

I also pay tribute to my friends at Diamond Aircraft Industries GmbH in Austria, and for all of the kindness extended to me by so many Austrians and Germans during my stay in those countries.

Of course, I credit my wife Judith for her support and patience as I finished the hapless ghost's novel. Most importantly I will always be grateful to my wonderful mother Florence, who was the real writer in the family.

What you can rely on:
- The Soviet Union was bankrupted in part due to an intentionally created oil glut engineered by *U.S. President Ronald Reagan* and the Saudi Family.
- Boris Yeltsin's successful plan to bail out Russia with the Loan for Shares deal is a fact.
- All latitude and longitude coordinates referred to in *Geocache* are real. Readers can use *Google™ Earth* to view the venues described in the novel.
- Theophile Bader was in fact the co-founder of the Galerias Lafayette in Paris in the early eighteen hundreds. It is the largest mall in the western hemisphere.
- They really did plan to tear down the Eiffel Tower after its twentieth anniversary.
- The Romans did establish Innsbruck Austria and the voters of Denver really did default the Olympics to Innsbruck.
- There are a million people who enjoy Geocaching the world over.
- The *American Tree* by the Piast Castle in Poland is real.
- *The Well of the Three Brothers* is real.
- The *Bomb Tree* in Wiener Neustadt Austria exists.
- The *Lignumvitae Tree* on Florida's Lignumvitae

Key is real.
- The *Furn winds* phenomena in the Austrian Alps is real. Only certified air crews can fly into Innsbruck Airport when the Furn winds cross the Alps from Italy.
- There are bootleggers at the Olza River foot bridge connecting the Czech Republic and Poland.
- The old museum in Ceski Tesin does have a still functioning, centuries old music cylinder.
- Young French Muslims did riot and light fires in the suburbs of Paris.
- De La Sierra exists and is in truth the direct descendant of the *Pirate of New Orleans, Jean Lafitte*. He is every bit the character described in *Geocache* and swears he knows where the old pirates treasure is really hidden . . . but that's another story.

Errol Bader

CHAPTER ONE

THE MEETING

November 15th – 06:30

The light November snow tailed off with only occasional snowflakes drifting down to contribute to the white blanket covering the foothills west of Denver. The morning sun was still low on the horizon with its orange rays lighting up the dark blue eastern sky. A local resident, a full grown grey wolf, sauntered down a hillside and stopped to survey his surroundings. The mountain air being still should have made it easy for the wolf to hear a predator, but the fresh snow's absorption of sound meant the wolf strained to listen. Something was different this morning; a deep vibration in the ground beneath his paws meant he felt the sound before he heard it.

Suddenly the wolf's hunt for his morning meal came to an abrupt halt. The sound became audible, and then deafening. He had stood motionless on a ridge when a, big turbine powered, Bell helicopter rose from the valley and stopped to hover at his eye level. The wolf's heart was pounding as his thick fur rippled from the wind produced by the whirling blades. The giant machine began to lumber forward, from right to left, in front of him. Then it abruptly headed for the Denver skyline at 2,000 feet above ground level. There came another helicopter and yet another. Finally, a fourth lifted off from the eastern slope of the Rockies.

Helicopters this large made for an unusual sight even to the human eye. From a distance, the unbroken chain of massive flying platforms looked reminiscent of an airborne combat mission.

These were not standard helicopters, and the men on board were anything but ordinary. Four of the wealthiest men on Earth were on their way, carried by their modern day chariots, to meet a fifth and equally extraordinary man. Alexander Maxwell waited for them in his boardroom atop the Maxwell Land Company Office Tower, one of the tallest structures in Denver. He dressed casually for the meeting wearing a thin, grey turtleneck sweater, black belt and black trousers. His relaxed dress belied his nervousness.

It was cool in the room so he pulled a maroon, long-sleeved, sweater over his turtleneck. A recording of soft instrumental music came from speakers hidden in the ceiling. From fifty floors above street level, he looked across to his estate on the western edge of the city. He knew the helicopters would be coming from that direction. He had been host to his wealthy, globe-trotting, friends at his hillside mansion the night before. As the four helicopters came into view he pivoted away from the glass curtain wall, took a few paces to the conference room phone and pressed the call button labelled "Marsha".

"Yes, Alexander," answered Marsha Thompson, Maxwell's executive assistant.

"They're almost here, Marsha. Do you have the disks?"

"I've already loaded them into the computers; they'll boot automatically when you deploy the monitors."

"How about the catering? Did the advance people get all that handled?" He was uncharacteristically tense.

"Yes. Alexander, it's all good. Stop worrying. Everything will go as planned," reassured his assistant. "How do you find the music? It's supposed to be relaxing."

"I appreciate the thought," he replied.

He leaned his full weight back against the edge of the conference table and continued to look toward the mountains. The boardroom table, though massive, was a thing of beauty. It weighed over four hundred pounds and would not move even a fraction of an inch. Built from the most rare of woods and polished to a high gloss, the wood came from a 1000-year-old *Lignumvitae* tree, found only on *Lignumvitae Key* in the Florida

Geocache

Keys. Botanists refer to it as the *"Wood of Life Tree"*. The dense and hard wood was used on WWII submarines to line propeller shafts. The craftsmanship, to build the table, was of such high quality it was difficult to see the thin lines, cut on the surface, that cloaked the computer terminals below.

The five sole members of the *Global Geocache Society* were about to convene their third annual meeting around the high-tech table. The decisions made during the meeting, being important only to them, would be hidden from the public. It was Alexander Maxwell's turn to be host.

He felt anxious again and got to his feet. This was the only meeting all year that would cause him to pace. Yet there was no need for him to be on edge. He should have been beyond the fear of financial loss that had plagued his youth. His corporate struggles were over. Maxwell had won the game of business. He anticipated no more hurdles to jump. Long life had seasoned him. He was adept at dealing with high-powered men and women.

However these were his peers and, in a couple of cases, perhaps a bit smarter. His executive assistant usually made things run smoothly. Maybe that was why he tolerated Marsha's independence from time to time. She was the only employee at the Maxwell Land Company who enjoyed a close working relationship with him. He trusted her, which in his world was no small matter. If she said all was well then it was. Occasionally she appeared cold, detached and emotionless, but she was efficient.

The men would work through breakfast and no unknown food allergies would cause medical problems for Maxwell's friends. Marsha would take into consideration preferences for special tastes: caviar for the Russian, wine for the Frenchman (even for breakfast), a hot sauce for the Mexican and Cuban coffee for the Japanese member. He had strange tastes that one. The helicopters were coming closer. Finally, they reached the top of the office tower and hovered in formation. The closest helicopter approached for landing, dropped off its influential passenger and departed the helipad to make room for the next.

Errol Bader

The five members of the *Global Geocache Society* were together again. Once in the conference room, they exchanged greetings in the way of their own cultures. One would bow and another would hug. They had much to talk about.

CHAPTER TWO

PREPARATIONS

November 1st – two weeks earlier

As with all heads of state, *The President of the United States* had three teams to go out in advance of a Presidential trip. The advance men and women handled logistical, political, and protocol arrangements. The Secret Service dealt with security, safety, and emergency medical needs. The third advance team was the White House Communications Agency whose job was to maintain worldwide communications for the President. Powerful, wealthy individuals who ran multi-billion dollar businesses also employed these kind of human assets when they travelled. Executives at this level do not reinvent the wheel. They hired government-trained talent, from around the world, to staff their own protection and logistical departments.

The members of the *Global Geocache Society* had dispatched their respective advance teams to Denver to prepare for their November 15 annual meeting. Advance people expert in security and communications to make sure their bosses would have an uneventful meeting. Many of them knew each other from past interactions at international meetings where heads of states gathered. One of them, Victoria Kavanagh came from *Bill Clinton's* Secret Service contingent. Maxwell had been impressed by her service record and she interviewed well. A facet of her personality reminded him of himself. When others underestimated him he used this to his advantage and perceived Victoria possessed the same trait. His first impression of her was that no woman this stunning could be tough enough to protect his life but realised he was wrong. By the end of their initial meeting, he was convinced anyone attempting to knife this lady would quickly hit steel. Victoria's physical appearance alone was disarming. Adversaries mistakenly underestimated her; as so many had done to him when he climbed to the top of the energy industry. Over time she proved his instincts correct about her. She was efficient and without compassion for anyone not equally committed to the mission.

Maxwell had but one frustration with his security chief. There were unintended consequences that came with her astonishing beauty. Her striking appearance disrupted business meetings. Her powerful physical stature and beautiful face caused both men and women to lose their focus whenever she entered his boardroom. While he found it amusing, just the same, it was unproductive. It happened so often he was forced to develop a strategy to deal with the problem.

"Okay, folks! Time for a rest room break," he would announce when she appeared. The two would briefly discuss the urgent matter for he knew she was good at determining which warranted his immediate attention. Then she would depart the room allowing his meeting to get back on track. Victoria could have owned Hollywood, if that kind of life had interested her, but serving her country had a higher calling. Working in support of a powerful leader ran in her genes. Her great aunt was Kay Somersby, the British aide to *U.S. General Dwight Eisenhower* during his D-Day preparations. In Victoria's thirty-three years she had developed a passion for physical fitness and sports. She was five feet ten inches tall perfectly proportioned, with a pinched waist, powerful limbs, and shoulder length naturally blond hair. She was blessed with laser-like, big baby-doll, blue eyes. Her heart shaped face was symmetrical, each half a perfect mirror of the other, a genetic marvel. She was astute to every pick-up line ever muttered.

Victoria's appearance made her Secret Service training at Quantico all the more difficult. Her training was anything but standard. Her drill instructor took one look at her and wanted her gone. She was, in his opinion, a sexual-harassment lawsuit waiting to happen. He saw her as nothing but a liability; a

Geocache

distraction that could cause the death or injury of another agent. This prejudice blinded him until the day she kneed him in the groin for calling her a piss-ant pinup. His painful underestimation then developed into a new found respect for her.

After graduation she was appointed to the Secret Service. She invested little time on her own personal life. A few dates here and there, but nothing memorable. Her profession required her to work as an equal to tough men both mentally and physically. But, disappointingly, she had yet to meet one who could relate to her. There seemed no male equal for her. Now, by virtue of her position as Maxwell's head of security, she was responsible for directing traffic among the all-male advance team members preparing for the annual meeting.

She was in her first year on the job and had developed a respect for the man whose life she had signed on to protect. He was fair and, in her view, unaffected by his wealth. She accepted her responsibility, of protecting this powerful old man, with a passion known only to the most committed of security professionals. Nothing bad would happen to Alexander Maxwell on her watch.

Victoria's Denver advance team meeting had gone well. She was pleased with the level of experience and soberness of the participants. A decision was made that the five executive helicopters should arrive atop of Maxwell's office tower helipad. Victoria settled the specific order with a random drawing.

The helicopter staging area would be the ramp at the *Jet Centre* at Centennial Airport. Centennial, one of the busiest general aviation airports in the United States, was known for its professional tower and ground control operators. There were usually five or six business jets parked on the tarmac at any given time. The *Jet Centre's* ramp was a familiar stop for VIP visitors to Denver.

According to the advance team plan the principals, scheduled to arrive on private jets throughout the day of November 14 at Centennial Airport, would immediately board their personal helicopters. The fifteen-minute trip to the Denver foothills would be followed by an evening at the Maxwell estate. The next morning, November 15, the helicopters would lift off from the estate and carry their owners on a similar journey to Maxwell's downtown office tower. Upon completion of the *Global Geocache Society* meeting, the board members would be picked up from atop the tower helipad by their helicopters. They would fly from the office tower back to Centennial Airport for departure in their jets.

As is standard operating procedure, the advance team arranged for substitute helicopters and pilots to fly the triangular route in advance of the actual meeting date. The only way to discover any unforeseen issues was to walk and fly through the trip in advance.

Victoria distributed a three-ring trip binder to each advance team member. The binders contained the minute-by-minute schedule of all the principals from initial landing at Centennial to departure. Victoria also provided the names and contact numbers of everyone remotely involved in the visit. As a precautionary measure, area hospitals were identified on city maps with emergency room phone numbers. Victoria had already been in communication with agents at *Interpol*, the local Denver police department, her contacts at the FBI and, her previous employer, the U.S. Secret Service.

As with all lead security agents her concerns were the obvious threats of kidnapping, assassination, and terrorism. All of the advance security representatives would collectively use their respective government contacts to discover any unusual travel by known miscreants to Denver.

Maxwell was a widower without children, making Victoria's job easier. She was not concerned about family members and their whereabouts. Even so, she was pleased to be reinforced by the additional security muscle supplied by the other participants. She was satisfied with the preparations for the board meeting.

There was one area of discomfort. Victoria would have

preferred all the helicopter pilots to have been present for the advance meeting but, being scattered over several continents, this was impossible. Instead she delegated Jim Stewart, Maxwell's own chief pilot, the responsibility to brief and support the helicopter pilots upon their arrival in Denver.

Jim, a former DEA and Customs pilot, had survived five Vietnam War helicopter crashes caused by small arms' fire. He was, a gritty 23,000 hour fixed wing and helicopter pilot, a very tough hombre — as professional as they come. Victoria would rely on him for the helicopter portion of the trip. She was ready now — or, at least she believed she was.

Errol Bader

CHAPTER THREE

A FATAL DISTRACTION

November 15th – 07:45

The last of the big helicopters discharged its passenger on the roof-top helipad. Travis Raeburn, a retired Royal Navy pilot, veered his helicopter down and away from the tower and headed south/southeast for Centennial Airport. Raeburn had never been to the Rockies before. The morning was crystal clear and crisp. As he looked off to the west, he thought to himself *it would be fun if he could play hooky with his twelve million dollar flying machine.* The foothills and valleys west of the city were an inviting sight, and he wanted to just play for a change.

The radio crackled with a transmission from Air Traffic Control. "Denver approach . . . helicopter X-ray five Lima cleared direct Centennial."

Raeburn's daydreaming stopped. "Denver approach . . . roger, helicopter X-ray five Lima direct Centennial," he responded. Perhaps there would be time later for a side trip, once his immediate task was completed, before he loaded the helicopter onto the transport plane for his boss's next destination. The idea of seeing the mountains close up was now an idea firmly planted in his mind.

"Hey, Travis, how about lunch?" suggested his co-pilot Joyce Lester. "I hear the restaurant on the second floor of the *Jet Centre* is a great spot; *The Perfect Landing.* If I don't eat soon, I'm really gonna crash."

"Hey, do all you army chicks think only of your stomach," Raeburn grumbled, "And will you quit using the word crash? It's bad luck!" Thoughts of a side trip to the mountains would have to wait, but they would not be forgotten.

CHAPTER FOUR

COLD WARRIOR

Alexander Maxwell was a product of post World War II and the Cold War. Born in 1936, now sixty nine, he was twenty years old when he served in the U.S. Army in West Berlin. At the height of the cold war, the *Berlin Wall* provided a stark contrast between the stagnant economies of the eastern block countries and the vibrant economies of the West. The young American soldier was assigned as a driver for a Full Bird Colonel. The Colonel had to be taken to meetings at odd hours, so he required two drivers. Maxwell looked forward to the trips across *Check Point Charlie* — at least those after the first one.

Leaving the safety of the West and driving through the Brandenburg Gate into East Germany was unnerving at first. The guards on the east side of the checkpoint were chosen for their dislike of Americans. They had to be trusted by their masters or they might defect to the West themselves; they were chosen for their loyalty. They were hard, dedicated communists. He could feel their icy stares as he drove slowly through the gates as they were opened. It was not general knowledge, but periodically, military officers and intelligence operatives from both sides met to work out issues that neither side wanted to make public. Spies, scientists, and other persons of importance to one side or the other had to be transferred across the barrier of *Berlin Wall*.

Maxwell was off duty when the second driver was on. He and his Russian counterparts, a few young Russian soldiers, were not technically at war. After all they were allies during the war and hostilities were over. The Russians liked the young man's bravado. They saw that he was unafraid of driving in the more hostile parts of war-torn Czechoslovakia. The Russians spoke just enough English and he knew just enough Russian to communicate well enough. Not to mention the way they all described the more shapely Czech girls needed no verbal explanation. So Maxwell and the young Russians ignored the politics of the cold war. The Russians did not want to be in Czechoslovakia anymore than he did.

The Colonel attended his meetings in Prague. There were no justifiable reasons for this other than the Soviets would rather spend time in Prague than East Berlin. It never failed to amaze him how cheerful people were in West Berlin and how grey and depressed they were in East Berlin. It was not lost on the young man that capitalism worked — communism does not. Later in life, he would give a speech, the theme of which was an argument that capitalism was an even greater agent for freedom than democracy itself.

He would argue that capitalism was a catalyst for peace, even among people who simply could not relate to the confusing politics of western-style democracies. Countries conducting trade with one another, he would say, tend not to waste money on missiles aimed at each other. Why kill your customers?

His time behind the iron curtain would leave a lasting impression on the young Maxwell and shape his views about his own country. The war had brought about his introduction to the magnificent city of Prague, the crown jewel of the three main castle cities built during the Hapsburg Empire, which had been spared by Hitler as well as by the Allies.

Few bombs fell on Prague. Its ancient castle, overlooking the city, was undamaged by the violence that befell other cities across Europe. The young soldier was enchanted by the place. More than a few Czech women were enchanted by the good-looking and fun-loving young American. He would return often after the fall of the Soviet Union.

After his Army service ended he returned to his hometown of Denver and landed a job as a land man for a large oil company. His job was to search out landowners in the oil and gas-rich ranch

Geocache

lands of Colorado and Wyoming. Maxwell negotiated land leases with landowners for mineral rights. The oil companies paid royalties for every barrel of oil and cubic foot of natural gas produced under the agreements. In many instances he arranged out-right purchases of large tracts of land in the Rockies. Then the energy boom collapsed in the early eighties. Texas and Colorado were hammered by an economic recession brought about by a glut of Saudi oil. Cold War politics forced oil prices to drop dramatically, hammering both states with an economic recession. Large oil companies began to abandon the oil patch.

Maxwell's employer made an offer that most would have refused at the time. The oil company offered him the lands he had purchased for them for ten cents on the dollar. He borrowed as much money as he could, took in a few partners, and managed to do the deal.

In the early years, it was rough. He came close to losing everything several times, but over time his land company grew. Problems in the Middle East drove oil above seventy dollars a barrel, a historic high. He continued to add to his holdings until he emerged as the largest privately-held owner of oil and natural gas lands in the world. Only the largest oil companies controlled more mineral rights than he did.

The long climb to the top had consumed Maxwell. He had no time for family and no desire to create one. His wife Jenny had been unable to conceive. Secretly, he was relieved at her inability to bear children. He knew he would be a deficient parent because he was married to his enterprise as much as he was to Jenny. It was true he missed her; she had died too young. Nevertheless, he had his interests, and now he had his special friends, the *Global Geocache Society*.

Today, he would break bread with them and catch up on things. The five members of the *Global Geocache Society* were in their chairs. Each sat in front of a plaque with his name on it. Maxwell took his seat, after the others, at the end of the table. He pressed a switch and five computer terminals rose silently through the boardroom table from underneath. When the terminals were fully extended the keyboards followed through the openings and were placed within reach of each participant.

The hard-drives began humming in unison. The disks were booting up. The Maxwell Land Company screen saver appeared first as the screens lit up. The image was of a beautiful Rocky Mountain skyline bordering Denver at dusk.

Shortly, the image switched to a picture of the Earth taken from a distant satellite. The green and blue orb displayed all of the continents as the planet turned on its axis. A digitally created and animated composite photo of the entire world revolved in front of each viewer. Superimposed over the big blue marble were twenty-four satellites in geosynchronous orbits. The satellites hovered at just the right altitude for their speed to matched that of the globe as it turned below. Thus the satellites were suspended over specific points on the Earth. The computer-generated graphic was only symbolic of the constellation of GPS satellites circling our planet. Without these satellites there would be no need for the *Global Geocache Society* to meet.

CHAPTER FIVE

NAVISTAR, A UNIQUE WEAPON

The largest global positioning system (GPS) in the world belongs to the United States. Its name is the *Navistar Global Positioning System*. The next largest is the *Galileo Navigation System* developed by the European Union; and then there is *Glonass*, a less-robust satellite constellation placed in orbit by the Soviet Union. The Chinese are about to launch their own Compass constellation, with over 30 satellites planned. Originally launched and used for military purposes, the *Navistar GPS System* was enabled for civilian use in 1983. The decision to grant civil use of the system was a result of an unintended tragedy. An inertial navigation system error by the pilots of Korean Airlines flight 007 resulted in the Soviet shoot down of their 747. They flew the aircraft into sensitive Soviet-restricted airspace. *U.S. President Ronald Reagan* determined that there was more to be gained than lost by providing the $400,000,000 per year navigation system to the civilian community. In the fullness of time, the United States military learned how to jam GPS signals on selective battlefields and, therefore, deny an enemy of the benefit of the system as a weapon. This advance in American GPS technical capability forced the Soviets to launch the *Glonass Navigational System*.

It takes 24 satellites (The U.S. has a spare three in orbit) to guarantee horizontal as well as vertical navigational accuracy. The Russians only have 12 satellites circling the earth. Without five satellites in view from horizon to horizon, navigational fixes are difficult to obtain.

The establishment of the *Navistar Global Positioning System*, once opened to the scientific, commercial, and industrial complex, changed the way the world navigates, listens to music, and monitors the weather. Subtle changes to the earth's surface can be measured in inches, objects located with great precision. At the turn of the century, the owner of a handheld GPS unit could find his way to within six feet of a set of coordinates. Now accuracy is to within a few inches. All a person needs to find ground zero (the cross hairs of two coordinates) is the latitude and longitude of the location on the earth.

For the wealthy members of the *Global Geocache Society*, the GPS system provided the perfect tool to afford them a pastime which they had elevated to an extraordinary level. Golf no longer held their interest. What, do some of the wealthiest men in the world do to get away from their businesses and enjoy a good competition? What activity could force them to abandon their familiar work environment and go on vacation? The root word of vacation is vacate, to vacate; that is the idea. To force oneself to break away from an all-consuming enterprise and recreate. The members of the Global Geocache Society had discovered the perfect sport, global geocache. The advent of the Internet coupled with the global positioning system had already spawned a worldwide network of people who enjoyed an inexpensive high-tech form of treasure hunting. Participants stashed objects in waterproof containers and noted the location's latitude and longitude as detected by a hand-held battery operated GPS unit. The coordinates are posted on an Internet website for others to see. Visitors to the site can read the coordinates and a rating for the difficulty of access to the cache - or hiding place. The rating system is a five level bifurcated system. A 1/1 rating means the cache is easy to locate and easy to reach, even by wheelchair. A 5/5 rating and the player had better buy a plane ticket and take special gear along, like oxygen and climbing equipment or possibly diving equipment. The rules of the sport require that the participant remove an object from the cache and replace it with their own contribution to the cache. These objects, deposited and retrieved from caches across the geography of the

Geocache

earth, seldom have any value beyond the reward of having hunted and discovered the cache. Special coins or medallions travel the earth, moved from cache to cache by the sports enthusiasts. Internet surfers participate for an afternoon of exercise and fresh air, a great family outing for the kids to spend time with mom and dad. But for the members of the *Global Geocache Society*, it meant the hiding and seeking of items worth millions of dollars across every continent on the globe. And to some players it would mean certain death.

CHAPTER SIX

GEOCACHE REDEFINED

"No, Jorge, I don't agree." Maxwell nodded his head from side to side. "It's just a little over the top — a million dollar geocache deposit! What's wrong with last year's cap of 250,000? That's $1,250,000 worth of geocache value for each of us. If the paparazzi find out about our game, we will never hear the end of it." Maxwell was replying to a suggestion by Jorge de la Sierra to raise the stakes of the game. Jorge laughed as he sipped a glass of 20 year old Scotch.

"C'mon, mi Amigo. Oil is at an all-time high. You can afford it. Besides, the paparazzi think we meet to plan world domination anyway. They will never figure out that we are just having fun. No?"

"*Oui*, Alex. Jorge has a point. If it were not so sad, I would laugh," responded Armand Belmondo, as he leaned back in his leather chair, put his hands behind his neck, and looked up at the ceiling. "In France, the conspiracy freaks write that we are secretly pulling the strings of some mysterious one-world shadow government. They focus on us and ignore the Islamic radicals who are disrupting France every day. We are losing our country to a visible invasion of people who hate our way of life and tell us so. The press would rather look for a few phantom conspirators to blame for the world's problems. Garbage, I'm ready to sneak away for a while and frustrate them some more. The month of June can't come soon enough."

Armand had touched on one of Maxwell's favourite subjects, Islamic radicals. Maxwell developed his own thinking about their growing militancy. He leaned forward in his chair and offered an unsolicited opinion.

Geocache

"The challenge," Maxwell never used the word problem, "posed by the Islamic fascists isn't endemic to France, Armand." Maxwell's bushy eyebrows raised, further defining the creases in his forehead. "30 years ago these same misfits would have embraced the politics of communism to use as the vehicle of their hatred of the West. The followers of radical Islam have simply replaced the politics of communism with extreme religious intolerance as the vehicle to attack Western values. Become a follower or disappear from the face of the earth, nothing has changed really. At least these new fascists give us a choice — convert or die. The Nazis didn't offer an option to become Aryan; they just exterminated everyone that didn't look or think the way they did. In the end, the conflict isn't over religious fervour at all. It's the age-old conflict between haves and have-nots.

"They want to shift wealth to themselves; they just hide behind an established and legitimate religion. The communists labelled us as bourgeois. Now Islamist radicals call us infidels. It's the same drum beat, just a different cast of characters. They have managed to frighten decent Muslims around the world into silence, just the way Hitler intimidated the German people in the thirties into looking the other way. That led to 6,000,000 Jews and millions of non-Jews being slaughtered during the war."

"You know what your problem is, Alex?" responded Jorge de la Sierra as he squinted his right eye and opened wide his left eye, pointing an outstretched finger toward Maxwell. "You don't have an opinion about anything; you're just a milk-toast kind of guy. What do you think, Niko?" He gestured with open, upturned hands and looked at Kobayashi for agreement.

"I don't know about France's problems, we have our own frustrations in Japan," responded Niko as he placed his elbows on the table and cradled his face in his hands.

"That fruitcake in North Korea will kill us all if he can figure out how to make his missiles get off their firing pads. I anonymously send him porn videos each month in the hopes he will die of a heart attack playing with himself." They all laughed.

"Press letting up on you over there, Niko?" asked Vladimir, the Russian Oligarch.

"In Tokyo, I am perceived to be too serious; they say I'm boring. They say this is a good thing and compliment me for being so conventional," answered Niko. "The press made a joke out of the outgoing Japanese Prime Minister's visit to *Graceland*. He loved Elvis but dare not make that visit until he's on his way out of office. So imagine, if the tabloids knew I met with you hoodlums just to plan my vacations around our geocache searches! As Armand says, it breaks me up when I read what the pundits think about my omnipotence. If it were not for this diversion once a year, I would go crazy." Niko lifted his face from his hands.

Vladimir Kornikova stood up from his chair and walked around the long, hard table to the window. He peered through the floor-to-ceiling glass curtain wall at the city below.

"Da, this is why it continues to be important that our cache locations be so remote that the paparazzi cannot follow and discover our game. It drives them nuts that we all disappear every June for a month without explanation. Even my senior staff do not know where I go. They know that on June 1, I depart St. Petersburg. After that all they know is they can only reach me by satellite phone on a secure line and only if necessary." He turned and looked at de la Sierra. "How about a compromise, Jorge, say, $500,000 for each cache deposit? You can send your minions to Mexico City to search out $2,500,000 worth of cache items, can't you? Good for the Mexican economy, what there is left of it after the Mexican leftists down there are done," said the powerful Russian.

"Alex, listen to Vlad. Can you believe it?" Jorge de la Sierra replied in his booming voice. "Putin just nationalized *Yukos* (the largest oil producer in Russia) and put its owner, Mikhail Khodorkovsky, Russia's biggest taxpayer, in jail. You call that glasnost, Vlad."

Geocache

Jorge pointed his finger toward Vlad and wagged it back and forth.

"If you're not careful, you'll be calling me to arrange your escape to Mexico from the new Soviet Union part two. At least in Mexico, we know what to expect from our Government. It is reliably undependable. We make our rules, and then we pay to make them work. It's all understood. I vote $500,000, Vladimir; you go to Paris to shop. I know we go on a world-class Easter egg hunt as the Americans say, but I can't believe you actually hid eggs in the caches last year."

"Jorge . . . you son of a pirate. Those eggs as you call them were *'Faberge'* eggs! Each jewelled egg was worth every bit of $300,000," replied Vladimir. "In so far as *Yukos*, the oil company is concerned, one man's loss is another man's gain."

Jorge hit a nerve when he mentioned *Yukos*, the giant Russian oil company. It was not public knowledge yet, but Vlad's own Russian oil company benefited greatly by the nationalisation of *Yukos*. *Yukos* had been a worthy competitor under Khodorkovsky's competent management. With him in jail, *Yukos* would no longer be a viable competitor.

"See, I knew it," said Armando. "You cheated last year, Vlad, and you busted the $250,000 cache limit two years in a row. I vote not a penny more than $500,000. Alex, we need a penalty designed just for the Russian; he cheats like it's a nuclear proliferation agreement."

Maxwell smiled. It was always like this, good-natured banter between friends. He could relax now; they were having fun. After all, this was what it was all about, just plain fun. The *Global Geocache Society* would take the month of June and travel the globe in search of bragging rights. They would travel from continent to continent in their jets. They would board their helicopters and fly to the most remote and beautiful locations where others seldom trod. They would follow their handheld GPS units adjusted to military satellite reception to a geocache site where they would find a clue leading to another cache location with another clue and so on. Ultimately, the hunters would locate the final caches which would contain objects — for these treasure hunters gathered valuable objects. Victoria and the other security agents would place the cache boxes in their secret places with their contents just hours before the assigned date and time of the game. Their job included watching and guarding the geocaches from a distance, the contents too valuable to leave unattended. Altogether, Victoria and a select few of her other expert security colleagues were to observe the deposit and collection of $6,250,000 worth of Easter eggs (figuratively speaking). These deposits and collections were to be accomplished by some of the most unlikely people ever to undertake such a task. That was the plan anyway. Maxwell pressed the intercom button.

"Marsha, better send lunch in before they eat each other."

Geocache

CHAPTER SEVEN

GLOBAL POWER PLAYERS

The pilot lounge at the *Jet Centre* was a popular place for professional pilots to hang their hats between flights. The private suite was an assemblage of three rooms: a darkened room with a bed in it and an exercise room. In the largest room, there was a couple of leather reclining chairs and a couch facing a large television. Along the side of the room were two computer stations, a phone, and a printer. Everything a pilot needed to catch up on E-mail, check weather, and talk to the local Flight Service Station about weather reports.

Pilots could file their flight plans by phone or computer. They liked to gather in such places. They enjoyed a special camaraderie shared by professionals who lived and worked in high risk environments. Soldiers, fireman, policemen, pilots, all those, whose missions expose them to a higher risk of death than the average person, shared an unspoken reality. A colleague may not survive his next mission. He or she may never be engaged in conversation again. It is one explanation for their gregarious traits best symbolized by the antics of WWI pilots just before engaging in aerial combat.

The five helicopter pilot-in-commands had returned from dropping their bosses off, at the office tower helipad, and settled into the lounge. The eight business jet pilots took over the second floor conference room. The five helicopter right-seat pilots were left to hang out in the Jet Centre lobby, but there were no complaints. The lobby sported a large TV, a bank of couches, and a warm fireplace. All wore the traditional uniform of professional pilots - white shirt with epaulets, black trousers, black belt, and black shoes.

Errol Bader

In the second floor conference room, the conversation between the jet pilots turned to a discussion about their powerful passengers. Pilots were always curious to learn about jet-setting VIPS. It was prudent to be aware of potential clients, if a job change became necessary. Jim Stewart had given them a short biography of Alexander Maxwell.

"What about Jorge de la Sierra? What's his story?" asked Jim, eager to deflect any more questions about his own boss. Jim had been in enough of these discussions to be ready to get on with the task. Today he would be flying Maxwell's helicopter. He was scheduled to be the last to depart for the Maxwell Land Company helipad to pick up his boss. He should have been down in the lounge interacting with the helicopter pilots; departure time was approaching. However, the jet pilots prevailed on him to talk about the new glass cockpit that he recently installed in Maxwell's Gulfstream Five. The aircraft had state-of-the-art avionics, and all of the other aircraft would eventually be similarly retrofitted.

"Comes from the wealthiest family in Mexico," said de la Sierra's pilot. "They own diverse companies. De la Sierra is a direct descendant of the pirate of New Orleans, Jean Lafitte. One of his companies supplies transportation on and off the oil platforms off the coast of Mexico. He's operating over 150 helicopters by last count. Jorge is a pilot himself and a damn good one.

"He owns and flies his own Extra 300 L, the hottest high-performance aerobatic aircraft in the world, a German-built beauty of an airplane. He regularly pulls more than ten Gs. Jorge is crazy that way; he even does inverted spins. If I had his money, I wouldn't be risking my neck doing five Gs let alone ten. Crazy SOB, but a nice guy once you get to know him."

"In France there is no one who does not know my boss," said Belmondo's pilot. "He owns the majority stock in the *French Aero Space Company*, the builder of the new 500 passenger airliner. His company is so intertwined with the government that he is more politician than entrepreneur. He treats us very well; we like him. An easy guy to work for, with a good sense of humour.

"Unfortunately in Paris, he gets nothing but grief in the tabloids. I feel sorry for him sometimes. Every June we take him to various places for private meetings. He always seems recharged by the end of the month."

"And Kobayashi?" asked Jim.

"Tough and demanding boss," answered Kobayashi's chief pilot. "Niko's at the top of a large group of high-tech companies in Japan. He built a research park in Tokyo fifteen years ago and negotiated a piece of the profits in lieu of real-estate fees. Then he lobbied the Japanese government to grant large subsidies and tax breaks for any research facility that relocated to his park. Several facilities hit some big tech breakthroughs and made Niko fabulously wealthy."

"I hear the Russian is a little rough on his pilots, is that true?" asked Kobayashi's pilot.

"Nyet, Vladimir is only difficult when he is awake," responded Vlad's pilot, followed by a momentary silence.

"C'mon," Jim says. "How did he make his money?"

"If I told you, I would have to kill you," responded Vlad's pilot with a smirk.

"How did he make his money?" shouted the group almost in unison.

"Okay, okay. To understand how Vlad became a Russian oligarch you have to understand the history of the Russian oil business. During the height of the cold war, your *President Reagan* did two things that bankrupted our country. One is well known and the other was a U.S. state secret until recently leaked to the public. In the mid-1980s, Reagan announced Star Wars and challenged the Soviets to try to outspend the United States militarily. Twenty years of war in Afghanistan had already decimated our treasury. Reagan secretly and successfully lobbied the Saudis to flood the market with oil. There was a glut of oil causing oil prices to drop. At the time the only source of revenue

Errol Bader

for the Soviet Union was from its oil fields. The low oil prices during the eighties brought our economy to its knees. Reagan strangled us with cheap Saudi oil.

"When all this was unfolding, Vlad was one of the new but struggling Russian entrepreneurs. He imported computers to Russia and starting to amass some money. He started a bank, as did another fellow by the name of Khodorkovsky. At the time Boris Yeltsin was trying to keep Russia from sliding back into the control of the communists. Workers were going unpaid for months. Yeltsin knew that millions of pensioners, who were not receiving payments, might bring the communists back into power. He needed cash desperately, so he devised a plan that eventually saved the Russian government.

"First, he created shares in Russia's two state-owned oil companies. He gave thirty percent of the shares to the oil company employees. The Government kept the balance of the shares. Then he went to the new home-grown Russian bankers and negotiated a *"loan for shares"* deal. He posted the Government's shares in the oil companies as collateral in return for bank loans from which to pay the countries pensioners.

"Vlad and Khodorkovsky used their banks to loan the Government the money. Yelstin paid the pensioners and was able to hold the communists at bay until the crisis passed. But Yelstin couldn't foresee how enterprising the two young capitalists would be. They both went to the oil company employees and convinced them to sell their shares for very little money. In the end the government defaulted on the loans at maturity and voila, Vlad and Khodorkovsky wound up owning the two largest oil companies in Russia.

"There are some who think that the government's default was intentional. The oil companies had been losing money under the management of the Russian apparatchiks. The theory is that once the companies were in the hands of the young capitalists, Yeltzin betted that they would be more profitable and able to pay more tax to support the Russian economy. In the fullness of time, that is

Geocache

exactly what happened and it is how Vlad met Alexander Maxwell.

"Maxwell employed two American petroleum engineers on staff in Colorado," Vlad's pilot continued with his history lesson. "These men were geniuses at getting low producing oil fields to be more productive. Vlad knew he needed western technology to turn his new oil company around. He met with Maxwell and worked an arrangement for special pricing on Russian oil in return for the loan of his executives in order to make his existing oil wells more productive.

"When the two Americans assessed the status of the Russian's wells, they discovered that they were only producing 10% of their potential. They devised ways to improve the production and achieved miraculous results. Vlad stopped spending money on new well-drilling and redirected his resources to the existing wells.

"It worked; and not only did Vlad become a billionaire, but with the new tax revenue coming in, our economy was given a huge shot in the arm. So that is how Vlad became an oligarch and a very good friend of Alexander Maxwell. You all do a lot of trips in June comrades?"

CHAPTER EIGHT

THE ACCIDENT

Travis Raeburn turned the collective in his hand and spooled up the turbines in the Bell helicopter. The ex-Royal Navy pilot was the next to the last to depart Centennial Airport for the office tower helipad. Only Maxwell and Jorge de la Sierra remained in the conference room.

"Hey, where you going, Travis?" asked Joyce, his young female co-pilot. "We need to go directly to the tower office building."

"I know," said Travis, "but I saw Jim Stewart still in the upstairs conference room jabbering with the jet jockeys when we left, so we have a head start. Let's just fly a little west and see what those mountains look like up close,".

Joyce felt uneasy about this. It was uncharacteristic of Travis to depart from a plan, but his reasoning seemed okay; and besides, Travis had been doing this kind of work a lot longer than she had; 30 years, in fact. Anyway, the snow-covered foothills were only a few miles off the direct path. It should not be a problem, unless they dwelled over there too long.

As the helicopter headed west, away from the city and toward the mountains, the land began to rise. Travis followed the undulating terrain remaining only one hundred feet above the ground. After passing over the first of the foothills, the pilot pushed the nose over and flew his craft down below the ridge tops.

"Now this is what it was like in the Falklands," Travis told his co-pilot as the hills sped by the side windows of the helicopter, referring to his experience flying in the Falklands' War. The two pilots flew through valleys and ravines until they reached the

Geocache

storied and beautiful *Red Rocks Amphitheater*.

Finally, Joyce turned to Travis, "Okay, Captain, if we don't break off now, we're going to mess up the pecking order over at the office tower helipad."

"Roger that," replied the senior pilot. "Time to go, but this side trip was worth it, don't you think?"

The co-pilot gave no response; her thoughts were elsewhere. She knew there was no way to make up the lost time.

Jim Stewart was running a few minutes late. He called his co-pilot by cell phone. The blades were already turning when he reached the chopper door. Five minutes behind schedule. They would make up the time by flying at full throttle, for ten minutes, to transit the airspace between Centennial Airport and the office tower. Jim was relieved to note the time when they touched down at the helipad. They were back on schedule.

Jorge de la Sierra stood, with Maxwell at the helipad, surprised to see Maxwell's helicopter arrive before his own.

The two men shook hands and Maxwell boarded, followed by Marsha Thompson; she had left her car at his estate earlier in the day. Normally, Victoria would have flown with Maxwell but elected to stay behind to make sure de la Sierra would be all right. *Perhaps there was a mechanical problem with his helicopter, she thought. Maybe the pilot had to turn back.*

Jim grasped the collective and the large blades began to speed up. The blast of the down wash forced de la Sierra and Victoria off the roof for the protection and quiet of the conference room just below the helipad.

"Travis, we're running late. Jorge will be ticked off," said the co-pilot. They were at 700 feet and clear of the last of the hills. Travis was more concerned about speed than altitude and opted to stay low.

"We need more altitude for the helipad, Travis; shouldn't we climb?"

"We'll trade speed for altitude when we get there," said Travis. She was irritating him.

Errol Bader

It is a commonly-used procedure to trade the energy of an aircrafts forward speed for an immediate gain in altitude. This plan would get them to the office tower a little faster, but unfortunately would not give them the bird's-eye view of a normal approach to a rooftop helipad. The co-pilot was thinking to herself, *this isn't the best of approaches*. A string of bad judgements by her pilot-in-command was beginning to bother her. She was uncomfortable; her military training taught her not to argue with a superior. Yet, she felt in conflict with everything she had been taught about cockpit management and decision sharing. When she finally decided to forcibly object, she looked towards the top of the office building, it was too late; their helicopter was closing on the tower low and fast. The pilots were committed to a steep altitude gain, very close to the building. Upon reaching the building, they began to climb vertically, watching the rows of office windows slide by them in what seemed like a downward motion. Both pilots were fixated on the sight and experienced the same optical illusion. Even though they were rising at 500 feet per minute, it appeared to them that they were stationary and the building was sinking into the earth at that speed. They watched their helicopter's reflection in the window glass as it slid by. (There is something in the human psyche that compels people to examine their reflections when confronted by a mirror. Man is the only animal to ponder a reflection of self.) This human frailty, momentary as it was, caused both pilots to lose focus on the dangerous task they were undertaking.) Three stories above Alexander Maxwell's helicopter prepared to lift off the helipad. The rotor blades turned so rapidly, no individual blades were visually distinguishable .

Unaware, Jim Stewart tightened his right hand grip on the collective and began to lift it. He twisted his left hand to throttle for more power. The big helicopter rose off the helipad, with its two pilots and two passengers firmly belted in. As the west side of the building was cleared the veteran pilot caught something in his peripheral view. Initially, he thought it was a large piece of

Geocache

cardboard flying up from below, but wondered how it got this high? Though he was having trouble processing the conflict between what his eyes were reporting and what his brain refused to accept as logical, his 35 years of flying, dodging ground-to-air missiles, made him react instinctively to the threat. He dropped the craft's nose and banked away from the object. Too late! The lower helicopter's large rotor blade tore into the hydraulic lines on Maxwell's aircraft.

"What was that?" Jim shouted.

Maxwell could see what was happening and shouted back, "Another helicopter from below."

Underneath, Raeburn was struggling to keep control of his machine. His heart pounded in his chest. He felt the impact of his main rotor blade as it hit Maxwell's helicopter. His helicopter, at eye level with the conference room, began to spin in a circle. He lost directional control; the tail rotor had been sheered off by a composite piece from his main rotor blade. Victoria and de la Sierra looked out through the curtain window wall of the conference room in horror. They saw the collision as if in slow motion. The lower helicopter spun closer to the boardroom. De la Sierra froze. but Victoria acted instinctively as her training, to protect principals, kicked in. She could do nothing to help Maxwell, but at least she could try to save Jorge de la Sierra. She tackled him and pulled him behind the *Lignumvitae* table. Somehow, despite the weight, the two of them managed to turn the massive table over to use as a shield. The sound was deafening as the massive helicopter blades cut through the window's thick panes of tempered glass. Pieces of composite blade, metal, and glass careened off the walls behind and around the two as they huddled behind the massive hardwood table. The conference room suddenly went quiet; the burning fuselage was lodged in the room's window frame.

Victoria knew the flames would soon ignite the fuel vapour, so she rose up from behind the board table and surveyed the scene. The two pilots struggled to free themselves from the burning wreckage. She ran to the edge of the conference room to help the trapped co-pilot. The helicopter door had ripped off, allowing Victoria to reach into the fuselage. She twisted the round buckled device on the co-pilots chest to release her from the seat. The only thing left intact was a two inch wide aluminium window frame running vertically from floor to ceiling. The frame bent inward half way up its length. Victoria braced her left shoulder against the inside of the narrow post, then reached over Joyce's right hand and grasped her wrist. Suddenly, the burning mass jerked and fell away from the gaping hole. The co-pilot hung in Victoria's grasp. Her weight pulled Victoria downward causing her shoulder to slide down the metal frame until her right armpit hit the floor. Victoria could see the fear in the young woman's eyes as she dangled from Victoria's right arm fifty stories above the street. Below her Raeburn screamed and reached out towards her as the wreckage accelerated towards the street. Joyce was flailing her one free arm and both legs making it harder for Victoria to hold onto her. De la Sierra came to the window and stretched out to reach the struggling woman.

"Listen to me, listen carefully . . . stop moving if you want to live!" Victoria shouted through clenched teeth.

"Don't let me die, please" Joyce pleaded for her life.

Even so, Victoria's reserves were being sapped, though a superb athlete, by the wild gyrations of the panic stricken woman. Joyce finally obeyed and stopped flailing, tears ran down her cheeks.

"Jorge, I'm going to swing her over your way, grab her waistband and pull."

"Okay, go" de la Sierra reached down towards the woman.

Slowly, painfully, Victoria began to swing the woman back and forth in a pendulum motion. The pain in her left shoulder was excruciating, pressed against the sharp edges of the aluminium extrusion. Her right arm burned from the exertion and the weight of the woman's limp body. Finally de la Sierra grabbed the woman just as the jet fuel in the falling wreckage reached its combustion point at the twentieth floor. The fuel tank exploded with an ear deafening sound. A plume of flames, ball bearings, and pieces of shrapnel shot upwards bouncing off curtain windows towards Victoria and the co-pilot as she strained to hold on to the young woman. The two pulled Joyce into the conference room just as the flames and shrapnel raked by the opening.

Victoria held her right shoulder with her left hand and lay exhausted, among the cube shaped pieces of fractured tempered glass, on the conference room floor. She rolled away from the windows edge and looked towards the conference room table.

There in the hard surface of the table was a portion of rotor blade lodged firmly in the *Lignumvitae*, the hardest wood in the world. *'The wood of life'* had been aptly named. It took 1,000 years for that seedling to grow into the tree that would ultimately save their lives.

Next to the tower, Jim Stewart was working hard to keep his big helicopter stable. The aircraft was losing power fast. *This was the worst place for an engine failure; nothing but office buildings everywhere* he thought. He reached a quick decision to make for the nearby downtown park. He could only hope the power would hold long enough to get clear of the office towers. His plan was to auto-rotate to a landing if he lost all power; but it would only work if he could clear the office towers that barred the way to the park.

Marsha Thompson clutched at Maxwell's hand in panic.

"It's going to be okay, Marsha. It's going to turn out okay. Jim will get us out of this," Maxwell assured her. In his heart, he knew better. He did not believe they would survive this day.

That was it. The last office tower was cleared, and it was a straight shot to the park. The turbine power plants shut down, demanding that the veteran pilot summon all the skill he possessed. He was determined to use the remaining energy left in the blades to the best advantage. Increase the pitch too soon and they would plummet; increase the pitch too late and the craft would hit too hard and explode in a ball of fire. He had to change the pitch of the blades at just the right altitude, and there would be no second chance at it.

At 50 feet, Jim began the auto-rotation procedure, and the craft began to slow. Another few feet and it would have worked out as planned. Instead, the helicopter hit a stand of trees and flipped on its back. The co-pilot died instantly. Maxwell and Marsha Thompson were trapped in the back, fuel spilling down through the inverted cabin.

A Denver motorcycle cop had watched the mid-air collision between the two helicopters. He had raced below the surviving helicopter as it made its way toward the park. The officer drove over the sidewalk and down an embankment leading to the park. He reached the scene and left his cycle on its side as he ran to the smoking wreckage. He had just enough time to drag Maxwell, Marsha Thompson, and Jim Stewart to a safe distance before the jet fuel reached its combustion point, and the wreckage burst into flames.

Victoria and Jorge de la Sierra rode the elevator to the street. There was nothing resembling a helicopter in the wreckage at the foot of the building. The sounds of sirens pierced the air around the base of the Maxwell Land Company building. Off in the distance they could hear another set of sirens. They hailed a cab and headed in the direction of the distant sounds.

"My God, Victoria!," Jorge said in a stressed voice. "Pray that Alexander is not in that mess at the bottom of the building. Damn, how could this happen?"

He slammed his fist on the cab's seat back in frustration.

Victoria had the same thoughts. Her instincts had warned her that there was a problem in not including the helicopter pilots in the advance briefing. However, Jim Stewart had shared with her the discussions and agreements he had with the other helicopter pilots. It sounded like he had everything covered. She was certain even now that the briefing had been comprehensive.

Geocache

"There it is, driver! Over there where the lights are." Victoria referred to the flashing red and blue emergency vehicle lights in the park. They approached the scene hoping to find Maxwell, Marsha Thompson, and the pilots in good condition; hoping at least this was their helicopter. If not, it meant, their bodies were in the wreckage at the bottom of the office tower.

Police cordons were not up yet. Victoria and Jorge found Maxwell, Marsha Thompson and Jim Stewart wrapped in blankets lying on the ground. Paramedics took their pulses while others took stretchers out of an ambulance that had just arrived. All of the injured were still alive, but none were moving.

"Have you got a pulse?" Victoria asked a medic leaning over Maxwell.

"Yes, but he has head trauma," answered the medic. "I checked the woman. She's still breathing. The pilot is hurt pretty bad, but he should be okay. We need to get them all to E.R. fast."

CHAPTER NINE

FAIRWELL TO THE DYING

The ambulance went ahead with a police escort. Victoria and Jorge settled for a cab. The paramedics warned University of Colorado Hospital of numerous casualties. Travis Raeburn's bad judgement had caused many injuries in Downtown Denver and the loss of his own life. It was a miracle there were not more deaths.

In triage, doctors worked to keep the injured alive. Victoria discovered Maxwell unconscious, lying on a gurney. Marsha Thompson was a few feet away, both had IVs started. Jim Stewart had been taken to a medical clinic as his injuries were not life-threatening.

"Who's that?" Jorge asked, as a young man walked through the emergency room doors and immediately made his way over to Marsha, who lay dying.

"That's Chandler Benson," replied Victoria. "Someone at Maxwell Land must have contacted him. He's going to be devastated if they lose Marsha; she's influenced his every decision, including his choice of pharmaceutical schools."

Chandler leant over Marsha, then looked over to both Victoria and Maxwell, before drawing his attention back to his mother. She was telling him something and he was listening carefully. Marsha's hand fell limp and Chandler straightened up. His fingers let slip his mother's hand and Victoria knew Marsha was gone. Chandler stared at Victoria for a fleeting moment.

It would be hours before the doctors would emerge from the operating room. Maxwell survived the crash, but he was in a coma. Jeremy St. James, Maxwell's personal attorney, joined Victoria and Jorge de la Sierra in a private hospital waiting room.

Geocache

Chandler was sitting in the corner of the private suite. Victoria pulled him inside the room to console him. They would receive the prognosis together. Victoria could hardly believe the circumstance confronting them.

She kept going over in her mind the preparation and cautionary measures she had taken to avoid this. How could this disaster happen? How could she have avoided this? Her responsibility was lying in post op in a coma.

"Hello, my name is Lomello, Christopher Lomello. I have been working Mr. Maxwell's file." The doctor entered the room and addressed the four without hesitation. He was a tall silver-haired man in his early sixties; he looked distinguished and had an air of sophistication about him. He seemed not to care about the formalities of introduction. His approach was direct with no small talk. Victoria liked this and had a good feeling about his competency. Characteristically, Jorge de la Sierra was impatient.

"How is he? Is my friend going to be okay? What can we do?" asked de la Sierra in an urgent tone.

"We have to get the swelling down in his brain. It's impossible to tell what cognitive loss he may suffer, if any. That is the immediate problem," replied Doctor Lomello.

Victoria was accustomed to reading between the lines — reading body language. She perceived there was more.

"What do you mean by the immediate problem?" she asked.

Doctor Lomello looked her directly in the eyes and responded, "Mr. Maxwell is dying of bone cancer, and he needs a bone marrow transplant as soon as possible. With a proper donor, I feel we can save his life. Ironically, his accident has resulted in an early diagnosis, so we have a chance. If we can get the swelling down in his brain, we can address the cancer threat later, if we get lucky."

"*If we get lucky?*" Victoria sensed there was more bad news yet to come.

"What do you mean, if we get lucky?" she asked.

"The preliminary blood tests indicate that Mr. Maxwell has a rare blood type. It will take a few days to determine just how rare; but right now, I would say that we are going to have to scramble to find a donor who will be an acceptable match. We have an excellent oncologist on staff, Doctor Levy. He should be here shortly. He will give you more details about the type of cancer Mr. Maxwell has and our treatment options. I can tell you that the diagnosis is multiple Myeloma. Multiple Myeloma is not usually detected in patients until they reach their late sixties and often too late to treat effectively," answered Doctor Lomello.

Victoria would not have to wait to discover how rare Maxwell's blood type was; she already knew the answer. She learned of his rare blood type during the normal course of preparing for her new job. She had him make donations of blood for his own future use in just such an event. Victoria knew that there were no relatives to call on. She knew his blood type was so rare that it would take a global search to find a match.

Doctor Levy knocked before opening the door. Doctor Lomello introduced the younger doctor as he entered, followed by a nurse.

"This is Doctor Levy, the oncologist I was telling you about; and this is Karin Rollins, the head nurse for this floor. I'll stop back later to check on Mr. Maxwell. Karin will be here looking in on him."

Doctor Lomello handed his card to Attorney St. James. "You can reach me at this number if you need anything,"

Victoria was accustomed to such slights, it came along with the curse of being beautiful.

After the usual introductions, Doctor Levy began his assessment of Maxwell's illness.

"Mr. Maxwell has a condition known as multiple Myeloma, or MM for short. MM is a form of leukaemia that usually raises its ugly head in later years. If detected early enough, we can treat it with a combination of chemotherapy and stem cell transplants; presuming we can find a match. The transplant procedure is called Peripheral Blood Stem Cell or PBSC. If it were not for

Geocache

recent breakthroughs in stem cell technology, this procedure would not be available to us. It isn't a slam-dunk cure by any means, but we are getting better at it. Fortunately, in Mr. Maxwell's case he has a cancer, which is chemotherapy sensitive. These patients have a greater chance of achieving what we refer to as complete remission. You see, this disease is not curable." Doctor Levy was looking at Victoria now.

"However, with complete remission, the patient can live out his or her normal lifespan with a good quality of life. I would say that he deserves the opportunity for this kind of treatment."

At least this doctor knows I have a brain, Victoria thought to herself. The doctor continued, "the best donors, of course, are donors who are related to the patient. These donors can give us a fully matched HLA, which is what we always hope for. If there are no fully HLA matched donors available, then we must find partially matched unrelated donors. I'm hoping you will tell me that Mr. Maxwell has some close relatives we can test?" This was more of a question than a statement from Doctor Levy.

"No, Doctor. There are no relatives, but we have his blood in storage. I can arrange to have it delivered right away." responded Victoria.

"I'm sorry, Ms. Kavanagh. Mr. Maxwell's own blood won't work for a bone marrow transplant. We need a live, breathing, healthy donor; and it needs to be soon."

Jeremy St. Vincent turned to Victoria; but before he could say a word, she spoke what he was thinking. There was no one else better qualified to conduct the search. Besides, his life was her responsibility.

"I'll find a donor, if one exists." Even as she spoke, she remembered a conversation she had with a medical researcher she had talked to earlier in the year. There might be four or five matches for Alexander Maxwell on the entire globe, a mathematical impossibility for any more than that. She would be looking for a needle in a thousand haystacks. However, if that needle existed, Victoria Kavanagh was determined to find it.

"I'm sorry to hear he has no relatives. This makes things difficult. We will contact the University of Massachusetts this afternoon. They have an excellent facility there, the Catherine Ryan International Registry. The registry communicates with most of the donor registries around the world. They can do searches for unrelated donors. It's our best place to start," said Doctor Levy.

"How much time have we got doctor?" Victoria asked.

"Two months, maybe three. Presuming the others here can defeat the head injuries that Mr. Maxwell sustained from the accident," answered Doctor Levy.

CHAPTER TEN

AN INVITATION TO DIE

Antoine Sandel had spent all of his 52 years in Prague. Orphaned at 12 after his mother and sister had died in a car accident. Of his father he only knew, from his mother's stories, he had been forced to join the German army and was lost in the war.

Antoine's mother had received an inheritance, but it had remained in a Prague bank account until her death. He had been too young to recall who the benefactor was, but the funds saw him through school, and he progressed to a lucrative career in accountancy.

Now on his way to work in his BMW, Antoine's journey had been interrupted by a short diversion to his local post office. The night before he had missed a parcel delivery and was required to collect it. The clerk handed the package to him through the window. He was surprised by the size and weight of it. The sender had wrapped the parcel in plain brown paper.

Antoine drove to the office in the lower parts of Prague, with the parcel in the passenger seat. Not far from the Charles Bridge, his curiosity got the best of him. He pulled onto a side street, parked, and stripped the paper away to reveal a rectangular cardboard box. Antoine opened the carton. Inside he found a fourteen inch laptop computer with a fully-charged battery and two spares. Along with the computer, there was a sealed envelope. Intrigued, he opened the envelope, which contained a cashier's check made payable to himself for $10,000 in US currency.

Antoine looked at the check. It must be a mistake — he was certain. This was a new computer and the check, drawn on the Bank of Prague, was undeniably authentic. Taped on the computer lid was a slip of paper with the words:

Username — *GEO*; Password — *CACHE*.

Antoine booted up the computer; its first prompt requested a 'user name' and 'password'. Antoine typed in *GEO* and then *CACHE*. The screen immediately changed to the traditional macro-safe screensaver. There was only one icon on the desktop and it was labelled '*GEOCACHE*'. Antoine placed the curser over the only choice given on the screen and triggered it. A word document filled the screen. It was a letter addressed to him on a very official looking letterhead. The Jack and Elizabeth Gielgood Foundation was printed along the top of the letter. The document had been scanned into the computer as Antoine saw the shadow cast by the embossment on the letter head. There was a watermark of the family crest covering the entire background of the document. He began to read it:

The Jack and Elizabeth Gielgood Foundation
New York, New York

Dear Mr. Sandel :

I am the conservator for the Jack and Elizabeth Gielgood estate. I know that the method used to introduce myself is very unorthodox; I must apologize. However, the method of selection, contacting recipients and communicating the information contained herein, was set forth in Mr. Jack Gielgood's Last Will and Testament. Mr. Gielgood lived most of his life considering the best interests of others. The foundation he formed, fifteen years ago, has contributed to the wellbeing of those in the poorest of countries.

Mr. Sandel, Mr. Gielgood was a sportsman. When not directing his philanthropic foundation, he was often found enjoying his favourite pastime; a sport called geocache. Mr. Gielgood continuously expressed disappointment that more people were not aware of the joys of getting out into the fresh air and going on a geocache hunt. You see, Mr.

Geocache

Sandel, the geocache sport is a wholesome way for families to spend time together, away from the vast wasteland that television has become. Geocache gets people away from the cities to enjoy what nature has to offer.

I know you are wondering what this has to do with you and why I have included a $10,000 check for you. The money is yours regardless of whether you accept the challenge bequeathed to you or not. There are no strings attached. The money is included to underscore the seriousness of Mr. Gielgood's posthumous wish. It is also to provide travel expenses should you decide to undertake his challenge to you.

In his will, Mr. Gielgood gave very precise instructions for the distribution of $24,000,000 of estate funds to some of the best charitable organisations in the world. This distribution, however, is dependent upon the successful completion of a promotional effort to make the existence and virtues of geocache known to millions of people. Following Mr. Gielgood's directions, we have established a robust publicity campaign to promote the sport of geocache. The campaign will centre on the geocache adventures of four randomly chosen individuals. The four are ultimately to become very wealthy in their pursuit of a very special geocache, a kind of a reality programme if you will.

You have been chosen, again purely by a random selection process, to be one of these four participants in what will surely be the most enjoyable and financially rewarding experience of your life.

Not only will you become wealthy by helping satisfy Mr. Gielgood's desire to spread the word about geocache as a wonderful sport, but your participation will also result in a substantial contribution to world charities. Here are the instructions and rules:

On November 28th at exactly noon at a given destination, you will locate a box which will have

$1,500,000 of cash in United States' currency. The money already belongs to you, bequeathed to you by Mr. Gielgood. Along with this money will be a certificate which will result in another $1,500,000 payment to you. You will receive the additional $1,500,000 when you present the certificate to me at a publicity event we have already scheduled. You will receive more information about this event when you return from your geocache adventure.

After you have removed the cash and certificate from the cache box, you are to replace them with the laptop you have received. This is in the spirit of how geocache works. One travels to a place on the globe by handheld GPS, finds a cache, and removes an object previously deposited there. The rules require that players leave something in the cache so that it is never empty. In fact, there are thousands of cache locations all over the world as you read this letter.

I have incorporated a global positioning system (GPS) receiver with moving colour map into your laptop. The receiver will take you to a specific spot on the earth. You see you will need this laptop to get to your geocache site. You must be prompt in arriving at the coordinates, we cannot leave a container with so much cash unattended for long. The money will only be at the location during a two-hour window. If you miss it, you will forfeit the contents as per Mr. Gielgood's instructions. The exact coordinates for your geocache will be posted on the Internet on the morning of November 28th at a website established just for you. The website is www.antionesgeocache.com.

Mr. Gielgood was adamant that no details of the event leak out before the date of the established publicity event. If you were to compromise the event by losing this laptop or otherwise discuss this with anyone, your coordinates will not appear on your website. You will be disqualified from the reward.

I must warn you that there are investigative reporters

Geocache

for a large tabloid trying to uncover details of Mr. Gielgood's will. If any individuals approach you, please avoid them. If you discuss this with anyone and they turn out to be media representatives, you will lose a great deal of money for having done so.

Mr. Sandel, you will need to make plane reservations right away for Basel, Switzerland. It is a city at the southernmost part of the Black Forest. Rent a car now; and dress warmly for your trip, you will be out-of-doors and it will be cold. There will be warm gluwein waiting for you at your geocache location when you get there.
All the best,
Alfred Sinclair ESQ.'

Antoine sat stunned by what he had just read. It was an invitation to wealth. His mind began to process the information. He read it again and then a third time. His first thought was that this was a set-up by some con man. There have been scientific studies done about how the mind works, given exposure to a shocking set of facts for the first time. The studies tend to substantiate that a person's first thoughts during stressful and unexpected situations are usually the correct thoughts. The brain is processing information subconsciously in rapid fashion without conscious understanding. In other words, go with your first instinct because that is the best you are going to get out of your brain when under stress. The longer a person ponders the information, the more blurred the best action becomes. Antoine's first instinct was to be cautious, but he would think on and start rationalising.

No. I'm not a rich person; I'm an average guy. No one would pay a ransom for me. Why would anyone give me ten thousand dollars and put me on a plane to the Black Forest? To rob me? Rob me of what?

Antoine was taking the bait. The author of the letter to Antoine Sandel, ignorant of his personality, appealed to the emotions of greed and philanthropic sentiments both at once. A diabolical mind wrote this letter. If greed did not set the hook, the prospects of helping people in poor countries would, or perhaps both. The concept of philanthropy intertwined in the enticement served as a psychological salve to mask Antoine's own innate greed.

Antoine continued on to his office and booted up the PC on his desk. He logged on to an internet search engine and started a search for the Jack and Elizabeth Gielgood foundation. The website began to load. There it was, that family crest again. An announcement appeared on the screen. "This website is under construction."

Then a personal message from an Alfred Sinclair. "Due to the untimely death of Mr. Jack Gielgood, we are preparing a special website in tribute to his past contributions to the health and welfare of people the world over. Please visit our website again in February."

Okay. Makes sense, he thought. He then typed in the address to his assigned website, *www.antionesgeocachesite.com*. The website opened up with a page covered with grey halftone Gielgood family crests. In the middle were the words "latitude and longitude" with blank spaces to the right of each word.

Okay. This is for real. My life is about to change, he thought.

Antoine picked up the phone and dialled it.

"Yes, thank you. I would like to reserve a roundtrip flight to Basel, Switzerland, near the Black Forest Region of Germany, for the 27th of this month. Yes, I will need a car and a room." Antoine was correct about one thing. His life was about to change.

CHAPTER ELEVEN

THE SEARCH BEGINS

"Yes, ma'am, this is the International Donor Registry. My name's Alice. How can I direct your call?" answered the receptionist.

"Hi, this is Victoria Kavanagh. I work for a gentleman who is in dire need of a bone marrow donor. He has multiple Myeloma. Can you connect me with the appropriate person?"

"Certainly," Alice reassured her. "You need to talk to either Doctor John Singh or his assistant, Mary Genevieve. They are in a staff meeting but should be back in about an hour."

Victoria noted the receptionist had a gentle touch with her callers. Her tone was soft and soothing. The girl did not come across as only filling a chair to bide time, but genuinely seemed to have a passion for her job. She seemed to sense the stress her callers were under. Most of the calls, Victoria assumed, must have been from medical professionals, but quite possibly one out of four would have been a relative or friend trying to find a donor, like she was, and working overtime at it. Alice seemed only too eager to alleviate the pressure.

"Victoria, do you have the donor match requirements from your family doctor?"

"Well, a . . . well, yes, I do," replied Victoria.

"If you can fax them to me along with your name and contact information, I will have one of them call you as soon as possible to go over the report. It should be this afternoon, if you can do it now. Is that okay?"

"It's on the way Alice," Victoria replied "I cannot thank you enough for your help."

It seemed like days but it was only hours when Victoria's cell phone rang.

"Victoria Kavanagh," she answered.

"Is it Ms. or Mrs. Kavanagh? This is Doctor Singh at the Catherine Ryan Registry."

"Please call me Victoria, Doctor. Thank you for calling so quickly."

"That's okay; we are accustomed to the time constraints patients and their families are under. I see you're in the 303 area code. Are you in Colorado?"

"Yes, in Denver," replied Victoria.

"Wonderful place this time of year. Have the resorts opened yet?"

Victoria sensed he was trying to take the edge off the difficult subject matter. He must have been accustomed to talking to stressed-out family members.

"Not until around Thanksgiving, Doctor Singh."

"Oh, yes, that's right. It's always Thanksgiving when they open, isn't it? Well, Victoria, I have read the work ups that you sent us on Mr. Maxwell. Is he your father?"

"No, Doctor. I work for Mr. Maxwell. He has no relatives."

"That is unfortunate, Victoria," the doctor replied. He seemed disappointed. "Finding a match for Mr. Maxwell will be very difficult. A relative would have been much better. How is he doing?"

"Mr. Maxwell was in an accident and has complications from head injuries," Victoria informed him. "We believe he'll recover from his injuries, but need to locate a donor for a PBSC transplant for him as soon as possible."

"That is what we are here for," reaffirmed Doctor Singh in a more positive tone. "The Registry is in telematic contact with over ninety blood donor organisations across the globe. I'll put some research assistants on the search when we hang up; maybe we will get lucky right off. Is this the best number to reach you? You might want to give me your E-mail address also. I will try to get back with you by late afternoon tomorrow."

"Thank you, Doctor. I appreciate what your organisation is doing for us."

"We'll do our best to help, Victoria," came his honest voice, but there was also a sense of defeat in Doctor Singh's voice. "I don't want to get your hopes up. This will be a tough search."

Errol Bader

CHAPTER TWELVE

THE PRAGUE DONOR

Prague, the Czech Republic

Marie Tereskova loved to take black and white photos of the many venues around her native Prague. She was really quite good, and many of her pictures won awards. She had a few favourites like the close-ups of tombstones taken in the Old Jewish Cemetery, which contained over 12,000 gravestones dating between 1439 and 1787. The ageing stone tablets tilted in odd and non-uniform directions from centuries of earth movement from below and being weather beaten. The Hebrew inscriptions had been rendered illegible making the identities of the inhabitants long lost to history. However, the family names of the deceased could be determined from carved symbols still visible on the stones. A lion symbolised the occupant was a member of the Levi family; hands were symbolic of the Cohen family. The cemetery provided Marie with some classic black and white photos.

Today, she was on holiday and doing her best to disengage from her work. Her camera loaded and slung over her shoulder, she was in search of that one great picture that would make her famous and maybe even rich. It was a cold, clear day, and the light modelled the stones in a way that pleased her. She was bundled up with a knee length tan woollen coat. This was complimented by a green and red woollen scarf flipped around her neck and shoulders with one end dangling in front to her waist. A blue beret topped off her oval-shaped face. She could easily have been mistaken for a high school girl on her way to school.

Marie had just celebrated her twenty-seventh birthday. It was the first without her father. Leukaemia had finally proven too

Geocache

much for him. Her grandmother had survived him by only a couple of months. It had been a tough year for losses. Her mother was in good health and lived nearby, but Marie rarely saw her after the rift between her parents. Marie was grateful to the medical staff who had worked to extend her father's life. Were it not for the fact that she shared the same rare blood type with him, he would have died years earlier. She had been the only known donor. Knowing how important her father's life had depended on her donations, she had registered with the Czech Bone Marrow/Cord Blood Registry in Prague in case another needed her rare blood type.

The commitment and professionalism of the doctors and staff at the Registry so impressed Marie, she offered to do voluntary work. When a permanent job arose, several months later, the Registry enthusiastically encouraged her to take up the post as she had proved herself a most competent asset but Marie was torn between her creative nature and the need to earn a living. With some reservations she accepted the post.

"Marie, Marie, there you are. I've been looking all over for you." Elli Troutner, Marie's best friend, approached as she aimed her camera. "Shh, Elli! This is it, This is the one."

"This is the one what?"

"This is the picture that will make me rich and famous. Be quiet for just a minute."

The two were standing on the edge of The Charles Bridge, next to the sculpture of St. Augustine, created in the year 1708. Construction of the famous bridge started in 1357 and was finished sometime in the fifteenth century. Marie had taken many pictures of the sculptures of the saints that line the length of the old bridge. Thirty on each side, every one made of Czech sandstone. The bridge carries the name of the Roman Emperor and Czech King Charles IV. Running perpendicular to and away from the bridge was a small waterway. On one side of the canal was a very old and very large wooden water wheel that last turned a gristmill stone in the year 1400. The Velkoprevorsky

Mill was the only Prague Mill still standing. The waterway was lined on both sides by centuries old two-story town homes. Marie framed the scene with the old sandstone statue on the ancient bridge itself. Elli saw it also; it would be a photo which would give one a sense of place. People would want to step into such a picture. The camera shutter clicked.

"Okay. You can talk now, my fortune is assured," said Marie with a smile.

"Ah, don't be daft," scolded Elli, "the truth is Marie Tereskova, you couldn't care less about money. You're not interested in material things."

"I know," giggled Marie. "But one can dream occasionally. Now what did you want?"

"We're all meeting at seven on the Prague Castle grounds." said Elli. "There is a great concert for tonight only. It's going to be in the square that surrounds the old church." Elli was referring to St. Vit's Cathedral where the remains of all the Czech Kings are buried.

"It's free. Want to come?"

"Sure, Elli. I'll be there," Marie replied.

"Good. Then I'm glad I found you," Elli gleamed. Then she had another thought, "Oh and that new guy, from the Registry, he's coming too. I reckon he likes you. So you need to be there." She turned and left Marie daydreaming.

Hmm, he is pretty hot, Marie thought. I'll wear that new tunic mother sent me for my birthday. Perhaps I should pay her a visit sometime?

"Oh, Marie, I almost forgot," Elli called back "I went by your apartment earlier. I found this postal note on your door. There's a package for you to pick up." She pulled the white slip of paper from her pocket and handed it to Marie.

"See you tonight. Don't be late and dress warm."

CHAPTER THIRTEEN

EUROPEAN BLOOD

It took three days for the streets at the base of the Denver office tower to get back to normal. The yellow tape, which had cordoned off the area around the main wreckage of Jorge de la Sierra's helicopter, was gone. The FAA safety investigators and the National Safety Transportation Board investigators were through with their interviews. It was not a difficult task. It was not a crime scene, and there were no mechanical failures, just a straightforward case of fatally bad judgement.

Victoria had just sat down at her desk on the fiftieth floor with a cup of black coffee when her cell phone rang.

"Victoria Kavanagh," she answered.

"Hello, Victoria. This is Doctor Singh at the Catherine Ryan Registry. How are you doing? How is Mr. Maxwell?"

"Oh, hello, Doctor," Victoria was a little startled. I'm well. Mr. Maxwell is comfortable. Have you anything for us?"

"My staff have exhausted the North American blood data banks," Doctor Singh informed her. " There are no matches in there. Our search is now turning toward Europe. The Europeans, fortunately, are very sophisticated and have very good international sharing arrangements. We have contacted the EMBT, the European Group for Blood and Bone Marrow Transplant Institute at the Institut Des Champlaine in Paris. The EGBT has the ability to contact all of the European Union G7 countries to conduct a search of data bases in their locality."

"How about Asia, the Middle East?" Victoria asked.

"Once you get beyond North America and the European continent, it gets dicey," the doctor commented. "Those bone marrow donor entities are not hooked up to each other telematically. It becomes a one by one phone call affair in those countries. Our best chance is with the Europeans right now." Doctor Singh was being very matter-of-fact, but it was not what Victoria wanted to hear.

"So there are definitely no donors to be found on this continent?" she reaffirmed.

"No. I wish I could tell you otherwise. If there is a donor in Europe, the Institut in Paris has the best resource to find them. I know the Institut Director very well — Doctor Jean Pierre Luc. I have already spoken with him. He promised me, personally, he would assign a team on this search. He has never misled me in the past. I trust him, but of course, they are a busy bunch over there."

"What if I went there myself, Doctor Singh, to see Doctor Luc?" asked Victoria.

There was a pause. Doctor Singh was pondering the question. If everyone who needed a donor showed up on the doorstep of the EGBT in Paris, that institution would be hampered in doing its job. However, something about Victoria's demeanour told him nothing bad would happen.

"Yes. I think it would help and do no harm. I'll call Doctor Luc myself and tell him you are coming. If we get some news while you are travelling, I will leave a message on your cell phone voicemail. Good luck. Please let me know how things unfold, after your visit to Paris."

"Thank you, Doctor Singh. With some good fortune, Mr. Maxwell will thank you personally some day soon."

CHAPTER FOURTEEN

DEATH IN THE BLACK FOREST

Antoine Sandel arrived at Basel Airport, on the Swiss border, in the early afternoon. He had purchased a ticket for a seat aboard a small Caravan, (a single engine commuter aircraft) to fly into Basel. The pilot dropped him off and departed immediately for the return flight to Frankfurt. Few small aircraft flew anywhere in Germany after sundown. There were only a handful of airports equipped with landing lights in Austria, Germany or Switzerland.

The only car rental service in the region could not supply a car until the morning but promised to have it delivered to his hotel first thing. The airport was 60 km from the Romantik Hotel Spieleg where he had made a reservation. He boarded the train outside the airport and disembarked at the Muensterland Station. From there it was a short five kilometre taxicab ride to the hotel.

Nestled in the lush green hills of the Black Forest, now covered with snow, the old historical two story, 42 room hotel was the place of many ghost stories. The hotel was just a few miles on the Swiss side of the German and Swiss border — the two countries separated by the Rhine River Valley.

The southern region of the Black Forest is seldom visited by tourists. Most travellers to the Black Forest region never make it that far south. They drove to the northern regions where there were lakes and taller mountain peaks. Perhaps it was also the road less travelled because of the folklore associated with Basel and more specifically Hotzenwald and the southern parts of the Black Forest. Stories of devils, sorcerers, witches, and other dark spirits who called the dense forest home, dated back to when legions of the Roman Emperor Titus governed the area. It was the Romans who named the Black Forest because of its dense carpet of trees. The folklore included sightings of elves and other light-hearted spirits who served to protect the locals who travelled through the dark forest.

Antoine checked in at the desk and confirmed that there was a personal computer available for him to use in the morning. He assumed that when he logged onto his website, the geocache coordinates would not be far from the hotel. He was tired but needed a drink to calm his nerves before going to sleep. He reasoned that he needed a good night's sleep. He was worried that something would go wrong: the GPS signal would be lost; the rental car might not show up in the morning; or he would have trouble locating the geocache. His mind was still racing when the young lady delivered a dry martini. There was only one other guest in the quaint little Bavarian restaurant.

"Where did you arrive from, sir?" asked the young woman. "We do not get many guests this time of year."

"I'm from Prague," answered Antoine. "I just arrived this afternoon."

"Are you staying with us for a while?"

"No. What's your name?" he inquired.

"Heidi."

"Heidi, I'll be leaving tomorrow or worst case, day after tomorrow. I'm not on vacation."

Heidi knew she was on thin ice asking such questions, but she was bored and the other guest was not very talkative.

"Will you be staying in the hotel tomorrow or going to visit someone?"

"I'm going for a hike, I believe, Heidi — a hike in the forest."

"In the Black Forest? Could I be so bold as to ask your name?" ventured Heidi.

"My name is Antoine, Antoine Sandel."

"Mr. Sandel, I do not mean to intrude, but I must tell you that hiking in the Black Forest at this time of year is not a good idea. Not unless you have a very experienced guide and are very well equipped. This is not a well-known area, and there are not many people in the forest to help if you have a problem."

"It's good of you to be concerned, Heidi. Don't worry. I don't believe in forest devils, if that's what is bothering you. Tell me, are there any snowmobiles for rent should I need one?"

"Ja, sir. You can arrange for one at the front desk. You may want to do that before going to bed." She knew any more warnings about the inherent dangers of the Black Forest in winter would be ignored.

"Thank you, Heidi. I may see you back here tomorrow night if I'm too late to catch the last plane back tomorrow."

"I hope so, Mr. Sandel. I hope so."

Antoine logged onto his website before he went to bed to see if the coordinates had been posted. The coordinates were not there.

The next morning, November 28, as promised, the coordinates were there. 47° 41' 08.40" N   7° 41' 48.20" E. This is where Antoine would find his wealth. He could not believe his eyes, it all seemed so surreal. So the foundation had not sent him on a wild goose chase after all. Here were the coordinates he would now load into the laptop GPS program.

"Good morning," the young man at the front desk greeted Antoine.

"Good morning. My name is Sandel. I have a car rented. Is it here yet?"

"Yes, sir. It just arrived. Just sign here. The fuel tank is full."

The morning was grey and overcast. Light snow fell as he left the hotel lobby and located the little rental car. Antoine had decided to check out of the hotel, hoping he could make the last flight of the day. He threw his small carry-on bag in the back seat and dusted snow off the front window. It was cold and the windshield was too fogged up to move until things warmed up inside. Antoine sat in the driver's seat with the motor running, taking the time to load the coordinates into his new laptop computer. The program displayed a coloured-moving map, a small circle represented the coordinates at ground zero. The map orientation was north up. The target was east through the little village and toward the forest. He decided to drive toward it and see if he could get there without the need of a snowmobile.

Leaving the village and continuing east, the snow was beginning to accumulate on the roads. Antoine's car had front-wheel drive, which was some help, but he preferred a four-wheel drive. No matter, he was getting closer and feeling better about things.

Doing his best, to head in the direction of the target, he turned onto a small road. Eventually, he came to a tree line and could see the dense forest beyond. He stopped while still in the clearing. The snow covered the road, but he could see the subtle indentations of tyre tracks disappearing into the trees.

Yes, of course, Antoine thought, someone was going before him to deposit the money at the coordinates as explained in the letter.

Everything was falling into place. Antoine continued down the road and into the darkness of the Black Forest. The snowfall grew heavier. The car became mired in snow only a mile into the densely packed trees. It was a heavy, wet snow — very large flakes. Antoine was too close now to sit in the car. He already knew there was no cell coverage, so he could not call for help anyway.

Antoine folded the laptop and tucked it under his arm. He began to walk in the deep snow. In the distance he could see that there seemed to be light interrupting the darkness of the densely packed trees. Eventually he came to a clearing — a mountain meadow in the summertime. An area about two acres large and rectangular shaped had been clear-cut from the forest. He looked at the moving map and saw he was only a hundred yards away from the coordinates. He found the spot by a tree at the edge of the clearing. Antoine had carried a soft cloth bag along with him in anticipation of filling it with cash. He used the bag to shield his eyes from the driving snow. He thought he would have to do

Geocache

some digging, but it was not necessary. There it was, marked for him by a thin six foot high plastic rod with a red flag attached to the top. There were only a few inches of snow on the container.

Interesting, he thought, it's just a piece of luggage.

He had imagined a large metal box.

Across the clearing, about a 100 yards away, and just inside the tree line, a deer bolted from the protection of the trees. The deer crossed through the clearing and back into the trees not far from Antoine. Something had startled the animal. Antoine turned and surveyed the clearing. It was too cold to dwell there much longer. He opened the case and saw a towel covering what had to be the money. The envelope he had expected to be there was indeed there, sealed and placed upon the towel. He read the words on the envelope:

'Start by opening this first'.

He pulled his gloves off so that he could rip the envelope open without tearing the contents inside. Instead of a certificate, there was a note.

'At least you have the one and one half million.'

Antoine, confused by the mixed message, reached for the towel. He grabbed it with his bare right hand, not noticing how wet it was, and lifted it from the case.

Nothing! Nothing but newspaper! How could this be? Why?

Antoine's peripheral vision was beginning to fade. His heart began to race. Breathing was becoming difficult. His legs were like rubber. He heard something behind him. He turned and fell to the snow. Looking up, he could make out the blurry outline of someone walking toward him in the distance. He felt like he had a 1,000 pound weight on his chest. The poison had penetrated his hand, travelled up his arm and reached his heart.

Errol Bader

CHAPTER FIFTEEN

PARIS ON FIRE

When the airliner carrying Victoria Kavanagh to Paris left the runway at Denver International Airport, it was already eight hours later in Paris. Another twelve hours in the air took its toll. Victoria knew she had to get some sleep or she would be worthless in the morning. It seemed like hours to clear customs and collect her luggage.

The Charles de Gaulle Airport is north-east and only a 35 minute ride from Paris. Victoria had made this trip before on White House advance trips. The prudent thing was to make reservations at the closest hotel to the airport. That was exactly what she had done, and now she was glad she had made that decision.

The Legion Hotel at the Charles de Gaulle Airport was conveniently located between the two main terminals. Victoria left her luggage with the concierge after checking in. There was no waiting for the glass-enclosed atrium elevator; it was already on the lobby floor. The trip to the 23rd floor was mercifully fast. It was now one o'clock in the morning in Paris, which made it 5pm the day before in Denver. Victoria placed a call to the hospital to check on Maxwell's status.

"I'm sorry, Ms. Kavanagh." answered the nurse. "Neither of the doctors are available this evening. This is Karin Rollins, we met when Mr. Maxwell first arrived at the hospital. I'm working the floor tonight."

"How is Mr. Maxwell, Karin?"

"No change. He's holding his own. His temperature has come down. That may be a sign that the swelling around his brain is reducing."

Geocache

Maxwell was fortunate to have this particular nurse looking after him. Karin Rollins had special training in brain injury and recovery. She had worked under the tutelage of an Indian doctor who taught alternative medicine and even hypnotism to help brain-injured patients recover their memories. Karin possessed a license to practice these non-traditional methods, although the hospital never officially recognised the methodology. On occasion, when traditional treatments were not getting the job done, Karin would quietly administer some of her own eastern methods. Doctor Levy was aware of this and seldom interfered with her unusual treatments. He had witnessed too many recoveries to question her unorthodox ways.

"We're doing our best, I promise you, Ms. Kavanagh," answered Karin.

"Thank you, Karin. I'll call back tomorrow. Thank you for your concern."

Victoria put the phone in its cradle and headed through the small hallway leading to the bathroom. She passed by the large wall mirror above the sink and stopped to survey her appearance. She was accustomed to the view. Victoria knew she was beautiful by contemporary standards. She had always taken her good looks for granted. However, this was a tired face looking back at her. It had been four days since the mid-air collision above Denver. She had been going non-stop and had not slept well. An odd thought found its way into her consciousness; it lasted only a few seconds.

How long will this face stay this beautiful? How much longer will this body be a body that a man would want? Damn, where did that come from? she thought.

Exhaustion sometimes strips away the mental fences that human beings put up to protect themselves. Victoria Kavanagh, professional as she may be, was still a woman with natural needs and wants. She had been suppressing these for too long in favour of her profession. Her body was telling her subconscious mind that her biological clock was ticking. Perhaps she was beginning

Errol Bader

to listen?

Another fifteen minutes and Victoria was in bed, dead to the world. At least she knew her boss was still alive, she knew her mission had to continue.

As luck would have it, Victoria's mission to Paris coincided with a campaign of civil disobedience across France. Young Islamic men were burning cars and generally causing havoc in large areas of Paris. Over several decades, the Muslim population in France had grown to 6 million. For a nation of 56 million, that was a significant impact on society. Mark Twain wrote; "East is East and West is West and never the Twain shall meet." The clash of cultures taking place across Europe was coming to full boil in Paris. The chief complaint of the young rioters was employment discrimination. However, the same tensions between Islamic peoples and the West that caused the Crusades, a millennia ago, were in Europe once again. Like waves of the ocean, Muslims from the Middle East had pressed toward Western Europe, and as with the tide there always came the inevitable push back from western cultures. The French may have waited too long to push back, not taking the threat seriously, perhaps too much political correctness. Now their beautiful city was burning. Not wanting to offend Muslim countries who they had trading agreements with, the French looked the other way as immigration went unchecked.

Victoria stepped out into the hotel breezeway to hail a cab. It was a chilly, clear morning in Paris. She heard a large number of sirens, some in the distance and some nearer. She was dressed in a dark blue business suit with a white blouse. The blouse had a frilly lace collar which had enough neck line showing to reveal a thin gold necklace draped high on her neck, but not so high as to be considered a choker. It was cold, so she was wearing a beige trench coat.

Victoria hailed a cab for what should have been a thirty minute, direct route to Downtown Paris. She had an appointment at 11 a.m. with Doctor Jean Pierre Luc, Director of the EGBT at rue de L' Ecole de Medicine. This was a community of medical office buildings not far from the Eiffel Tower. Victoria was aware of the riots as this was the third day of the disruption. She boarded the first cab that arrived. The driver spoke first.

"My name is Pierre." The taxi driver spoke better English than he wanted Victoria to know, he was a Parisian after all. Victoria gave the driver the address but failed to ask him if he was having a good day, a mistake in Paris most Americans make. Parisians view North Americans as condescending and an impolite bunch that are always in a hurry and could not care less about them. Cab drivers make snap judgements in Paris about Americans. If an American climbs into a Paris cab and says something, anything that indicates they appreciate the driver, things tend to go well. Pierre nodded that he understood where the address was located. He had made up his mind about Victoria. Despite being pretty, she was just another ugly American as far as he was concerned.

They were only two blocks from the hotel when the cab screeched to a halt. A Molotov cocktail landed in the road 20 yards in front of the cab. Victoria's head swiveled. She surveyed their situation and understood the threat while the driver sat motionless.

"Pierre, let's go," shouted Victoria. "Drive!"

Angry young men were emerging from side streets.

"This is no place to be. We need to move, now," Victoria shouted.

It was becoming clear that Pierre was having a panic attack. She had no choice; but to get out of the car. She reached the driver's door with the intention of pushing Pierre aside and taking his seat, but it was too late. The first of three young rioters reached Victoria and swung her around before she could get into the car. The fellow must have been very surprised when in a split second his testicles were relocated in a northern direction.

Victoria was not the typical victim of random violence. If she was going down, a lot of over confident people were going with her. As usual, she was being underestimated.

The second and then third assailant had their noses smashed. She hit them with the heel of her hand but with measured blows. She could easily have pushed their noses into their brains, killing them instantly, but she held her blows back to disable and not kill.

The fourth assailant managed to grab Victoria around her throat from behind. He was strong, and Victoria was losing the fight for air. Suddenly, strangely his grip relaxed, then loosened altogether. As she turned, an unexpected sight stunned her. A tall, well-built man was standing over the now limp body of her assailant. She looked into his eyes and saw intelligent, intense, blue eyes — the eyes of someone who has been in conflict before. A full head of wavy brown hair so dark it was almost black. Her gaze went unreturned. The man was looking beyond her.

He pushed her aside to block the swing of another onrushing attacker. Victoria watched as her defender used the forward motion of the assailant to his own advantage. He catapulted the attacker into the air and slammed him against the roof of the car. There were more assailants coming.

The man was wearing a grey sport coat. He reached his right hand behind his back and inside his coat. Pulling a 9mm Beretta from his belt, he fired three shots into the air. He pushed Victoria into the car and shoved her over. The man was reacting instinctively. She knew he was a professional — military, law enforcement, protective agency, something. The man put the cab in gear and gunned the engine. The gunshots froze the assailants. They jumped out of the way, as the car sped from the quickly, degenerating neighbourhood. Victoria looked behind her and saw many cars on fire. Another few minutes and she would have been the subject of front-page news stories.

"Hey, slow down with my cab," shouted Pierre in perfect English. "I just finished paying for this thing."

"Shut up" Victoria and her rescuer shouted in unison, at the cab driver.

"Okay, Okay," Pierre replied.

Geocache

"So do you speak English?" Victoria asked the stranger. She was collecting her wits now, taking a closer look at this fellow who just saved her life. Apart from *shut up*, he had not uttered a word since the conflict began just a few moments earlier. One thing she knew, he was strong, determined, quick-thinking; and it was not lost on her that he was ruggedly handsome.

"The Queen's English . . . you almost broke a couple of those blokes in two all by yourself," he answered in a Scottish Brogue. "What's your name?"

"Victoria Kavanagh," she reached over and shook his hand.

"Kavanagh, you could be a relative. I'm Sean Mason."

"Oh, so you're not French," Victoria said.

"Well, neither are you with an Irish name like yours," responded Sean. "That makes us even.".

"Not sure, specially with a Limey name like that," Victoria seemed briefly lost in thought. Then asked, "where did you come from?"

"From Scotland, not England. From the clan of Sinclair, can't you tell?"

"No, that's not what I meant. What were you doing in that street back there?"

"Saving your life, it seemed to me," answered Sean, "and kicking the stuffing out of those gits giving the Frenchies bother."

"Let me try this one more time. Why were you in that neighbourhood? Where did you train in the Martial Arts?"

"I'm in Paris on assignment," he answered. "I work for Interpol; you know that stands for International Criminal Police Organization."

Victoria gave him a cutting stare. "Yes, I have heard of Interpol, Mr. Mason."

Sean realised she was not just a dumb blond and became more serious.

"I'm visiting the Interpol National Central Bureau here in Paris. My office is at the General Secretariat in Lyon. Your cab happened to stop right in front of me. I watched the melee unfold, and I was expecting that fellow sitting next to you to take you out of there. But I guess the poor bloke wasn't up to the task."

"Okay, that's better." Victoria turned her piercing blue eyes away from Sean's right cheek and looked forward at the oncoming traffic.

"So," Sean decided to break the ice once more. "Do I look like I'm over the hill?"

The cool blue eyes were upon him again, this time looking him up and down. A smile twitched at the edge of Victoria's mouth.

"No. Why?

"You shouldn't call me Mister then."

"Okay, I'm sorry," she smiled. "You can call me Victoria."

"Ah, I'm honoured," he grinned. "Okay Victoria..." He paused to cherish the moment. "You can call me Inspector Mason".

Victoria's eyes flared at him once more.

"I'm just kidding; call me Sean."

"You have a weird sense of humour, Sean." she replied, then smiled. "Anyway, I suppose you saved my life. I can give you that. Oh, and this, worthless SOB, cab driver." She nodded towards Pierre. "So thank you."

"What do you mean worthless SOB cab driver?" Pierre declared defiantly.

"Shut up," Sean and Victoria answered in unison, and then laughed.

"Where were you going, Victoria? Sightseeing or just out to rough up some future suicide bombers."

"I'm on my way to see a doctor, a blood specialist. I'm running a little late. Can you drive me there?"

"You're arranging transfusions for all the men you've beaten up?"

Victoria rolled her eyes.

"All right, sure. Do you have the address?" Sean asked.

"15 Rue de L Ecole de Medicine."

"Driver, tell me how to get to that address; or I'll break both your knees, rip off your left ear, and make you sing both the Scottish and American national anthems," demanded Sean.

"Right turn next street," the cab driver answered as he looked straight ahead.

Victoria smiled to herself. She liked Sean Mason. Another one of those strange and new thoughts popped into her mind. Hmm, thank God I'm not related to this guy. That would never do. She turned to hide the smirk that had formed across her face.

They arrived at the EGBT only forty five minutes late. Victoria had to run, but hoped she would see this man again before she left Paris.

"How long are you here for?" she asked as she got out of the cab.

"Another week and you?"

"I'm not sure yet," she answered.

"Here's my card." Sean handed her his business card. "Call me on my cell phone if you get in trouble again. Come to think of it, look me up if you think I'm in trouble." He smiled.

"Hey, who pays me?" Pierre the taxi cab driver asked.

"Shut up," Victoria and Sean shouted in unison.

CHAPTER SIXTEEN

DATA BASES COMPLIMENTS OF BIG BROTHER

Victoria walked across the wide sidewalk toward the medical office building, leaving the cab behind her. She found herself turning back to watch as Sean and Pierre drove away. She was still processing the events of the past hour. Typically, when about to enter an important meeting, Victoria would mentally prepare and review what she planned to say. This would have happened in the cab on the way to the morning meeting with Doctor Luc, but the attack interrupted her routine. Victoria tried to switch gears, but images of the violent confrontation kept interrupting her train of thought. She had images of Sean Mason, the Interpol Agent, burnt into her brain as if written to a computer disk. *C'mon Victoria, focus on the task, she told herself.*

The building was a large stone and masonry structure reminiscent of the Parthenon, ten large stone pillars holding up a portico. The tops of the columns were of the Corinthian variety, flowery and decorative, as opposed to the typical and simple opposing scrolls or squared-off column tops. She noticed them and thought it to be a clue to the architect's personality. He was, in Victoria's opinion, not afraid to make a fashion statement. Most visitors would not notice such detail. However, Victoria's training had made her much more aware of her environment than the average tourist, in case of possible threats.

She climbed the stone steps to the open doorway and entered the atrium of the building, a cavernous lobby with a vast marble floor. A kiosk with a large black glass panel, sat in the centre of the lobby, listed all of the offices in the building. There it was, "European Group for Blood and Marrow Transplant Institute des Champlaine - Suite 315." With a bank of six elevators, all with copper door fronts, Victoria assumed this building was a well-populated one. The elevator doors opened on the third floor, to a lobby with a receptionist who greeted visitors for all entities situated there.

"Oui, mademoiselle, how may I assist you?" asked the receptionist, a middle-aged woman who appeared not to have missed a meal in some time.

"I have an appointment with Doctor Jean Pierre Luc of the EGBT. I'm running a little late."

"Down this corridor," she pointed to her right, "Suite 315. Mademoiselle, are you all right? Do you need a drink or anything?" Inquired the receptionist.

"Well, no, I'm fine. Why do you ask?'

"You look like, — well, like you have been in a fight, Mademoiselle."

Damn, she thought. She was in such a hurry, she had paid no attention to her appearance after the tussle in the street. No time to do anything about it, she was late.

"Oh, yes, thank you. I have had a rough morning actually, but I'm okay," Victoria responded.

She entered through the door to the EGBT suite and met with a similar look from the young girl behind the lobby desk.

"Are you, Ms. Kavanagh?" she asked Victoria.

"Yes, I am. Sorry I'm running late."

"That's okay," said the young girl. "Doctor Luc has been expecting you and was getting worried. He mentioned you might have been delayed by the problems we have been having in Paris. Are you all right? You look like you have been in a fight"

"Yes, I was in a fight but I'm okay."

"Oh, should I call the police?"

"No. A police officer was there."

The young girl opened a door for Victoria to enter. Doctor Luc was sitting in a swivel chair with his back to the door. Victoria could see smoke rising from behind the chair's back. The sweet smell of pipe tobacco filled the air. Hearing his door open, the doctor swivelled his chair toward the door as the receptionist announced Victoria's arrival.

"Mon diu, What has happened to you, mademoiselle? You look like you have been in an American football game!"

"Hello, Doctor Luc. I'm pleased to meet you," she smiled "I'm very sorry for my appearance. My taxi cab took a bad turn, and I had a first-hand experience with some of your unhappier citizens."

"My God! Denise, take Ms. Kavanagh's coat and please show her to the rest room so she can freshen up. What can we do to help? I feel terrible about this. Are you sure you are all right? Do you need any medical attention? If you do, we have facilities here in the building."

"No. It's kind of you. I'm really not hurt. Perhaps I should freshen up, though. I'll take you up on that."

Denise led Victoria to the women's room. The mirror revealed that it was obvious she was in a fight. Her frilly white collar was so torn it was not fixable. It hung from her blouse by a thread. Her hair was a mess. Her lipstick was smeared, giving her lips a strange two-tone appearance.

Lord, she thought, I look like hell.

It took a few moments to fix her face and hair. Fortunately, her Cover-Girl face had not been marred.

There was little to do but just rip off the frilly collar and throw it away.

"Doctor, thank you for your patience," Victoria said upon re-entering Doctor Luc's office. "I'm afraid I have already taken up much of your morning, and we have not even had a chance to discuss my mission,"

Doctor Luc, a man in his late sixties, was a product of a Vietnamese father and a French mother. His father was a supporter of the French in South Vietnam during the time that France maintained troops in the embattled country. When the French pulled out of Vietnam, Doctor Luc's father left the country and emigrated to Paris to practice medicine. His father met and

Geocache

married his mother in the south of France. Doctor Luc was not a Parisian by birth. He was born in the southern rural part of France. He followed in his father's footsteps and became a specialist in the field of bone cancer.

Doctor Luc was a hard man to meet. When he granted appointments, they seldom lasted more than fifteen minutes. Usually these meetings were the result of special searches for blood marrow matches, delegated to him for being to difficult to obtain by others. This time, however, was different. He was genuinely upset at the treatment Victoria had received earlier in the day. He wanted to hear details of what had happened. Doctor Luc was a proud Frenchman and felt in someway responsible for the outrageous treatment she had received. He apologised repeatedly for the incident.

"Have you had lunch yet, Ms. Kavanagh?" Doctor Luc enquired. "Let me take you across the street and buy you lunch; it is the least I can do. We can talk about your mission then."

"Well, no actually I haven't eaten today. Thank you. That would be nice."

A short walk and Doctor Luc and Victoria were in the Saint Germain des Pres section of Paris. The doctor was a regular for lunch at the restaurant Brasserie Left. The two-story restaurant was a favourite hangout for literary figures, editors, authors, and an occasional movie star. Diners of lesser fame were escorted to a table on the second floor. However, frequent guests, like Doctor Luc, received a table on the elegant first floor dining room.

"This is a beautiful room," Victoria observed. "Look at those tile murals on the walls. They're exquisite."

"Yes. I come here often, not necessarily for the food, although it's quite good," Doctor Luc answered. "I often meet friends here for lunch. It's convenient and relaxing. My day can be stressful. People's lives are at stake or they would not be using our resources."

A garçon de café approached their table and took their order. Victoria chose the soupe du jour to start with, followed by an omelette aux armillaire dorées et arpins. Doctor Luc ordered risotto aux crevettes et au pamplemousse for starter and filet de bar rayé cuit au sel, laitrue rôtie au lard et jeunes carottes for his main course.

"Que voudriez-vous boire ? S'il vous plaît." asked the waiter.

"Sparkly Water, Merci," replied Victoria.

"Coffee," said Doctor Luc.

Once the garçon de café was out of ear-shot, Doctor Luc continued.

"Ms. Kavanagh, I have been in contact with Doctor Singh at the University of Massachusetts. Doctor Singh forwarded the test results for your Mr. Maxwell. His blood type and cell structure are extremely rare. I have to say that finding someone with his criterion will be difficult, if not impossible. The probabilities of there being perhaps ten people on the globe that are a match are good. However, for those people to be found in any of our ninety data bases would come as a surprise."

"I know, Doctor. I know what the probabilities are, but we have an obligation to do everything we can. Can you help?"

"We have already run a program on our own data bank for France; nothing surfaced," answered Doctor Luc. "Please understand the search process requires drilling down into the data. It's not like typing in the parameters and printing a report. It takes some time and effort to do a thorough search of a data bank. We will revisit our own data several times before I'm satisfied that there is no match here in France. The best chance of success, however, is to query all of the European donor data banks. There are over ninety across Europe. That is where we need to go, out to the other donor organisations,"

Victoria had been wondering how helpful Doctor Luc would be. The events of the day had caused the director to take a special interest in her mission. He wanted to help mitigate the damage done to France's image. This was important to him, he possessed a great deal of national pride. She was feeling good about how the meeting was going.

Geocache

Not too soon, the garçon de café came over to their table with Victoria's soup-of-the-day and Doctor Luc's shrimp and grapefruit risotto.

Her mind soon came back to her mission, as the waiter placed their drinks alongside their starter dishes.

"Merci," smiled Victoria to the waiter. When he began to walk away, she turned her attention to her dinner companion once more. "I would guess that the larger databases in the western European countries would be the best place to start?"

"Most lay people would think that, but it could not be further from the truth.

Countries that have had socialised medicine for longer periods of time have bigger databases. Even more surprising is that countries who are either communist or are from the former Soviet Block nations have the largest databases of all."

"That is a surprise. Why is that?" asked Victoria.

"Apart from the negative aspects of central state control, communist nations can collect and store information about their citizens that western democracies cannot, at least not without their permission. Central control is what communism is all about. Communists are always eager to collect information about people without their permission or even knowledge. Knowledge is power. The communists provided free health care when they were running things. The results of blood tests performed on patients while receiving medical care became the property of the state. The patients themselves may as well have been property of the state. Therefore, large collections of information exist on European Union citizens who are not aware of this fact. This is particularly true of Russia and its former satellites like Poland and the Czech Republic."

"So there is data on people who did not volunteer it?" asked Victoria.

"Yes, and in most cases the former patients are unaware of the existence of that data. This issue is becoming more and more controversial among the former communist block countries. As time goes on, privacy issues are becoming more important in these new democracies Some former communist countries are further along in debating this topic than others. The data exists, but some donor banks in these countries refuse to let us mine into these banks of data if the information was originally collected without the knowledge of the patient. Some will allow it in the interest of saving lives. How do you say — it's a mixed bag. I think that at some point this information will be lost to us altogether, lost to either privacy protection legislation or death," answered Doctor Luc.

"Funny," she said, "I never thought I would have a mission that was helped by the Big Brother mentality of communism."

"Well, Ms. Kavanagh, in the end that little known vestige of communism may turn out to be very helpful in your mission to save Mr. Maxwell." Doctor Luc spotted the waiter just as he finished his risotto.

"Ah, garçon, may we have our main course?" Then remembered he was speaking in English. "Pouvons-nous avoir notre plat principal? S'il vous plaît."

CHAPTER SEVENTEEN

THE AUSTRIAN DONOR

Fifty miles south of Vienna and the landscape starts a gradual rise toward the Austrian Alps. This is where the city of Wiener Neustadt is located. More Allied bombs fell on Wiener Neustadt than on any other Austrian city in WWII, more even than Vienna — the cities larger namesake to the north. More Messerschmitt ME 109 fighter aircraft were built there than in any other Axis factory. The German's three Wiener Neustadt Flugzeugwerke factories drew Allied bombers to the beautiful Austrian city. Little evidence of the violent bombings remains there now, with the exception of "The Bomb Tree."

German and Austrian towns are built around quaint little town squares. At the centre of Wiener Neustadt's town square is a long dead tree. The citizens of Wiener Neustadt drove fifty thousand nails into the tree: one nail for every bomb that fell on the city. The tree serves as a reminder of the many citizens who were lost to the madness of the Third Reich and the ferocity of the bombings.

It has been said that this city was the cruelest toward Jews before and during the war. The passage of time can produce ironic change in places and people. Few people in Europe, or for that matter in Weiner Neustadt itself, knew of a small church in the town with a quiet but profound mission. The church searched across Europe for survivors of the holocaust. When the church located a survivor, even if in the farthest reaches of Russia, that person is invited to the church in Wiener Neustadt, all expenses paid. En masse the church members offered their deepest regrets for the torture of millions of Jews at the hands of the Nazis. In its own way, the little church served as a proxy for the people of Austria in offering an apology to these ageing people.

Finding survivors of the holocaust had become more difficult than in the past as almost all have died. Peter Leisel had been contracted by the church to find the few remaining survivors. Leisel had a reputation in the city for being the best computer technician around. He developed a speciality for internet website creation and computer database research. He looked at finding the old Jews as nothing more than a business enterprise. Leisel had located nine survivors over a three months search, for which the church was grateful, but he did not share the same passion for the mission as the parishioners possessed. He was busy word-processing at his downtown office when the post man knocked at his office door.

"Hallo, Peter. How are you?"

"Hallo, Frederic. I'm well. What brings you to my office?

"I have a package addressed to your home, but I had other deliveries closer to here and thought I might catch you."

Peter signed the receipt and accepted the package, which was wrapped in plain brown paper. It was heavy and he was intrigued by the unexpected delivery. He could not remember ordering any computer — related equipment. As soon as the door closed and Frederic had departed, he sat down to remove the wrapping paper from the box. A laptop computer was inside with a note taped to the cover:

Username—*GEO* Password—*CACHE*.

Peter booted up the laptop and read the letter from the Jack and Elizabeth Gielgood Foundation. There were the family crests and the $10,000 certified check. Peter thoughts began to gyrate. *Why me? Why would someone select me to receive a check for $10,000, let alone one for $1,500,000 now and another $1,500,000 later,* he wondered. *Picked randomly?*

"No, there must be something else going on here," he whispered to himself — his first instinct was suspicion.

He immediately went internet surfing as the package sender knew he might. The search engine found the Jack and Elizabeth Gielgood Foundation website in a few seconds, where he read an

Geocache

announcement that the site was under construction. There was also an announcement of Jack Gielgood passing and the promised return of the website in February.

Hmm, that's what usually happens when a webmaster is told he has to prepare a massive change to a website, Peter thought to himself. A lazy webmaster would just shut the website down rather than make piecemeal changes while keeping the site supported and running.

"It's not the way to do it. You are a lazy SOB aren't you," Peter said out loud.

Sometimes ignorance is bliss. Leisel knew too much about website creation and support. The superiority complex he sometimes exhibited was coming home to roost. Yes, of course this was for real. This is the way other less competent webmasters would handle the circumstance.

Besides, he thought, *I'm not kidnap material. I'm not wealthy or well known. $1,500,000! No, $3,000,000 after I deliver the certificate. Maybe there will be even more money if this becomes a reality television show. No more hunting for old Jews.* Leisel's greed baited him, the hook was set.

Leisel's instructions were to fly to Innsbruck, Austria, the host of the Winter Olympic Games in 1964. He was well familiar with Innsbruck, it was one of his favourite places to visit. The mountain valley city of 250,000 became the host for the Olympics again in 1976, by default, when the voters of Denver refused to support bond issues needed to fund the games. Now Peter Leisel was being summoned to the wintry city by an irresistible enticement. He would rent a hotel room and log onto *www.petersgeocachesite.com* for the coordinates to find his personal fortune. From there he would make his way to ground zero and his destiny. He located his personal website, just where the letter indicated it would be, eager to believe everything he had read — and so he would.

Dress warm. It would be cold in Tyrol this time of year, the letter cautioned.

Errol Bader

How nice. The writer was concerned for his health. I'm looking forward to meeting this fellow, Peter thought.

Leisel would indeed meet the person who sent the package, this was a certainty. However, the meeting would not be at a publicity event. They would meet at ground zero. Being a pilot familiar with mountain flying, he placed a call to the local flying club.

"Diamond Flying Club, can I help you," answered the young man. "Yes, this is Peter Leisel. How are things going today? Anybody flying in this scud?" In November it was common to have low overcast clouds in the region.

"No. It's a slow day, seven hundred foot ceiling," answered the dispatcher. "It will be better tomorrow."

"I need to reserve a Diamond Twin Star for December 1st, returning on the 2nd, any availability?" Leisel asked.

The club had seven such planes, all recently built in the same factory as the WWII German ME109 fighter planes. The Diamond Twinstars, the most modern all-composite twin engine aircraft made in the world, were new high-tech diesel engine powered aircraft replacements of the older metal airplanes of the 1950s still being manufactured in the states. Leisel knew the more modern glider-like craft would handle the high altitude of the Innsbruck Airport better than the older shorter winged metal aircraft."You're in luck," answered the dispatcher. "OE72JP is open — just coming out of its annual inspection, and it will be ready to go back on line at the end of the month."

"Okay. Write me in for December 1st and 2nd. If the weather goes down while I'm up at Innsbruck, it may stretch it to December 3rd."

"Okay, Peter. It's your plane from the 1st to the 3rd."

"Thank you, all the best."

Peter hung up and smiled to himself. He would reserve a car and be good to go.

CHAPTER EIGHTEEN

GERMANY'S COLUMBO

Not far, across the Swiss boarder, from the city of Basel, in the German municipal of Hägelberg, the Hotel Spieleg's restaurant had finally closed after breakfast. Heidi had two hours before the lunchtime opening, so made her way to the front desk in the hotel lobby to continue her duties as a receptionist. The mid-morning light was quite strong, coming through the main door windows. Even so, the heavy snow fall, the previous night, would keep most people inside.

The phone rang. Subconsciously she reacted — "Hotel Spieleg, Heidi speaking."

"Good morning, Fräulein Heidi. This is Adolph from the car rental. How are you this morning?"

"Hallo, Adolph," Heidi replied. "I'm good. The snowstorm was bad last night but we have the lobby fire blazing, so it's comfortable here. How can I help?"

"I was wondering if I could pick up Mr. Sandel's hired car later?" asked Adolph. "It's just a bit too cold to come out at the moment."

"Didn't he return the car the day before yesterday?"

"No, Heidi," Adolph's voice seemed agitated, "I assumed the car was with you?"

Heidi felt a pang in her heart, a sense of dread came over her.

"I'm worried Adolph. Mr. Sandel planned to walk in the forest. He didn't come back to the hotel. I warned him that it could be dangerous. I think we should call the police."

"All right. I'll call Marcus Webber, he's a friend," Adolph replied.

Marcus Webber was a competent policeman who had been

trained in Stuttgart. He could have been working in a large metropolitan police department, but preferred the small municipal of Hägelberg. This is where he grew up, and his wife and two children had a good life. His law enforcement training was comprehensive but seldom needed in this quiet place. He worked alone and depended on volunteers when necessary. The same men and women who volunteered to search for the occasional lost tourist also volunteered for the fire department. He pondered over the call from Adolph and the one he had made to Heidi at the Hotel Spieleg. Antoine Sandel had come to the region to go for a hike and then was to have returned to Frankfurt. He had hired a car and a snowmobile, and, though warned about the dangers of being alone in the forest at this time of year, had gone on with his foolish endeavour.

Something was wrong. Visitors to the region at this time of year were usually visiting relatives. A few salesmen came through Hägelberg from time to time, but never did they go walking in the forest alone, especially in the middle of a snowstorm. Why come to such a remote region of the Black Forest for only one night?

Marcus called police departments in nearby towns on both sides of the German border with Switzerland. He also called area hospitals with no result. It was time to call out the volunteers and start a search. A dozen men and women fanned out in groups of two, searching the region around Hägelberg. They walked through the snow for two days. The killer had drawn Antoine so deep into the forest that it would be a long time before his remains would be found, if ever.

Marcus walked through the Hotel Spiegel's lobby and into the restaurant looking for Heidi. He waited until she finished serving a guest.

"Hallo, Marcus. Any news about Mr. Sandel?" Heidi inquired.

"No, I'm afraid not, Heidi. Would it be possible to look at the hotel guest register?" he asked.

Geocache

"Ja, sure. Come with me."

They walked to the lobby desk and she opened the register. There was little to look at, only Antoine Sandel's signature and Prague listed as his address.

"Heidi, think about your conversation with Mr. Sandel again. Is there anything you missed telling me about him." Marcus was searching for a clue, any clue, and Heidi was his only link to the mysterious visitor.

"Oh, ja ! There was something. He asked if the hotel had a computer that he could use the following day. I showed him where the computer room is, and he logged onto it the morning he checked out," answered the young girl.

"Show me the computer please, Heidi," Marcus asked in a respectful, but urgent tone.

They entered a small office off of the lobby. The computer had to be booted up as it was seldom used. In this out- of- the-way place, there were not many computers with internet access. The connection was a dial-up, and so the computer was slow in displaying its home page. Heidi sat at the computer and followed his instructions.

"Okay Heidi. Please open the address bar history. That will display the websites recently visited by the computer," directed Marcus.

There it was — the clue Marcus had been looking for. The last six websites visited were listed. It was not hard to pick out the one Antoine had visited. Its address was *www.antionesgeocachesite.com*. It had been visited twice.

"Open up that website, Heidi, please."

As Heidi's hands moved toward the computer keyboard another set of hands reached for another computer keyboard. Sandel's killer was logging onto the same website, his goal — to delete the coordinates for Sandel's geocache site. The killer watched the website page slowly build on the screen. Finally, he reached for the delete key. One final keystroke would eliminate the potential for anyone finding Sandel's body unless by a stroke of luck.

The Hotel Spieleg's computer was building the same website page. A split second before Sandel's killer could accomplish his task, the web page containing the latitude and longitude of Sandel's geocache site loaded into the cache memory of the hotel's computer. It could no longer be erased. Latitude: 47°41' 08.40" N — Longitude: 7° 41' 48.20" E. Heidi's last keystroke was lucky. In the blink of an eye, Marcus Webber won a race he did not know he was in. He wrote the coordinates down on a Post-It note. In another second it would have been too late. Future visits to the website would have yielded nothing but blank spaces for the Latitude and Longitude of the cache site.

"Thank you, Heidi; you've been most helpful."

Marcus left the hotel and returned to his office to call Adolph at the car rental office. It was late in the day, but Adolph was still at his desk.

"Adolph. You know those new portable GPS units that you have for the rental cars? Can I borrow one?"

"Ja, of course, come by," Adolph suggested. "I will charge one up. Why do you need a GPS unit, Marcus?"

"I'm going for a snowmobile ride in the Black Forest, Adolph. I have a specific place to find." *Hopefully, I will find nothing when I get there,* Marcus thought to himself.

CHAPTER NINETEEN

THE BODY AT GROUND ZERO

Marcus attached a stretcher sled to the back of his snowmobile. He knew that if he found Sandel at the coordinates, he would not be alive. No one could survive in the forest for four days in a winter storm. The sun was shining; the storm had finally broken and there were only a few cumulus clouds scattered across the German sky. Nevertheless, it was still cold. Marcus followed the GPS signal just as Antoine had done. He came to the tree line and saw the snow — covered road leading into the dense forest. It was not long before Marcus came upon the rental car now covered in snow up to the wheel hubs. Finding no one inside, he decided to continue in the direction the car had been heading. He was driving toward the coordinates, when he came to the clearing Antoine had discovered before him. The forest was eerily quiet, the only sound — snow melting off the tree limbs and falling to the forest floor around Marcus.

The handheld GPS unit guided him to the edge of the tree line. The snowstorm had deposited a foot of drifting snow. At ground zero Marcus turned in a three hundred sixty degree circle looking for any sign of Antoine. Then his foot hit something beneath the snow.

Marcus kept thinking about the bizarre circumstances surrounding the death of Antoine Sandel. There were no marks on Sandel's body, no obvious signs of a struggle. The man had travelled from Prague for a day trip. He had logged onto a website to discover a set of coordinates leading to a place labelled, "*Antoinesgeocachesite*". It was exactly at this site that his body was found. Marcus was certain that the victim had been compelled in some way to find this place in a driving snowstorm.

What could be so important to Sandel to cause him to walk deep into the forest in the dead of winter by himself? It was so bothersome to Marcus he decided that an autopsy should be performed. Someone or something had lured Sandel to his death. A stroke of luck had led Marcus to ground zero, but those geocache coordinates had been erased by someone other than Sandel. This was not suicide.

Marcus needed help in discovering more details about Antoine Sandel. Interpol was his next phone call. He had a friend he had met in Stuttgart when he was in training, an Interpol agent from Scotland assigned to the Interpol General Secretariat in Lyon France. Perhaps Sean Mason should know about this, and perhaps he could help Marcus discover more about Antoine Sandel.

CHAPTER TWENTY

INTERPOL CODE PURPLE

The city of Lyon, is located in east central France and dates to 43 BC. Lyon started as a Roman colony. The hills overlooking the city provided an ideal site for a fortress. In time Lyon became the hub of the Roman road system connecting northern and southern France. Midway between Paris and Marseille, the city is formed by the juncture of two winding rivers. The Rivers Rhone and Saône flow on a path from south-west to north-east, creating a peninsula in between the two rivers. Both rivers are navigable, so Lyon became the centre of commerce in France. Claudius Caesar as well as Caracalla Caesar were both born in Lyon. During the Nazi occupation of France, the Germans used Lyon as a centre of control for the occupied country. The French are proud of the resistance that the citizens of Lyon put forth during the occupation. Lyon has a resistance museum memorialising the heroic history of the French resistance during those difficult times. In 1989, Lyon became the headquarters for Interpol.

The Rhone River is on the right side of the peninsula as one travels north. East of the Rhone and its peninsula is where the main concentration of the Lyon populace reside. Part-Dieu is the urban centre and the location of: the city's rail station; Lyon Part-Dieu; and Credit Lyonnais Tower, the only office tower in Central France. To the north of Part-Dieu and along the river is the wealthy Sixth Arrondissement District, and one of Europe's most beautiful parks, the Parc de la tete d'or. The park is a large triangular oasis of trees and grass bordered on the north by the Rhone and a large lake lay parallel to the river. Where the southern tip of the park triangle meets the Rhone, stands a large square glass-encased modern office building.

Errol Bader

If it were possible to view all communiqués regarding international crime as lines running across the earth, most would intersect this building. This is the home of Interpol. The building houses the General Secretariat of Interpol and the office of Sean Mason. Mason is a key official of the Command and Coordination Centre. The Centre operated twenty-four hours a day, seven days a week. It is the job of the CCC to provide law enforcement officials around the globe with emergency and operational support for the 184 member countries of Interpol.

Inspector Mason sat at the heart of the organisation's intelligence depository. The serenity of the park spreading out in front of the large building lay in stark contrast to the violent subject matter flowing into Interpol's computers. The data banks contained information about terrorists, cross-border criminal activities, illegal drug production, smuggling, weapons dealing, human trafficking, art theft, and crimes that are characterised by unusual modus operandi.

The crime-fighting organization was the world's second largest international organisation behind the United Nations and had survived numerous threats to its existence. Originally located at Vienna, when the United States refused to share intelligence with the organisation in the years immediately preceding World War Two. The release of intelligence regarding individuals in pre-war Europe subjected Interpol to charges of political crimes by the Nazis, who then took control of the fledgling organisation and moved it to Berlin. Interpol was initially dismantled after the war by the Allies, for being used by the Gestapo as a tool for malicious activities. However, out of necessity, the organisation was reformed with a new constitution, forbidding it from being used for political, religious, racial, or military matters.

Similar fears remained today because of Interpol exchanged intelligence with Iran and Syria. Regardless, the flow of information into Interpol from its members, including the United States, multiplied. Ease of international travel and lightening fast communication had shrunk the world and expanded the horizons

Geocache

of international criminals. If not for Interpol's sophistication and growing international police co-operation, local police forces would be outgunned at every turn.

All of Interpol's 184 member nations had National Central Bureaus, which received coded notices around the clock from the Lyon facility. These notices are colour-coded. Black for searches to identify corpses, red for wanted individuals sought for extradition, blue for individuals sought as witnesses in criminal cases, green for persons of interest in criminal cases, grey for organised-crime intelligence, and purple to notify police of murders which involve unusual modus operandi.

Sean Mason just sat down at his desk with a cup of black coffee when his phone rang.

"Good morning. Inspector Mason," Sean answered, "You stab 'em, we slab 'em."

"Sean, they put you in the morgue, my friend?" said Marcus Webber.

"Hey, Marcus! How are you? How's the family? Everything covered in white in Hägelberg?" asked Sean.

"Yes, lots of snow here this time of year, Sean, but right now the colour that interests me is purple."

"Purple? Why purple? Your wife beating the hell out of you again, Marcus?"

"No, Scotty, no bruises. She uses a rubber hose. The kind of purple I'm referring to is the colour that Interpol uses to code murders with an unusual modus operandi. I have one of those I'm investigating here."

"A murder in Hägelberg, Germany? You're joking, Marcus. There aren't enough people in Hägelberg to generate a murder."

"I think the victim and the murderer were both imports, Sean. This appears to be an international crime, and it has a bizarre twist that I'm having trouble with."

"What have you got," asked Sean.

"A man by the name of Sandel, Antoine Sandel, travelled from Praha (Eastern European for Prague), to Hägelberg, via

Basel, on the 26th of November. He checked into our local hotel and told an employee that he was only staying one night. He said he planned to return to Praha the next day, but two days later we found him frozen solid in a remote spot in the Black Forest."

"Cause of death?" inquired Sean.

"Poison, but not just any poison. I sent his body to the morgue at Saint Louis, in the French quarter of Basel to have an autopsy done. They found Aconite in his blood."

"That's a new one on me, Marcus. Is it metallic-based?"

"No plant-based. I've been researching this poison. It's been around a long time. The Greeks used it. Its fast acting and with the right dosage, always fatal. The stuff is so toxic that if you get a drop of it on your skin, you may last two minutes before it shuts down your heart. It has the same effect whether ingested or absorbed through the skin. It comes from a simple garden plant by the name of Monkshood. Its leaves and roots can be ground into a white powder, add alcohol and there you have it. One tenth of a grain will kill any living thing it's put in contact with. The poison targets the cardiovascular system.

"There was evidence that the poison entered his system through his right hand. I logged into your data banks and searched for crimes under the purple code and associated with Aconite poisoning.

"The KGB, Secret Service, and Mossad all had murders or attempted assassinations with Aconite as a feature of the modus operandi. It appears to be a favourite of contractors if they have to travel by commercial airliner. It's a powder that doesn't trigger metal detectors and doesn't take up a lot of room in baggage. A few grams of this stuff in a baby-powder bottle and airline security is defeated. The only challenge for the killer is to find a way to get the victim close enough to get his skin exposed to the poison."

"Well, okay," replied Sean. "So this fellow was poisoned to death. While the poison isn't your everyday rat poison, Marcus, it still isn't so unusual for someone to die this way. So why do you

Geocache

consider this to be a code-purple murder?"

"Actually, it's not just the type of poison that makes this murder unique, Sean. It's the strange way he was lured to his death."

"Ahh, Marcus," Sean interrupted. "You said he was found in a remote forest. How was the body found?"

"Well, that's just it Sean; this fellow Sandel logged onto the internet on our hotel computer and surfed to a website named *www.antionesgeocachesite.com*. The website had only one thing displayed on it, the exact latitude and longitude to his body."

"Sounds like he committed suicide and wanted his body found," offered Sean.

"No, this was no suicide, Sean. There were no signs of poison anywhere near the body. Also, after I found the coordinates on the website, someone removed them just as I was copying them down on paper. Whoever it was, missed deleting the evidence by a finger stroke. If you log onto that website now, you won't see them anymore."

"C'mon, Marcus. You been reading those Black Forest ghost stories at night? Are you saying that someone convinced this guy to chase those coordinates into the Black Forest in a winter blizzard and then deleted the coordinates?"

"Yes, that's exactly what I'm saying, Sean," stated Marcus "I don't know what the motive was, but this fellow was determined to find that spot regardless of the weather. There was a driving snowstorm at the time, but he still went anyway. If that isn't a novel way to murder someone, I don't know what is. There was a guarantee that there would be no witnesses to the killing. If I hadn't gotten lucky, we probably would not have found the body and known it was a murder. By spring, if found, we would never have suspected anything other than an unfortunate tourist lost in a snowstorm."

"I see what you mean, Marcus. Yes, we'll come onboard. I'll disseminate this one on our new I-24/7 com system. It's as fast as satellite communication. You'll see it on your computer yourself.

It's a cross-jurisdictional crime if he came from the Czech Republic into Germany via Switzerland. By the way, Marcus, what is a geocache site anyway?"

"It's a game of hide and seek," answered Marcus. "My kids play. They go out in the neighbourhood and hide some object in a waterproof container. Then they log onto a website they and their friends created and leave clues where the items are. Their friends do the same thing; only I'm about to put an end to their game."

"Why? It sounds like they're having fun," Sean replied.

"Ja, they are, too much. I went with them last time. They found a marijuana joint,while I was standing there watching. This is all I need; the little smugglers found a way to hide and trade their contraband. There goes my neighbourhood."

"Sounds like you're cloning yourself, Marcus," quipped Sean.

"I'm going to contact the Praha police and let them know about our dead man. We need to conduct a dual investigation. I'll copy you on the report that I send them. Sean, let me know if you find any similar MO's in the files over there. Keep up your strange sense of humour. Auf wiedersehen my Scottish friend"

"I'll get back to you if I find anything, Marcus. Ciao."

CHAPTER TWENTY ONE

THE PRAGUE CONNECTION

Victoria heard a knock.

"Room service," the hotel's maid announced through the door.

"Coming. Just a second," answered Victoria. It was early, and she needed coffee and a good breakfast. Victoria had rolled out of bed and put a hotel bathrobe over her lithe body. She opened the door.

"Good morning, mademoiselle," announced the young woman in halting English, a pretty Eurasian with an easy smile, as she pushed the cart into the parlour-like sitting room."It is a beautiful day in Paris, no?"

Victoria opened the sheer, white curtains, to reveal Paris at sunrise. The tungsten lights of the city were succumbing to the morning sky.

"Yes," answered Victoria, "you live in a beautiful place."

"Thank you," replied the maid as she departed the room. "Is there anything else I can get for you, mademoiselle?".

"No, thank's. I'll leave the cart outside in the hall later," Victoria smiled and closed the door. *Six in the morning here,* she thought, *10pm in Denver.* Victoria dialled the direct line to the nurse's station on Alexander's floor at the University of Colorado Hospital in Denver.

"Hello. nurse's desk, Karin speaking."

"Hello, Karin. This is Victoria Kavanagh"

"Oh, yes, Ms. Kavanagh. Are you still in Paris?"

"Yes, I'm calling to check on Mr. Maxwell. How is he?"

"Well, Doctor Lomello is here at the desk. Would you like to speak with him?"

"Yes, please," answered Victoria rubbing the sleep from her eyes.

A male voice came on the phone."Ms. Kavanagh, how are you? How's the search going?"

"Well, Doctor Lomello. How is Mr. Maxwell?"

"He is responding to light directed into his eyes and is showing some signs of feeling in his hands and feet, which is good. Presuming we locate a donor soon, we still need him in better condition. Right now we'd be unable to perform the bone marrow procedure. "

"Keep working on him, Doctor," answered Victoria shaking her head. "I'm still in Paris. Nothing yet on a donor though".

"Keep the search going and call as soon as you have some good news," Lomello tried to sound positive, then remembered something. "Ms. Kavanagh, there is one thing you could do for us, if you would?"

"What's that, Doctor?"

"Well, we're really busy on this floor. We only give this number out to close relatives or individuals such as yourself. Our floor nurse has had to answer numerous calls every day from several of Mr. Maxwell's friends."

"Doctor, we haven't given out your phone number to anyone."

"Well, the calls have been coming from Russia, Japan, Mexico, and France, I think. Also a fellow by the name of Benson calls daily. They all seem able to cut through our screening procedures without much trouble. If you know these fellows, do you think you could ask them to call every other day and not daily?"

"Okay. I'll see what I can do, but no promises. These folks don't follow convention very well. I'll call again tomorrow."

Victoria placed the phone on its cradle triggering a blinking message light. She listened to the message:

"Ms. Kavanagh, this is Doctor Luc. I have some information for you. I must say unexpected information. I have some time at two this afternoon; please let my assistant know if you can come by. All the best."

Unexpected information — what could that mean? Maybe Doctor Luc had some success, she thought.

Victoria's breakfast looked cold but though the hunger pangs were strong, there was a greater urgency to relieve her bladder. She danced into the bathroom to do her business then flushed the loo, washed her hands and dried them intent on returning to her meal, but as she passed the mirror she saw her reflection and saw something, something she had not seen before. Yet she could not quite discern what. She was analysing the beautiful face in the mirror as though observing someone else. She realised it was not so much the face she was looking at but the eyes, the dark pool leading to the soul. Then a thought deep within clawed its way into her consciousness. *What's that Interpol fellow doing right now? Is he still in Paris?*

The Scotsman was not intimidated by her. He appeared overconfident and foolishly fearless but she sensed something different, and was intrigued.

"Oh, I need to stop that," Victoria whispered to herself.

She chastised her own absurdity. Romance was deadly in their business and Sean had no other good reason to call. It was time to suppress her girlish fantasies.

I'll never see him again, she reminded herself. Besides, his humour sucks. I need to focus.

• • •

It was lunchtime. Victoria sat, in a large leather chair, in the lobby reading the "*America Today*" newspaper when the concierge approached.

" Mademoiselle, your taxi has arrived."

Victoria thanked him, left the paper on a small table and made her way through the main double doors. At the curbside, the hotel doorman opened the rear door for her and tilted his peak cap. She nodded and gracefully glided into the back-seat.

"Bonjour, mademoiselle. Où allez-vous aujourd'hui ?" The

Errol Bader

driver asked.

"Pierre, is that you up there?" Victoria asked.

Pierre turned to see what passenger would know his name.

"Mon Dieu! Not you again! My heart cannot take another trip with you, mademoiselle. I had hoped you would be gone from Paris by now. Look, look at this!" He pointed to his temples with both hands. "My hair is white overnight from your adventures. How much can I pay you to find another cab?"

"Tell you what, Pierre, why don't you get in the back seat and let me drive. That way maybe we'll get there in one piece."

To her surprise, Pierre got out of the cab, circled to the other side, and took a seat in the back with his arms folded and looking straight ahead.

"You think you are so smart, mademoiselle — the keys are in the ignition," replied Pierre.

The doorman looked puzzled watching the two exchange places. His mouth gaped as Victoria gunned the engine pulling away from the curb, with Pierre in the back.

She knew the way and today the route was peaceful. Thirty minutes later, they were in front of the Institut.

"I hope you are not expecting a tip, mademoiselle," Pierre announced from the rear seat.

"I hope you don't expect payment for the trip, Pierre. I did all the work. Have a nice day."

Victoria left the Frenchman sitting in the back of his own cab.

"Wait! You did not pay me for the last cab fare!" Pierre cried out as Victoria disappeared up the stairs and into the building.

Doctor Luc happened to be walking by the elevator as the door opened and Victoria stepped into the lobby.

"Bonjour. Welcome back, Ms. Kavanagh. Can we get you anything? Coffee? Tea?"

"I'm fine, thanks."

"Come into my office then. How was the cab ride today? I hope uneventful."

"Yes. I was in safe hands."

Geocache

"Good. Now, Ms. Kavanagh, since you last visited, my team has searched Europe hoping to find at least one potential donor. Even one would have been difficult to find."

"You found a donor for Mr. Maxwell?" Victoria asked with excitement in her voice.

"No . . . we found three," answered Doctor Luc.

"Three! But I thought —".

Doctor Luc interrupted Victoria by raising his right hand.

"Ms. Kavanagh, I have no explanation for this. It is totally unexpected and unlikely. It is wonderful news, but puzzling. This is not what we thought the results would be, but there is more."

"More?" Victoria was surprised. "All three potential donors are men whose last known addresses are within a five-hour drive of each other. Two are from Prague; the third is currently living in a small city in Austria called Wiener Neustadt, which is near Vienna. If you were to ask the odds of this happening, I would have said too long to calculate. Frankly, I am astounded. Your Mr. Maxwell is fortunate to have so many donors so close together. This is better than I could have hoped for."

"I can't thank you enough, Doctor Luc. How did you discover them?"

"All three were found in the Czech Bone Marrow/Cord Blood Registry in Prague. Just astounding." Doctor Luc leant back in his office chair, smoking his pipe, and just repeating the word astounding to himself. Then he sat forward and grabbed a sheet of paper from his desk.

"Here, Ms. Kavanagh, take this. It's a printout listing their names and last known addresses."

Victoria took the paper and scanned the names:

Antoine Sandel – Prague

Peter Leisel - Wiener Neustadt

Dieter Manheim - Prague

"I suggest you start the search for these men in Prague. Perhaps the people at the Czech Bone Marrow/Cord Blood Registry can help? Maybe they have an explanation for these rare donors in their database."

Victoria turned to leave after shaking the doctor's hand and thanking him again for all his help.

"Ms. Kavanagh —" Doctor Luc had something on his mind. "Never mind. Good luck. Please let me know how it turns out."

Victoria noted the furrows in Doctor Luc's brow deepen. *He knew something was missing,* she thought. It was odd for all of these rare donors to reside in one single region in Europe and all roughly the same age. But she put these thoughts to the back of her mind, thankful to have this lead. Perhaps his counterparts in Prague could explain it.

"Well," Doctor Luc's smile had reappeared, "I am expecting a gentleman to arrive shortly for a meeting. He may be waiting for me, so I must excuse myself. All the best, Ms. Kavanagh, Au revoir."

CHAPTER TWENTY TWO

FLYING THE DANUBE

Peter Leisel was a pilot in the best Austrian tradition, learning to fly sail-planes before he transitioned to powered flight. He had exceptional stick and rudder skills, as most sail-plane pilots did. Pilots who started out their flying careers by flying powered aircraft more often than not failed to learn how to make efficient coordinated turns. Experienced sail-plane pilots refer to the sloppy piloting of some powered aircraft pilots as *feet-on-the-floor* pilots, forgetting they even have rudder pedals. Peter understood that stall spin accidents killed pilots because of laziness far more often than mechanical failures.

After the First World War, Germany was forbidden to train pilots in powered aircraft. To overcome the restriction, the sport of gliding became an important training tool for the German army. Gliding as a training program for primary flight students eventually became institutionalised in Europe. The Austrian Alps to the south-west of Wiener Neustadt made a perfect learning environment for glider pilots. Peter learnt how to take advantage of the winds as they crossed the Alps and formed lenticular clouds known as mountain waves. A good glider pilot could ride a mountain wave to thirty thousand feet or higher with an oxygen bottle. A novice could enter that same cloud in the wrong place and have his craft torn to bits by its violent turbulence.

Peter Leisel understood these matters. He respected the mountains and knew the limitations light planes had. He would leave Wiener Neustadt in a new twin engine Diamond Twin Star despite the high winds and mountain ridge clouds predicted for the morning. He had a choice; stay on the ground, wait until midday for the weather to improve or take off and fly north for some sightseeing. He decided to enjoy the day and fly up the Danube at low level. This side trip would give the Alpine mountain weather time to improve.

"Hallo, Peter. Your tanks are topped up with diesel fuel," the young man working the flight line reported. He was disconnecting the grounding wire from the exhaust pipe on one of the aircraft's engines.

"Hallo, Paul," Peter smiled. "Good. You're certain it's diesel and not aviation gas?"

"Absolutely, diesel fuel. Can't you smell it?" answered the lineman.

"Ja, smells like my old sailboat," Peter laughed.

"I know," laughed Paul. "These new aircraft are the first of a new class of high-tech light airplanes equipped with diesel engines. I've been on several staff development courses about them. They're great planes, with liquid-cooled diesel engines, more fuel efficient than gasoline ones."

"That's right," interrupted Peter. "And I can fly much further. I prefer them, you just have to be careful not to put the wrong fuel in. Placing aviation gasoline in diesel engines would severely damage them. These things normally have piston engines taking Avgas."

"It's okay, Peter," reassured Paul. "We take all the precautions here. We like to ensure our pilots come back again."

"Well, okay," Peter nodded. "I'll see you in a couple of days then."

"Where are you off to?" Paul enquired.

"Innsbruck by way of the Danube River and the Vilshofen airport"

"Okay. Be careful of the Italian winds up there." Auf wiedersehen."

"Auf wiedersehen."

Peter taxied the plane past the lines of newly manufactured sleek Diamond aircraft and onto the sole runway at Wiener Neustadt. Cleared for takeoff, he departed eastbound and turned north for the Danube.

He climbed to 5,000 feet, then halfway between his departure point and the Danube, he could see Vienna off the Twin Star's right wing. The magnificent city spread out as far as his eye could see, a symbol of civility, art, and music. After a few minutes, the Danube loomed in the distance. The aircraft headed north, perpendicular to the river. The blue waters of the famous river were unmistakable as he joined the Danube at Tulln and followed it westward.

Peter moved the two power levers back and the nose dropped gently toward the earth. Descending to two hundred feet above the river, he soared quietly over castles built on the high overlooks along the river. The craft's two new diesel power plants whispered quietly, compared to their old gasoline predecessors.

Peter could see from his airborne chariot the logic used by ancient architects to select building sites for castles. The best ones were usually on a bend of the Danube so that the view would be both up and downriver. These were the easiest sites to defend. Some of the castles were but a skeleton of what they once were, lying in ruin, ignored and forgotten by passing generations. Some castles, however, had been preserved and were still occupied. Leisel thought to himself as he glided passed them, *it's good that not all of these had been lost*.

His journey continued west along the river, towards the industrial city of Linz. He was in Germany now and would soon need fuel. However, Linz was a busy industrial city airport — a real bother to land at and not very pleasant. Just a few miles further he would reach Vilshofen, a beautiful small German town along the Danube that still looked much as it did five centuries ago. All the little villages and towns that attach themselves to the winding river were like grapes on a vine, drawing life from the river's waters. Their survival would always be tied to the Danube.

The Vilshofen Airport runway was situated just a few feet off and parallel to the river. Peter reported on a five-mile final approach and was cleared to land on runway three zero. Reporting his location and asking for permission to land at such a small airport was an irritant to Peter as it would have been to many other European pilots. Small airports, which make up the vast majority of airports in the world, are uncontrolled. Pilots often question the wisdom of placing controllers at airports where there are no towers. The usual practice when approaching non-towered airports was for the pilots to broadcast on a common frequency and announce their intentions and location all the way to landing. The system of plane-to-plane communication worked everywhere except Germany and Austria. Literally, every airport in these two countries had a paid government employee who directed traffic and granted permission to land, even though he had no radar and no tower from which to see the aircraft traffic. (48° 38' 09.13" N 13° 11' 41.62" E).

The expensive system, is a holdover from the late 1930s. Few people in pre-war Germany owned airplanes for private use. A good percentage of those who did were wealthy Jewish bankers. The Nazis were eager to monitor the Jews, wanting to know their whereabouts at all times, such was their burning desire to eventually exterminate them. The emerging Nazi party posted paid party members at every airport to monitor all aircraft movements, especially those with Jewish owners. After the war the practice of posting a human being on every airport carried on as if it were standard operational procedure. Bureaucrats tended to protect themselves and strive to survive long past their usefulness. Few of the present day air traffic controllers at these little Austrian and German airports knew about the ugly historic reasons their jobs existed.

The Vilshofen Runway threshold passed beneath the sleek glider-like airframe of the Austrian designed and built Diamond Twin Star. The pilot taxied his aircraft up to the self-serve fuel island, parking the craft's shark-like nose toward the fuel pump. The Vilshofen Airport was too small to justify a fuel truck. Leisel was accustomed to fielding questions from pilots about the new,

Geocache

high-tech aircraft, and today was no different. Three men emerged from the airport restaurant and approached the aircraft.

"Hallo. A new Diamond Twin Star?" asked the youngest of the three local pilots as he extended his hand in fellowship.

"Ja. Just went on line at the Diamond Factory Aero Club" answered Peter as he shook the young man's hand.

"Diesel or Avgas?" asked the young man. "Diesel. I'm filling it with Jet A fuel. This thing flies further than my bladder will take me," answered Peter. The three younger men laughed.

"Here for the day or continuing on?" asked the most experienced pilot as he looked inside the cockpit at the new high-tech glass avionics panels. "I see the builder has replaced the old-style round steam gauge dials with two ten inch glass computer screens."

"That's right, they have" Peter answered. Then replied to the first question. "I'm going south to Salzburg, and then over the Alps to Innsbruck,".

"*Vorsichtig*, mien freund; I just checked the weather," remarked the experienced pilot, his concerns for his fellow airman outweighing his curiosity for the plane. "And there is mountain obscuration along the ridges. Also, the Furn winds are blowing hard from the Italian side."

"Thanks for the warning," remarked Peter as he shook the man's hand. "I read the weather report before leaving Wiener Neustadt. I'll be careful. Danka. Would you mind giving me a hand?"

Together, all four pilots repositioned the aircraft away from the fuel pump.

"Auf wiedersehen," Peter called as the other three walked away from the plane. They turned and echoed his parting gesture.

Peter lifted the hinged canopy up and forward and climbed into the cockpit much the way a horseman would mount his steed. Seat belt harnessed and headset secured, he started the two quiet diesel engines and taxied out to the runway.

In November and December, strong winds cross the Alps

from the Italian side of the mountain chain. After crossing the Alps, the winds come crashing down vertically into the centre of the valleys on the Austrian side of the mountains. Pilots unfamiliar with the phenomenon of the Furn winds often fall victim to the downdrafts and crash onto the valley floors. So dangerous are the unexpected downdrafts, that all commercial airlines flying into Innsbruck certify specific flight crews for operations in and out of the mountain valley airport. Not just any pilot can fly there safely.

Leisel understood his fellow pilots' warning. He was an experienced mountain pilot himself. Under normal circumstances this would not be a day he would choose to enter the mountains. However, this was not just another day; his mission required him to be on the ground in Innsbruck by nightfall. It was too late to rent a car and drive there. The distance was too great. He planned to fly up to the mountains and survey the weather once he arrived. There was no point in worrying about it now. He would decide whether to enter the mountains when he had more information.

He would depart towards the castle city of Salzburg — his next checkpoint. From there he would turn south to approach the mountains. With a little luck, the weather would improve by the time he arrived.

CHAPTER TWENTY THREE

UNWANTED DISTRACTION

Victoria walked out of the ground floor elevator of the medical office building and briskly made her way across the expansive marble floor of the lobby. Uncharacteristically, Victoria paid little attention to her immediate surroundings as she pushed through the tall exit doors and began a fast clip down the stone stairs leading to the sidewalk. Inwardly, she pondered on what she had learnt from Doctor Luc. Mentally detached from her external environment she collided head-on with someone halfway down the stairs, who had been ascending at full stride. It was like running into a large rock. She bounced off the man and fell backward landing on the step. She sat stunned, hair tousled and her skirt revealing her long shapely legs up to mid-thigh. She looked up and saw the silhouette of a tall man standing above her. With the sun behind his head she found it hard to distinguish his facial features.

"Damn, Victoria! What have you been eating woman? That hurt!"

"Sean?" Victoria, felt her heart thumping, forgot her compromising position, more concerned with concealing her emotions than her torn hosiery. Her eyes were big now and watering from the sunlight.

"Yeah, it's me. Sorry. I should have looked where I was going. Looks like I hurt you. You're crying."

"No, no. It's the sun in my eyes. Are you just going to stand there, or are you going to help me up?"

"Well, actually, I'm in no hurry, and besides I kind of like the view."

Like a jolt of electricity, she realised how exposed she was.

"Oh, damn! Never mind!" Victoria began to lift herself up as Sean reached down and grabbed her arms to help. She found herself standing face-to-face with him. Their eyes locked. Victoria saw Sean pupils dilate. There was a connection. Victoria tensed, involuntarily gasped. Victoria pulled back, fearful her own eyes had given too much away.

"Seriously, Victoria, are you okay?" asked Sean. "You took a pretty good spill there."

"It's okay. We're in Paris, and I should be able to find replacement silk stockings."

"So you're following me, Sean?"

"No. I have an appointment in this building, and I'm running a bit late. What about you?"

"I just left a meeting; doing a little research."

"Okay. So you're being mysterious. I'm a cop. Eventually you'll tell me everything I want to know. How about a late lunch? I'll only be about an hour. I owe you at least that for ruining your stockings."

"Okay. I'll wait at the base of the Eiffel Tower. See you shortly," answered Victoria.

Descending the stairs, she stopped at the bottom and turned to look back. Sean was entering the door she had just exited. Just before disappearing into the building, he stopped and turned to look back also. He smiled and had a devilish look in his eyes. *Trouble*, she thought, *he's trouble*.

CHAPTER TWENTY FOUR

UNDER SUSPICION

Sean saw Victoria disappear amongst the tourists on the street below. It was an unexpected encounter but not an unpleasant one but made him late for his appointment with Doctor Luc. He was aware of the Institut and the famous doctor but had never needed to visit the facility. The receptionist led Sean into the doctor's office.

"Hello, Inspector. It's a pleasure to meet you; please have a seat." Sean took the same chair Victoria had used only minutes before. Doctor Luc sat back in his chair.

"Inspector, do you mind if I light my pipe?" inquired Doctor Luc.

"No, go ahead," answered Sean. "I tried a pipe once but I could never keep it lit,"

"Well, actually, the main idea is to just chew on the pipe and look as if you are a deep thinker," Doctor Luc laughed "What brings you to visit me, Inspector?"

"I'm investigating a murder. The circumstances that surround the killing are unusual, and you can help us with your expertise." Sean leaned forward.

"On November 28 a man's body was found in a distant part of the Black Forest just along the German/Swiss border. He had been killed by a poison called 'Aconite'."

"I don't understand," Doctor Luc puzzled. "Poison's are not my area."

"I know doctor" interjected Sean. "The investigating officer sent the body to the closest morgue to the crime in Saint Louis, Switzerland. The autopsy discovered the method of murder. However, the autopsy also revealed the victim had a rare blood type. I have the report with me." Sean pulled it from his brief case and handed it to Doctor Luc. "I'm hoping you can search your database to see if you have a record of him and his address. His name was Antoine Sandel. We believe he is from Prague."

Doctor Luc looked at Sean, removed the pipe from his mouth and placed it in its cradle on the desk. Sean sensed an awkwardness.

"Is there a problem, Doctor Luc?"

"No, Inspector. Just a coincidence about Mr. Sandel."

The doctor handed a slip of paper he had been writing on to Sean.

"I already have his address in Prague."

Sean looked down at the paper. It had Antoine Sandel's name and address.

"How come you already have his details, Doctor Luc?" Sean was surprised.

"We have been conducting a search for individuals with Mr. Sandel's unusual blood type. His name was uncovered along with two others of the same type here in Europe. I was amazed to discover not just one person of that blood type, but three. Now you are telling me that one of them has been murdered. I was thinking about retiring in a couple of years, but I may move that schedule up a bit."

"Why were you searching for these people?" asked Sean.

"There was a helicopter crash in the United States — in Denver," Doctor Luc explained. "A very wealthy man by the name of Alexander Maxwell was nearly killed in the accident. Mr. Maxwell, it has been subsequently discovered, has a rare form of bone cancer and this same rare blood type. No donors were found in North America, so Mr. Maxwell's employee came to us to enlist our help in looking for a donor in Europe."

Sean digested this information, his brain calculated the chain of events as he knew and understood them.

"Is Mr. Maxwell's employee a woman?"

Geocache

"Why, yes — unmistakably a woman," answered the Doctor.

"Is her name Victoria Kavanagh?"

"Yes, that's correct. How did you know?" puzzled Doctor Luc as he shifted forward in his chair. Sean's mind was racing.

"Doctor Luc, you said there were three possible matches. Can you give me the names of the other two?"

"Of course, I will give you the same printout I gave Ms. Kavanagh."

Doctor Luc opened the Maxwell file and removed the printout. Then called his assistant on the intercom. Moments later the assistant came into the room with a copy of the list and handed it to Sean.

"What can you tell me about Ms. Kavanagh, Doctor?" asked Sean.

"I received a call from a colleague in the States asking me to help Ms. Kavanagh find a donor for Mr. Maxwell. Ms. Kavanagh came to Paris and met with me twice, once to discuss the process and once to receive the results. She just left here a little while ago. Other than that, I cannot tell you much about her. She does seem very professional and very mission-oriented. Quite a woman though," the doctor smiled.

"Yes, I know. She can be very disarming in more ways than one."

"Other than the phone call from your colleague, do you have any other third-party confirmation of the information Ms. Kavanagh gave you about Mr. Maxwell and about herself?" Sean was having doubts about Victoria Kavanagh.

"No, what is this all about? Why do you think this man was murdered?"

"I'm not certain, Doctor. If there really is a Mr. Maxwell, perhaps someone would like to make certain he doesn't survive." Sean excused himself and left the building, headed for the Eiffel Tower and Victoria Kavanagh.

Errol Bader

CHAPTER TWENTY FIVE

FLYING THE ALPS

Banking twenty degrees left and turning south at fifteen hundred feet above ground, Leisel departed Vilshofen. He left the Danube behind as the river continued its way north. Salzburg loomed on the horizon, dominated by its single, large castle, high above the city, on a ridge with a commanding view of the surrounds. As the aircraft drew closer, he could see the old town just below the famous Castle Salzburg. Like so many cities, the central city clings to the bank of a wide river flowing along the ancient buildings. From here it is a straight shot to the mountains.

Peter shoved the two levers forward to increase the power of the diesel engines. The aircraft gradually climbed. He needed altitude to survey the weather along the mountains. The peaks of the Alps were visible, 50 miles away. The mountains still had clouds around them. It was too early to determine how dense the cloud bank was. At this distance he could see the peaks clearly above the clouds and knew they could easily be avoided. However, he could not determine if there was an impenetrable cloud deck below the peaks.

The aircraft's two; ten inch glass avionics panels incorporated a GPS receiver. The right panel was a colour display of the map of the area with a little airplane displayed at the centre. Peter could tell exactly where his aircraft was on the map in relation to the mountains, airports, and cities. He could also see the elevation of the terrain below him and in front of him. The new panels made cross-country flying easier than the old round dial systems. He could see exactly the distance between his aircraft and the mountains. He could also see where the valleys between the peaks were. Terrain below the aircraft and within one thousand

Geocache

feet would bloom yellow. Terrain within one hundred feet beneath the aircraft would bloom red.

The left glass panel displayed the flight instruments, an amazing amount of digital information built into the new avionics suite. Previously, only military aircraft had such equipment. At ten miles distance Leisel saw what he had hoped would be a different picture. The peaks were clear, but below them was a solid deck of clouds that obscured the canyons and valleys below. He flew between the first two peaks and found himself skimming above the clouds and flanked by a line of ridges on both sides of the aircraft. He knew by looking at the little airplane on the moving map, that he was flying above the valley of the Inn River. Further up the cloud-covered valley was his destination airport of Innsbruck. By staying between the mountain ridges that formed the valley below and watching the moving map, he could fly down the valley toward the airport. Under ordinary circumstances Leisel would not be flying in the mountains in these conditions, but he felt compelled to get to Innsbruck. He had an appointment he could not miss, so he would continue down the valley looking for a break in the clouds. He knew that the ceiling beneath a cloud deck would not usually go all the way to the ground. In all probability there was at least five hundred feet of clear visibility beneath the cloud layer. If he could find a way to get through the four or five hundred feet thick layer he would break out of the clouds, and land at Innsbruck.

To drop through clouds when not on an instrument approach, is not only illegal but dangerous. Over flat lands the risk is diminished, but dropping through a cloud bank in the mountains is suicidal. Two miles down valley from the airport, Leisel saw a hole in the clouds. According to the moving map, the aircraft was in the middle of the valley. He decided to chance it and dropped the nose of the aircraft toward the hole. What he was contemplating was folly.

He pulled the levers back and slowed the aircraft. As he entered the small opening in the clouds, he could see the valley floor below him. A good sign, he thought. He relaxed and felt he had made a good decision as the plane descended beneath the surrounding clouds. It was a succour hole; he was descending into grey cloud and losing view of the terrain. He thought this is not a good idea. At four hundred feet above ground, he broke out below the overcast. At this altitude he expected to have good forward visibility, instead what he saw made his heart pound. Suddenly, he was confronted with a large hill rising up out of the middle of the valley. He yanked back on the centre stick to avoid hitting the ridge; and in an instant he experienced two positive G forces on his body — a doubling of his weight. He went from 180 pounds to 360 pounds in a split second.

As the aircraft cleared the hill, it entered the clouds again. Leisel was losing control. He could tell that vertigo was setting in — a confusion of up from down. Peter began to experience a spinning sensation. He pushed the stick forward and the G forces went negative as quickly as they had gone positive, just a second before. Peter's body went from 360 pounds to zero pounds in an instant. A pen and pad of paper were suspended weightless in front of his eyes. Finally he broke out below the ceiling, levelled the Twin Star, and collected himself. He looked down the valley toward Innsbruck, hoping to see all the way to the airport. Nothing doing, the clouds dropped all the way to the surface in the direction of Innsbruck.

Peter could not continue in that direction. The walls of the valley were only a few miles apart, and the ceiling was rapidly dropping. There was no choice but to turn around and fly back up the valley. He needed the full width of the valley to accomplish the 180° turn. He banked right and flew to the edge of the valley. Upon reaching the valley wall, he began a 15° left bank. With only 400 feet between the ground and the aircraft, the risks were no longer acceptable. He thought to himself, *this is crazy. Why did I make this stupid decision?* With the turn completed, Peter's worst fears were realised. He was boxed in and the void in the clouds he descended through was no longer there. He had three choices: he could crash-land on the floor of the valley — not a good choice as this was rugged country; he could keep doing turns and risk running into something or perhaps suffer a further degradation of the weather; or he could climb up through the clouds and try not to hit rock.

He opted for the climb. It was safer up in the clouds than the scud-running he was doing. Looking at the moving map, he positioned the aircraft in the middle of the valley and began a blind climb up through the clouds. Peter was a good pilot but not an instrument-rated one. It is said that VFR or non-instrument rated pilots, who are lost in clouds without reference to the horizon, survive an average of twelve seconds. They lose their sense of up and down. In obscured weather a pilot cannot rely on his sense of balance; only the instruments can be trusted. Leisel knew this and was determined not to be a statistic. He focused his eyes on the artificial horizon on the glass panel, knowing he had to keep the wings level or he would enter a spiral and crash into the terrain below. Looking at the clouds outside as he climbed, would expose him to a dizzy confusion between up and down. It seemed like hours, not minutes, when he broke out above the cloud tops. He had survived, beaten the odds.

Peter climbed above the peaks and circled to calm his nerves. His heart had beaten hard and fast, and he was covered in sweat. He settled himself and began to analyse his situation. He could scrub his mission and walk away from millions of dollars, or he could look for another way to get to Innsbruck. He looked at the moving map and began to develop a new plan. He could see on the screen where the canyons exited the mountains and joined the flatlands to the north. He reasoned that he could fly back the way he came — away from the mountains. Then he would turn and approach the mountains again. This time he would fly back at 200 feet above ground level and approach the mouth of the largest canyon. The canyon would be perpendicular to the larger valley where Innsbruck Airport would be found. He decided to execute this plan.

Errol Bader

Flying to the north, he left the mountains travelling back in the direction of Salzburg. He descended to 200 feet and turned back toward the mountains. The moving map showed the canyon entrance right where it should be. As he approached he saw that the horizontal cloud had capped the top of the canyon and inside the valley visibility was good. *It's now or never,* Peter thought. He knew that to enter was unsafe. The canyon was too narrow to reverse direction once inside, and if the ceiling came down even 10 feet he would die. He hoped he could negotiate the winding turns along the canyon walls and once in the main valley, the ceiling would be high enough for an approach to Innsbruck's runway. The glider-like Twin Stars' wing span was 42 feet, eight feet wider than the average light aircraft. A perfect design for high-altitude flying, but not designed for this mission. It was like flying a U2 spy plane under the London Bridge. He made his decision and took a deep breath, pointing the aircraft into the dark triangular tunnel that the canyon had become. The steep slopes became a blur in his peripheral vision. Peter lowered the flaps and landing gear and throttled back to fly as slow as he could. The Twin Star cooperated. Its slow stall speed allowed Peter to decelerate to only 55 knots. No other twin-engine aircraft would cope this slowly. He banked left, then right and then left again. The wing tips brushed the canyon walls. There was no margin for error. The canyon became a tunnel, the edges grew darker. His field of vision narrowed. He began to see yellow, white and then pinpoints of light. He was losing consciousness. He was blacking out from oxygen starvation. He wasn't breathing! His body was being pumped full of adrenalin, and at the same time, he was unconsciously holding his breath. Forcing himself to breath, his field of vision expanded. He saw a ridge loom towards him, that seconds earlier could not be seen. One last steep turn and he was through. The airplane shot out of the canyon like a bullet leaving a gun muzzle. He entered into the main valley and turned toward Innsbruck Airport — his body soaked and cold. He was exhausted, as though he had been in a

Geocache

fight. He could see the airport in the distance. In fact, he had been in a fight — for his life. He set up for the approach to Innsbruck's runway and called the tower.

"Where did you say you are?" asked the Innsbruck tower controller in disbelief. He was the only controller in the tower, and trying to stay awake. There had been virtually no traffic for two days. The only radio traffic was a pilot friend of his crossing high overhead the airport at 32,000 feet calling to chat on the tower frequency. Not even scheduled airliners could land at Innsbruck when the sky was overcast.

"Two-mile-final Innsbruck," responded Peter.

"Are you VFR?" asked the tower controller.

"Affirmative, on VFR, one-mile final approach," answered Peter.

"Cleared to land; suggest you go have a beer," answered the tower controller, knowing there was no way to fly into Innsbruck on a day like this and be legal.

The Twin Star's wheels kissed the runway. Peter Leisel had cheated death, at least for this day.

Errol Bader

CHAPTER TWENTY SIX

GALERIES LAFAYETTE

Sean decided to walk to the Eiffel Tower instead of taking a cab. He needed time to think about what Doctor Luc had said. He wondered if he was on his way to have a late lunch with a killer or a beautiful woman who was on a mission to save her boss? How should he play this — confront her right off or hold his cards close to the chest? *What lousy luck*, he thought. *I finally run across a woman who can hold her own in my world, and I might have to send her to the clink.*

The thought process continued as Sean walked toward the historic tower. *Okay, innocent until proven guilty. The thing to do was what he had been trained to do, conduct his investigation without telegraphing to her what he was doing. Besides, there was one fact in her favour. Antoine Sandel died before Doctor Luc handed Victoria the list of the three donors' names and addresses. Damn!*

His mental ramblings were interrupted by a random incongruous thought. *I'd hate to see that body in orange prison garb; now that would be a crime.* His brain returned to its analytical side again. *On the other hand, she may have known about Sandel and was looking for other potential donors that needed dispatching. She arrived in Paris after the 28th of November; it would be interesting to discover where she was before arriving in Paris. If Germany or Switzerland, that would be the smoking gun, unless, of course, she had an accomplice.*

There may be a wealthy man by the name of Alexander Maxwell lying in a hospital bed in Denver. If this were true, then there might be a financial reason why one or more people might not want him to recover. Interpol would have the resources to uncover the truth about these matters.

Right now there was no time to clarify things; he was entering the large square plaza beneath the Tower. He could see Victoria standing in the sunlight by its southeastern base leg — framed by the massive lattice work of the steel structure. She was looking off toward the mile long grassy promenade that serves as the spectacular approach to the Eiffel Tower.

The ornate structure was built to celebrate the centennial anniversary of the French Revolution. Finished in 1889, there were plans to dismantle it twenty years later. Fortunately for the French, the tower's designer, Gustave Eiffel, lobbied successfully for its survival.

The tower was a work of art. As Sean approached, he could not help but see a relationship between it and the statuesque beauty before him. It was as if the tower was built to showcase Victoria. She stood beneath the soaring spire as though it was a monument to her and her alone. She could easily have been a French movie star waiting for the next location scene to be filmed.

He glanced around the base of the tower and estimated that there were 200 or more tourists waiting to tour the facility. He thought it interesting that perhaps a score of men standing with their wives or girlfriends were focused on Victoria.

Who could blame them, Sean thought to himself. *Just because she may be a cold blooded killer didn't change the fact that she was one of the most beautiful women in Paris.* He hoped it wasn't so. He liked Victoria — a lot. There was a good chance his attraction to her was more than physical. She was tough, smart, strong, quick, and determined – all the ingredients it takes to produce a professional killer. What Sean failed to see in this assessment of his attraction to Victoria was that these were also his own traits.

As if sensing Sean approaching, she turned towards him. Seeing him approach, she smiled and it seemed to Sean to be genuine. She appeared happy to see him; if she was evil incarnate, her expression hid it. He felt disadvantaged. She knew more about him than he of her. She knew he was a cop but gave no signs of stress in her body language.

"Hello, Victoria. Sorry it took so long over there," Sean apologised. "Have you been under the tower all this time.

"Yes. I've been right here."

"You must be cold?"

"It's pleasant though," her smile broadened "The sun is warm and there's no wind but I'm getting a bit hungry, though." Victoria slipped her purse over her shoulder. "And don't forget you owe me a new pair of stockings."

"Tell you what," Sean back tracked as the two of them moved off. "I know a place where we can kill two birds with one stone. We can replace your stockings and have a bite to eat at Galeries Lafayette. It's a popular shopping mall in the ninth Arrondissement not far from here. There's a very good restaurant on the roof. You can see all of Paris from there."

Kill two birds with one stone — what a poor choice of words, Sean thought.

"Sounds nice. Galeries Lafayette it is," answered Victoria, still smiling at him. In fact, she was smiling more than usual. She seemed to put her serious side on hold around Sean. There was no inkling on her part that she had just become a suspect in an international murder case.

They walked side by side toward the curb, neither of them feeling pressured for time. Their earlier collision was down to haste in pursuit of their respective missions. Now, uncharacteristically, they were in slow motion as they approached the curb. Their strides were out of synch causing their shoulders to touch twice along the way. Each time they bumped into each other, Victoria felt what seemed like a mild electrical charge flowing from her thighs and up through the base of her spine. The sensation continued up into the base of her neck and settled in her inner ears — a tingling, flushing sensation. She knew what this was. She remembered feeling this way at the top of the Maxwell

Geocache

Land Company Office Tower as parts of a disintegrating helicopter flew about the conference room. This was adrenalin being released into her bloodstream. The unintended connection with Sean's body had triggered the fight-or-flight defense mechanism in her brain. She had no intention of fighting with this man; she had even less desire to run from him. Victoria was surprised by this unexpected and primitive reaction. No man had ever had this kind of affect on her. It concerned her, and she wasn't easily disconcerted.

A cab stopped by the curb as Sean held his hand up. They both stooped over to peer into the cab, half expecting to see Pierre behind the wheel. No luck or very lucky depending on the way they looked at it. They had fun harassing Pierre, the cab driver.

The cabbie had been driving with the passenger side window open. It was a mild day for December in Paris.

"Madam Goldblatt?" the driver was looking past Sean and Victoria. Before they could respond to the strange question, a portly, extraverted, woman broke through between Sean and Victoria from behind. Mrs. Goldblatt grabbed the rear passenger door handle, opened the door, and jumped briskly into the cab, closing the door behind her.

"Yes, it's me. Driver. I'm Mrs. Goldblatt. Bonjour. Take me to the Arch De Triumph please," demanded the lady.

Sean and Victoria looked at each other and laughed. He turned to the oncoming traffic to hail another cab. It only took a minute and the next cab pulled up next to them.

The window lowered as Sean and Victoria leaned in as before. Lo and behold it was Pierre, the French cab driver.

"Pierre!" they announced in unison.

Pierre had put the car in neutral and pulled on the handbrake to lean over and receive his instructions. When he discovered who they were, he reached for the column-mounted gear lever wanting to make a hasty departure. Victoria jumped in front of the cab barring Pierre's escape.

Errol Bader

"Whoa, whoa, whoa, Pierre. Take it easy," Sean tried to calm the nervous cab driver. "We promise not to hurt you. It's okay. We need your services."

"What did I ever do to you? Am I the only cab driver in Paris? Why do you follow me everywhere?" Pierre was pleading. "You want me to die! I have a wife, five kids, and a mother-in-law. Isn't that enough punishment for one lifetime?"

He pointed through the front window at Victoria.

"Listen, lady. I'm going to run you over. So I go to jail – at least I get three meals. The jails in France are very nice; I will never have to see the two of you again."

Finally, Pierre's protestations were put aside. Sean and Victoria were in the back seat of his cab and heading toward the Ninth Arrondissement and the Galeries Lafayette.

"All right. So you want to go to the Galeries Lafayette," said Pierre. "I will make a deal with you. If you behave as normal tourists and cause me no trouble, I will behave like a proper French taxi driver, and I will tell you about the Galeries Lafayette. But first, you must agree to prepay for this trip. The fee for normal passengers is €18. Please note that I did not say the 'normal fee' for passengers is €18. I said the fee for 'normal passengers' is €18. You are not normal. For you, since you are such special passengers, the fare is €25. I trust neither of you. You are both radin? (French for skinflint). You get no credit."

"Pierre, where is your sense of adventure?" asked Victoria.

"Okay. I'll pay your surcharge, Pierre; but you have to accept my credit card when we get there. Deal?" Sean said.

"All right. But you promise to pay?" insisted the driver.

"Of course, you can depend on me," answered Sean.

"Okay. The Galeries Lafayette Mall is a very old landmark in Paris. It was founded in 1893 by Theophile Bader. His first name means 'friend of God' in ancient Greek.

He selected the site of the first building because of its nearness to the Paris Opera. The building is now six stories high with a glass cupola at the top and houses some of the finest shops

Geocache

in Paris. More people visit the Mall during the course of a year than visit the Eiffel Tower. Are you looking for something specific to purchase at the Galeries?" asked Pierre.

"Yes. I need to replace my stockings." answered Victoria. "They were ripped to shreds earlier today,"

"Why I am not surprised," answered Pierre, as he continued.

"On the third floor of the Mall, you will find the lingerie department. It is called the Seductive Fashion Store."

"How would you know such information, Pierre?" asked Victoria.

Silence."Pierre?" she repeated.

"Well, if you must know, my wife is from New York — from the Bronx. She lives at the mall. I work like a dog to pay for her shopping addiction. Now you know why jail is so appealing for me."

"Oh, sorry, Pierre," replied Victoria.

"Okay. We have only three blocks to go," announced Pierre. "Please give me your credit card now before you make a run for it. We have to stop for this traffic light anyway."

He was impatient and wanted to make sure he was not short-changed by them again. The cab came to a halt and Sean reached for his wallet. In an instant, Sean and Victoria were shoved backwards then thrown forwards against the front seat . It only took a second for Sean, Victoria, and Pierre to realise they had been rear-ended. Another cab had failed to stop and hit Pierre's, a fair amount of damage was done to the trunk and bumper.

Pierre pulled his five-foot-three frame out of the car, to confront the offending driver. Screaming, he waved his short arms in the air, calling the other cab driver every name in the French dictionary, at the driver's window. The other taxi driver slowly opened his door and stood at least six-foot-six, weighing roughly 132 kilos. A mean-looking fellow with tattoos on his neck, the giant looked down at Pierre and said five words:

"Voulez-vous mourir?" Meaning: Do you want to die? Pierre put his hands in the air and backed away.

"Ah, correct. Désolé. Aucun problème. My fault. Have a great day."

Pierre turned back and saw an empty cab. Two blocks away and barely within the sound of his voice, Sean and Victoria were completing their trip to the mall on foot.

Pierre yelled as loud as he could in their direction. "Hey, hey, where are you going? You owe me my fare! You owe me for the last three fares! Radin, pauvres con! Brûlez dans l'enfer."

The mall entrance was large and elegant, a rotunda that climbed six stories to a domed glass cover.

"Lunch first or would you like to head to Seductive Fashions?" asked Sean.

"I want to get these stockings off first, if that's okay with you."

The third floor of the mall is Paris Central for woman in need of lingerie. Not the kind of shopping Sean was accustomed to. He found himself in tow behind the tall beauty. Victoria was not exactly an avid shopper herself. It only took a few moments for her to locate the acceptable replacements and hand the package to Sean.

"Okay. There's the cashier over there." She pointed him in the direction of the nearest cash register. He stood in line behind two women waiting to be served. Victoria stood with him smiling as she had all day, as though she belonged next to him.

Sean had other thoughts. *How could this woman, I feel comfortable with, poison someone with Aconite?* He was spending the afternoon with a woman he hardly knew but was strongly attracted to. She was like a magnet. It was too early to jump to conclusions, not enough information. But his gut told him she couldn't be a viper. An hour before he felt she could be guilty of murder, and now he wasn't sure.

Sean paid for the stockings and handed them to Victoria.

"Thank you. You're a man of your word. I'll be right back." She disappeared into the women's dressing room, emerging in a few minutes.

"What do you think, Sean?" Victoria posed like a model, displaying her lithe legs.

"Lady, you need a bodyguard."

"No, I am a bodyguard." She turned and began walking toward the exit without further explanation. Her comment was intriguing, but it was obvious it was all he was going to get out of her right at this second.

"Yeah, and I'm a Sumo wrestler," he replied.

"C'mon Sean, I'm starved." Victoria grabbed his arm and pulled him into the glass enclosed elevator. "Top floor?" she asked.

Sean nodded in affirmation and pushed the sixth floor button. The lift began its trip up the side of the large rotunda. Victoria looked through the glass wall of the chamber and down on the floor below. The mall had been decorated for the Christmas season. It looked like a six-story cylinder filled with giant, colourful large glass balls. A thousand shoppers walked along the terraces that spiralled up the centre of the massive mall.

Sean watched the woman as she studied the scene below them.

"Started your Christmas shopping yet?" inquired Sean.

"No. I've been preoccupied with other things, but hopefully by Christmas I'll get a break," she answered.

"And you, Sean? Do you have anyone special you have to shop for?"

Victoria turned her face toward Sean to make eye contact. Sean leant against the hand railing and looked across the mall.

"Let's see, there's Elizabeth. She likes perfume. Rebecca — she's into earrings, and then Jocelyn. Now Jocelyn — that one is really tough to shop for."

Victoria tilted her head and smiled from the right side of her mouth. She just stared at him, smiling and saying nothing.

"Okay then. Why would I buy Christmas presents? I'm a Buddhist," he answered.

She continued her silence, staring into his eyes. He stared

back.

First one to speak loses, he thought.

"Okay, Okay. I don't have anyone special to shop for." He lost.

Victoria had hoped this would be his answer.

"So no one special in your life, Inspector?" she asked.

"Well, you know, after my third divorce, I thought I would take a breather," he answered with a grin. She parted her lips, forming a slight smile and raised one eyebrow.

"Okay. I've never been married and I love my freedom."

Rescued by the arrival of the sixth floor, he led the way out of the elevator and into the lobby. The large glass double doors of the *Galeries Café* were propped open. White tablecloths and silverware decorated the room beyond the doorway. They were met by a young man and escorted to a booth flanked by a window with a view of the city below. The Eiffel Tower loomed in the distance.

"Can I get you something to drink? Water? Perhaps some wine?" asked the young man.

"Do you have any truth serum?" asked Victoria. The young man gave her a puzzled look.

"Water with lemon," Sean volunteered.

"Perrier," answered Victoria. "Can you tell me which way to the rest room?"

"Just next to the entrance, mademoiselle. I will get your beverages."

"So, Victoria, what did you mean by that?" asked Sean.

"What did I mean by what?" she answered.

"You said you were a bodyguard."

"Oh, yes, and you're a Sumo wrestler. What a coincidence. But you know, Sean, I have to be honest. You don't look like a Sumo wrestler."

"And you think you look like a bodyguard?" asked Sean.

"Never judge a book by its cover; you might miss a pretty good read. Ah, nature calls. I'll be right back. Watch my purse,

Geocache

will you?" She stood up from her chair.

"Why, what's it going to do?" he quipped.

"You know you have a weird sense of humour, Sean. Just keep an eye on it for me; there's a gun inside."

"Oh, right. I forgot you're a bodyguard, I'll take good care of it."

Victoria turned and headed for the rest rooms. Sean watched her every move; it was impossible not to. For the second time in one day, he saw her make heads turn. Men and women alike seemed hypnotised by the tall beauty. One woman leaned over to another, whispered something and nodded in Victoria's direction. The women watched Victoria disappear from the dining room. It wasn't that she walked in a feminine way; she didn't. Her cadence was deliberate, business-like, but she oozed charisma. Charisma is genetic; it can't be learned or feigned. Certain people can enter a room, speak nothing, and command attention. Sean witnessed the power Victoria had over people. He was curious to learn whether she was abusive of the gift she had been given. He needed more time to judge whether she was someone who would use her charm and beauty to manipulate others – possibly victims. Every bone in his body hoped that this lady would not be a human version of Venus's-Flytrap. He wanted to know the truth about her. He reached across the table and laid his right hand on Victoria's purse. The hard shape inside was unmistakable; the dog leg of a small handgun.

She wanted Sean to know it was there. It was her way of slowly educating him to who and what she was. She already knew he would not be intimidated by her looks, and she appreciated this. Telling him she was a bodyguard was a measured and intentional delivery of a small piece of information. She was slowly feeding Sean bits and pieces about herself. She had no way of knowing that he suspected her of murder.

Sean opened her purse. Inside was a 9mm Walther PPK/E semi-automatic handgun. In addition to the standard magazine inserted in the base there was a larger, custom made, fifteen round magazine — more bullets than needed for self-defence. This was a weapon that could serve a bodyguard well, but it could easily serve a murderer. As a suspect, Victoria was not cooperating. *Too many layers to this onion*, he thought. *I'm not gaining on this*. He picked up the purse intending to close the clasp but something caught his eye — a folded piece of paper nestled among her lipstick, female pads, and other unfamiliar feminine paraphernalia.

He pulled the paper out and unfolded it. The same three names and addresses were scribbled down, of the blood donors Doctor Luc had given him. The list included Antoine Sandel. Victoria turned the corner and saw Sean putting her purse down on the table. She took her seat and placed her elbows on the table. Resting her chin on the backs of her hands with her long fingers extended in opposing directions, she smiled and looked directly into his eyes.

"Are you in need of a pad, Inspector?" she asked.

Sean placed his elbows on the table and clasped his hands together in a ball. It was a more masculine version of her pose. He placed his chin on the backs of his clasped hands, smiled, and looked directly into her eyes.

"No. Actually I'm running a little low on 9mm rounds."

They sat in silence staring at each other for what seemed like hours. He was determined not to lose this time.

"I'm a professional, Sean." She was ready to give him all the pieces now.

"I know," he answered. Sean saw, from the corner of his eye, the sun was setting on the Parisian skyline, and darkness was falling on the city but he refused to let his gaze stray. The young waiter approached their table again, this time armed with a butane lighter.

"May I light the candles for you?" he asked.

Victoria broke the stare to nod her consent. The task completed, the young man moved on to the next table. Sean and

Victoria resumed eye contact. The flickering orange flame complimented Victoria's flawless complexion. Her astonishing blue eyes were hypnotic. It seemed like years since he had fought to save this woman's life in the streets below. He remembered how she had disabled so many on-rushing attackers in just a few seconds. Her visage was so different now, soft and relaxed. He arrived at the conclusion that whatever her mission in Paris, she would complete it in a way that was satisfactory to her. She would get what she wanted; she probably always did. She was well-armed to either melt a man's heart with her eyes or put a bullet in his head.

"Where were you trained?" he asked.

"Quantico. I'm ex-secret service." She was ready to finish his education.

"And now?" he inquired.

"I'm responsible for the protection of a very wealthy American businessman in Colorado."

"Is his name Alexander Maxwell?" asked Sean.

Victoria was caught by surprise.

"You've been investigating me. How much do you know? Do you understand why I'm in Europe?"

"I know you visited with Doctor Luc." He had decided to confront her and watch her reaction. "He gave you a list of three men who all share the same rare blood type. One of them was found murdered a few days ago in Hägelberg, near the German-Swiss border."

"One of my donors is dead? Murdered? Where? How?" She was clearly upset. Her right hand reached for her purse, an instinctive reaction to threat.

One of my donors is dead — that was a reactive response, Sean thought. *Good answer.* Her first thought and angry reaction revealed her immediate assessment of her mission status. She had lost a donor, and it was placing her mission at risk. Her emotions were real. He was convinced now she was not a professional killer but a professional bodyguard.

"Which one is dead? Wait a minute. You suspect me, don't you?" She was beginning to understand — beginning to realize his motives.

Sean lowered his hands and folded his arms on the table cloth before replying,

"Antoine Sandel's body was found in the southern region of the Black Forest near Hägelberg. He died of poisoning. And, yes, you would qualify as a suspect. You're carrying a list of three people from across Europe. One of whom has recently been lured to his death in the middle of a snowstorm. And did I mention you have demonstrated a mastery of the martial arts? From what I witnessed the other day, you don't need that arsenal in your purse. You could kill a large man with your bare hands."

"So you think I'm his killer?" she asked. She was still processing what he had just said to her, angry that one of the donors had been eliminated but also annoyed about his suspicions. Though Victoria had to admit she was a prime suspect. In Sean's shoes she would have thought the same, had their roles been reversed.

"So you suspect me?"

"I did but I don't now," answered Sean. "I believe you're in a race with someone who wants Mr. Maxwell dead."

"What makes you think that?" asked Victoria.

"Mr. Sandel was lured to a dense forest in a snowstorm and murdered. The autopsy revealed that he had been poisoned with Aconite."

"Aconite. He didn't have a chance. You can kill an elephant with a thimble full of Aconite," remarked Victoria.

"You're familiar with this poison?"

"We caught a waiter with the white powder in a vial. He was headed for the kitchen where the President's meal was being prepared. At first we thought it was cocaine – until the tests were completed," answered Victoria. "The KGB also foiled an attempt on Gorbachov's life. Aconite was the weapon of choice. You said Sandel was lured to his death. How?" Victoria was playing catch-

Geocache

up. She wanted to know what Sean knew.

"Sandel travelled from Prague to Basel on a commuter airline then by taxi to Hägelberg. He had no friends or relatives in the region. The weather was bad — a blizzard from what I'm told. Sandel checked into the Hotel Romantik and told a waitress that he would be leaving the next day.

The next morning Sandel went online using the hotel's computer and logged onto a website to find the latitude and longitude coordinates of a spot twenty five kilometres inside the Black Forest. The snowstorm that day was the worst so far this year. Sandel drove his rental car toward the coordinates until his car axels were buried in snow. He walked the rest of the way to the coordinates. For whatever reason, Sandel felt compelled to travel to a location that would be far away from any residents or tourists.

He was found in the forest covered in snow. We were lucky to discover the body before it decomposed. The body was recovered so quickly, there were no other victims," explained Sean.

"No other victims?" asked Victoria.

Sean smiled, "If any of God's little creatures had decided to feast on the corpse, they would have died of Aconite poisoning. We would have had dead bunnies everywhere." Sean intentionally injected some of his dry humour into the discussion. He wanted her to know that he was serious when he said he no longer suspected her of the killing.

"Are you ever serious? One of my donors is dead, and you're talking about bunnies in the forest?" she asked.

"Hey, when was the last time you read about a bunny blowing up an airliner?" asked Sean. "Bunnies are a symbol of non-violence. We can't have homicidal maniacs running around the forest leaving corpses with Aconite in their bodies. Too many innocent lives are at stake out there." He winked at her; trying to take the edge off the bad news he had delivered. It was true, he did have an odd sense of humour; however, he knew how to use it to its best advantage. Right now he needed Victoria's help to unravel the mystery surrounding Antoine Sandel's murder. He needed to settle her.

"How do you know all this?" asked Victoria. "How was the body discovered so quickly if Sandel was killed in the forest?"

"Marcus Webber was one of the best local law-enforcement investigators in the area. He works in Hägelberg near Steinen in Germany and is way overqualified for a place as small as that. Marcus discovered a website that Sandel had visited just before his death. The website contained the latitude and longitude of a clearing in the Black Forest. Marcus wrote the coordinates down before the killer could erase them and found Sandel's body at the site after he had been missing two days, so we were lucky."

Just as Sean was finishing, the young waiter approached their table.

"Can I take your order, mademoiselle, monsieur?" the waiter asked.

The menus had been in front of them, but they were too busy to look at them.

"I haven't looked at the menu, but I know what I would like," answered Victoria.

"Oui, mademoiselle?" the waiter asked.

"I would like some rabbit. Do you have rabbit?"

"Ah, no, I'm afraid not, mademoiselle."

"All right! Give us a few more minutes, please."

"Oui, mademoiselle," smiled the waiter, who then trotted off to serve another table.

Victoria immediately turned her attention back to Sean.

"How did you become involved in this investigation? Why would Interpol get involved with a murder in Hägelberg?"

Sean turned serious again.

"Marcus is a personal friend, he rang me up after he found Sandel's body," Sean continued "Marcus felt the modus operandi was so unusual and as the victim had crossed international boundaries, Interpol should assist in the investigation. After speaking with Doctor Luc and now yourself, I believe there will

Geocache

be more victims if we don't act quickly." He paused for a moment to gauge Victoria's emotions.

"Victoria, I know this is sudden, but can you think of anyone who would benefit from your boss's death?"

"Alexander Maxwell is a powerful businessman. Over the years, I'm sure he has angered some people, but I doubt to the point that they would want him dead. He has no children or other family members – just some very powerful and influential friends. His closest assistant was in the same helicopter crash and died."

"Tell me about the accident." Sean was searching for clues in her answer.

"Mr. Maxwell has four wealthy friends who live outside the United States: a Russian, a Frenchman, a Mexican, and a Japanese. All five men were meeting in Denver in mid-November. Mr. Maxwell was hosting the event at the top of his office tower. Each attendee arrived in his own helicopter, which were sequencing onto the helipad when one of the pilots caused a midair collision. Four people died."

"Why were they meeting?" asked Sean.

"Only a handful of people know this. They meet once a year to plan a sporting event for themselves" Victoria explained. "Each June they play the game for several weeks. The sport is called geocache. Only for these guys, it's a big-league game, the biggest playoff of all geocache sporting events,".

Geocache, Sean thought. *What was it about this word that was familiar?*

Victoria continued her explanation.

"Each of the group selects five items worth 500,000 dollars a piece. These items are then hidden in watertight containers somewhere on the earth, usually in exotic and remote places. In June the latitude and longitude of each location are posted on an internet website for each of the players. For example, the Russian has his own site where five sets of coordinates are posted. He then takes a portable GPS unit and goes on a hunt for his five geocache sites."

"Geocache sites," Sean interrupted. "Did you say geocache sites, Victoria?"

"Yes, why?"

"The website that Antoine Sandel logged onto at Hägelberg was *www.antoinesgeocachesite.com*," answered Sean. "Victoria, Antoine's murderer knows of Alexander Maxwell's pastime. There's a connection. The killer is using Maxwell's game to kill the donors who could potentially save his life. And you think I have a strange sense of humour."

Sean reached into his shirt pocket and pulled out the list of donors Doctor Luc had given him and placed it on the table. The light from the candles flickered on the paper. Antoine Sandel's name was at the top of the list. Victoria reached into her purse and pulled out her identical list. She placed her slip of paper down next to his.

"Have you got a pen, Victoria?" he asked.

She gave him one from her purse. He ticked Sandel's name. Victoria took the pen back. She drew a line through Sandel's name. They had the same mission and yet divergent missions. He viewed Sandel as a victim, and he was planning on finding his killer. To Victoria, Sandel was a rare blood donor.

With his death, Sandel no longer held any importance to her. But, helping Sean find Sandel's killer had a benefit. She could not afford to lose another donor. She needed Sean's help.

"I'm a little thirsty," she announced.

"See, that comes from eating too much rabbit," Sean opined. "You really should cut that stuff out of your diet — too salty."

Victoria was enjoying the fencing with him. She even appreciated his oddball humour. He had given her the news she needed. He had judged her a colleague and not an enemy. Sean had even uncovered a diabolical plan to kill the people she needed to keep alive. He did all these things and still kept a sense of humour. She was impressed. The only thing about him that concerned her was something that other women would find appealing he was magnetic. She couldn't walk next to him without feeling it. It concerned her as this distraction could be the difference between life or death for her boss.

"I promise I'll never eat rabbit again. Feel better now?" she asked.

"You know, I think this is a break-through. We need to celebrate. How about a glass of wine?" Sean smiled cheerfully.

"Great idea. Something from Napa Valley."

Errol Bader

CHAPTER TWENTY SEVEN

CONCERT AT PRAGUE CASTLE

Marie Tereskova was in a hurry. She had an invitation to a 7 p.m. concert on the Prague Castle grounds at St. Vit's Cathedral. She stopped at the post office on the way. Marie was surprised at the size and weight of the package when the postal clerk handed it to her. Her camera was already taking up one shoulder. The package was bulky and she was on foot so carrying the package was difficult.

"Marie, let me help you with that," suggested Jan Neruda as he entered the street from a nearby shop. This was the young man Elli, Marie's friend, had mentioned to her earlier in the day. "It looks heavy," he commented.

"Oh, Jan, thank you, answered Marie. "I could use the help. My house is just down the block." She found herself smiling girlishly.

"Are you going to the concert tonight, Marie?"

"Well, I don't know. I'm pretty busy." She did not want him to know how interested she was.

"It's a beautiful evening. C'mon, it'll be great fun. The cathedral will be lit up like a Christmas tree, and the music will be great." Jan was working hard and Marie was enjoying the spectacle.

"Well, Okay," Marie replied, trying to hide her expression. "I'll have to put something warmer on."

They arrived at Marie's apartment.

"Jan, would was you like to come in and wait while I change?" Marie's suggestion was put in a way hard to refuse. "Then you can walk me to the concert." How could he refuse and leave her to walk alone?

Geocache

"Sure, of course," he answered.

Marie unlocked the door and they entered a vestibule. Once inside Jan placed the parcel on a side table and took a seat on Marie's sofa. She offered to serve him a glass of wine while he waited. He declined but agreed to a cup of hot tea. Marie glanced at the parcel sitting on the side table and for a brief second thought she would take a look at the contents. Most recipients would have immediately dropped everything to satisfy their curiosity, but Marie saw no importance in material things. Right now her concern was to change, freshen up, and look pretty. The package could wait; it would be there when she got back.

Marie came into the parlour wearing a herringbone long-sleeve coat and a black skirt. Under the jacket she had a purple, silk high-collared blouse with a white scarf wrapped loosely around her neck, one end forming a tail hanging down in front of her coat. "All right. How do I look?"

"You look very pretty, Marie."

She got what she wanted; he had meant what he said. She smiled and grabbed his arm.

"Let's go ... time to take in a concert."

She led Jan past the side table and then momentarily glanced at the mysterious package. No, the concert was more important; her company took precedence. The package could wait.

Prague or Praha, as Europeans call the city, was spectacular at night. The streets are cobblestone. Illumination came from glass street lamps on top of tall poles, reminiscent of the gas lights of a century ago. The exteriors of the city's grand old churches and administration buildings were lit with high-intensity lights, causing the structures to glow bronze and subtle shades of gold. Some copper spires and roof features had oxidized to a wonderful patina. The city was one of the three jewels of the Hapsburg Dynasty. Budapest and Vienna, the other two cities, lie to the east along the river Danube.

Marie and Jan walked briskly through the downtown streets and along the Charles Bridge, crossing the Vltava River, which separated the old town from the modern expanse where Marie lived.

It was a clear night as they walked across the centuries' old bridge. A work of art in itself, the bridge was perhaps the single most romantic place in the world. The old bridge, somehow had its own soul, wishing to be traversed only by young lovers, putting a sole pedestrian out of place. Marie and Jan would contribute to its joy and dwell for a while among the sixty sandstone saints guarding the ancient land-link.

Halfway across the bridge, they stopped to look up at the brightly-lit castle on the hill. It was a vestige of power and elegance from a time long ago. Leaving the Charles Bridge, they climbed the cobblestone streets leading up to the castle and entered the castle's open square which surrounded St Vit's Cathedral. (50°05' 26.28" N 14° 24' 02.20" E)

"Elli! Hi, over here." Marie waved to Elli in the gathering crowd, who in turn motioned Marie to join the small group of young people. Elli saw Jan Neruda was with Marie.

"Hey, where did you hook up with him?" Elli asked.

"An act of God, I think," she whispered.

The evening of entertainment was perfect for the young people. The Dan Mathews Band from America played a blend of blues and rock. The large crowd pressed in close raising the outside temperature to a comfortable level. A good time was had by all.

When the concert was over, Jan walked Marie back to her apartment. He stopped at her front door, intending to wish her a restful night but after she unlocked the door and turned to face him, she reached out and grasped his coat pulling him inside the vestibule. Inside Marie's warm sanctum, their outer garments littered the hallway and an inner door was closed, muffling playful giggles. The package would wait another day.

CHAPTER TWENTY EIGHT

BRIDGE OVER THE INN RIVER

Peter Leisel enjoyed a good night's sleep. The flight into Innsbruck Airport the day before had exhausted him. The bed at the Vornehmes Hotel was unusually comfortable as hotels go. The thick down comforter and large, soft pillows made it difficult to roll out of bed.

He had worked hard to be in Innsbruck this morning. When he checked in at the front desk the night before, he confirmed that the hotel's flat screen computer was functioning. His instructions from the Jack and Elizabeth Gielgood Foundation required that he log on to the website *www.petersgeocachesite.com* and record the latitude and longitude of his geocache site. Peter had to arrive at the coordinates by two o'clock in the afternoon or risk missing the prize.

The wakeup call was prompt if not annoying. He staggered to the bathroom sink and splashed cold water in his eyes. He then pulled open the window drapes to reveal the kind of day it would be in the mountains.

The sun was rising and the streetlights were fading out. The morning sunlight streamed through cirrus clouds on the eastern horizon. Golden rays of sunlight blended with streaks of orange and together they splashed across the cobalt blue of the Austrian sky. Innsbruck's mountain ridges were still dark and silhouetted by the celebration of colours in the sky. It would be clear and crisp this morning. A good morning to become wealthy, Peter thought.

He looked down on the River Inn, as it flowed through the centre of the historic city, forming the Inn Valley and spawning the city itself. Roman soldiers were here first. Fifteen years before Christ's death, they were using the River Inn to travel northward on their way to the Danube. This wide part of the valley was a favourite staging area for the Roman army as it expanded its control over all of Tyrol.

At this site, close to where Leisel was standing, the Roman Legions built a fortress called Veldidena, which is now known as the district of Wilten. Slowly a village formed around the fortress. South of the fortress a marketplace had grown. Commerce across the river became more and more important. By 1187, Innsbruck or the "Bridge over the Inn" became central to the moving of goods north and south along the Austrian Alps.

By the fifteenth century, Emperor Maximilian I had claimed Innsbruck as his capital and financial centre. From his window Peter could see Maximilian's gift to the city, The Das Goldene Dachl — a beautiful example of Renaissance architecture replete with gold-lined copper shingles. The Dachl had survived 21 Allied bombing raids on Innsbruck during the Second World War. *Time to get going,* Leisel said to himself. He showered and dressed. He put on olive green woollen trousers, a white turtleneck sweater, with a red and white heavy knitted pullover. He pulled on his hiking boots and a dark brown beret to cover his straight blond hair. He looked more like a local than a visitor as he picked up his knapsack and threw it over his shoulder. The knapsack had enough room to handle most of the cash he anticipated. Inside the sack was another nylon bag which he was certain would expand enough to carry the balance of the cash.

Leisel had reserved a rental car he would pick up in Centre City, but first he needed to obtain the coordinates from his website. A pretty, young Asian girl at the front desk was on the phone taking a reservation as he approached. He stood by and waited patiently. There was a basket of fresh red apples sitting on the counter. He thought about taking one; but then again, he would need a good breakfast. He could not tell for sure how long his trip would be or how much energy he would expend getting to his geocache site. He decided to log online and get the

Geocache

coordinates first and then have a good breakfast.

"Yes, sir, I'm sorry I had to take a reservation. The closer we get to New Year's Eve, the busier the telephone gets." Leisel saw engraved on her plastic nametag, pinned to her blouse, her name and hometown. Jade was from the United States; Melbourne, Florida. Leisel discerned that she might be the offspring of a Cuban father, possibly of Chinese origin, and a mother of Russian ancestry. "What brings you over from the States, Jade?" Leisel asked.

"I took a year off from college to work in Austria," she answered. "I love it here, but I'm not used to the cold yet."

"Well, get ready, because in a few weeks this city will be jammed with people celebrating New Year's Eve. Especially the Italians — they take over Innsbruck on New Year's Eve, and the Italians know how to celebrate."

"Ah, you must be a regular visitor?" smiled Jade.

"I like to make New Year's Eve celebrations in Innsbruck a regular event; I know the old city well. Innsbruck was one of my favourite places," Leisel smiled back. Then his composure became more serious.

"Jade, I need to use the hotel's computer to go on the internet. Can you arrange this please?"

"Sure. It's just to the left of the bellman's stand. There is a small room with a computer, printer, and telephone. You will need this key."

She handed him a key attached to a large, flat piece of plastic. The fact that Jade had the key at the desk meant there were no other guests using the little office.

"Thank you, Jade. I won't be long."

The computer was already running a screensaver on the flat screen. It was a picture of the Baroque church Domkirche St. Jakob built in Innsbruck during the reign of Empress Maria Theresia. Leisel typed, *"www.petersgeocachesite.com"* into the address line. The connection was slow; it seemed to be taking months to build the page. Then the header splashed across the

Errol Bader

screen – *petersgeocachesite*. The coordinates followed: 47° 21' 42.49" North; 11° 11' 59.50" East.

Leisel had what he needed. His heart skipped a beat. He closed the site and then opened a search engine. He found and opened a global search program which utilised satellite photography to locate and zoom in to any spot on the earth.

He loaded the coordinates and soon the site was pinpointed, the top of a mountain next to a small village called Leutasch. It was perhaps only a 45 minute drive from Innsbruck. But he could see a climb would be necessary from Leutasch.

The program provided a feature enabling him to put a place mark on the location. He decided to mark the spot and print out the page. It would make it easier to travel to the area. He would only need the laptop's GPS guidance when he reached the mountain to the east of Leutasch. His task complete, Peter closed the program and left the computer.

"Thank you, Jade. I'll be back in a few hours." He handed the computer-room key to Jade but had planned to come back and stay one more night. The flight from Wiener Neustadt had almost taken his life. Now he was so close to his goal he was through taking chances. Flying in the mountains at night was a good way of dying young anyway.

"Where are you headed today, Mr. Leisel? Sightseeing?" asked Jade.

"Going for a hike in the woods today, Jade."

"Great. You have a good day for it. The weather is nice for being outside."

Breakfast only took him fifteen minutes to wolf down. The hotel restaurant offered the convenience of a full buffet. It was only three blocks down Main Street to the car rental office. He walked by five- and six-story apartment buildings that lined the wide street full of shops facing the Main Street. The car rental office was at the base of a clock tower. He had reserved a four-wheel drive just in case it was needed. The attendant was an older man with a silver handlebar moustache and a pleasant smile. He

Geocache

wore traditional Austrian garb, a decorative tan vest over a white shirt and grey flannel trousers. His silver hair was covered by a felt Fedora hat with a colourful feather on one side.

"Hallo. My name is Peter Leisel. I have a car rented for today and tomorrow."

"Hallo. I'm Hans. Well, let me look you up," Hans answered. "Ja, here it is; a four- wheel drive Jeep. Will you need a map, Mr. Leisel?" asked the old man.

"No, danke. I know the way."

"Gut, then just go through the back door. The car is in the parking lot behind our building. I will see you tomorrow. Here is our card with our phone number if you have any problems. The car is full of benzene."

Peter headed west through town, passed the Vols District by the Innsbruck Airport. He could see his Twin Star aircraft tied down on the ramp as he drove by the airport on his way out of town. The road hugged the River Inn on its winding course through the city. The river road passed by the airport and crossed by the end of the runway, giving him a view of its entire length. He thought about the departure he would make the next morning.

The Furn winds were blowing over the mountains from Italy, and so he would bank left immediately upon takeoff and hug the mountains on the north side of the Inn Valley. This would avoid the extreme down-drafts in the middle of the valley.

He was getting ahead of himself. He continued to drive along the river until reaching Zirl. Just past Inzing, the road crossed over the river to the north. He found a road that cut northward into the mountains. It climbed up the side of the mountain until it levelled off above the valley. He drove the Jeep onto a plateau and passed by a narrow but long mountain lake on his right and on through the small village of Auland.

Continuing north through the valley, he passed through Krinz and then into the large Olympia Region of Seefeld. A big open plateau, the region was a well-populated winter wonderland. The tall, jagged, grey mountain peaks of the Wetterstein Range serve as a backdrop for the splendid panoramas that could be seen from the plateau.

Leisel had been here before to ski with friends. The views from Seefeld are believed by many to be the most spectacular anywhere in the world. He drove past the Seekirchl or Lake Chapel just as the church bell began to ring. The sound of the old bell echoed through the mountains. Bell-ringing was an age-old tradition in the region's Karwendel Alpine Park.

The road became narrower as it continued in a northerly direction from Seefeld. He finally reached his destination, at least as far as he could travel by car.

Leutasch, a village of twenty-four small hamlets, was nestled in a quiet and little-travelled area of the Alps — a place where locals go to find beauty and peaceful vistas away from large numbers of tourists. Leisel parked the Jeep and pulled the backpack over his shoulders, inside was the laptop.

He started up a path leading towards the mountain peak where he would find the coordinates — for ground zero. The wind had blown the snow, from the last storm, into the tall pines that covered the mountain sides. The trail was exposed, though covered with a carpet of pine-needles. He walked through an open field until he intercepted a trail which travelled straight north almost to the mountain top. Then the trail turned east running along the ridge crest a few hundred feet below the peak. One last switch back and Peter reached the top.

He took a minute to catch his breath. He had a 360° view of the Alpine region. Off to the northwest, he saw the village of Platzl and to the east was Glessenbach in a quiet valley. Turning to look south, he had a birds'-eye view of beautiful Seefeld and its dark blue lake.

Peter knelt down on one knee and removed his backpack. He was in a small clearing on the tree-covered mountain top. Thoughts of what one and a half million dollars might look like entered his mind. He was on time. It hadn't been easy to get to

Geocache

this remote place at the appointed hour.

The computer had plenty of juice left in its battery. It seemed so long ago since it was delivered to him in Wiener Neustadt. He turned it on and opened up the GPS program. The moving map appeared. The target was nearby – 50 metres west along the ridge. Peter began walking towards what he thought was the target. It never crossed his mind that he might be the target. He entered the trees and the environment changed. It was darker here and the temperature dropped ten degrees. He was alternating his attention between the laptop screen and the view ahead as he drew nearer to ground zero. There was wildlife all around him; he could hear them moving through the trees. Even with the sounds of the animals and the occasional bird chirping, it was quiet. He stopped and looked up. He had a feeling he was being watched. He turned around, looking through the trees in all directions. Perhaps it was the person who placed the geocache here. He remembered that his instructions warned that if he were late arriving at the site, the geocache would be removed. Someone must still be up here monitoring the site, he thought.

"Hallo," he shouted. "Is anyone here?" The silence of the forest was broken by Peter's voice. There was no answer. Regardless, he was not alone; he could sense it. He turned back to his mission, and then he saw it, a thin, plastic rod sticking up six feet above the forest floor with a red flag atop the rod. The flag pole was exactly at the coordinates as promised. He had arrived at last.

Odd, unexpected thoughts go through a person's mind when confronted with life altering events. Peter Leisel thought to himself, *I'll never waste time searching for old Jews for the church again.*

He ran to the flag and found an aluminum suitcase-like container on the ground at the base of the flagpole. He unlatched the two latches and lifted up the top half of the case. The contents were covered by a towel, and on top of the towel, was an envelope. He was not wearing gloves, but he should have been. It was getting colder, and he had wished he had brought a pair. Like Antoine Sandel before him, he lifted the envelope up and opened it. He read the type-written words, "Willkommen, Peter. We are happy you made it to your Geocache site. Congratulations, we will see you soon."

Hmm, he thought, *where is the certificate for the second one and a half million dollars?* Peter reached for the towel with both hands to recover his treasure. The towel was soaked with something that had a sweet smell to it, almost like a flower in springtime. The towel was removed revealing nothing but newspaper. Peter threw the paper out onto the forest floor. Why? He thought, *why would someone go to —* ? He stood up. Something was wrong. Breathing was becoming a chore. He felt like he was suffocating. He fell to his knees grasping at his heart. The pain was like nothing he had ever experienced. His heart felt like it was exploding. He fell on his back. The last thing Peter saw before he died was light streaming down on him through the treetops, slightly blocked by the shadow of a figure standing above him. One thing Peter Leisel was right about, he would never again waste his time searching for old Jews for the church in Wiener Neustadt. This wasn't a life-altering event; this was a life-ending event.

CHAPTER TWENTY NINE

THE BOOTLEGGER

Český Těšín - Czech Republic
Czeski Cieszyn - Poland
49° 44'51.29" N 18° 38'06.54" E

Dieter Manheim called Prague his home, but he made his living performing transactions in an area unknown to most tourists travelling to Eastern Europe. In point of fact, few Europeans would think of the divided cities of Český Těšín and Czeski Cieszyn as a prime tourist destination, unless the tourist had a penchant for early European history.

Tesin was founded, as legend has it, by three brothers long before the nations of Czech Republic and Poland existed. According to legend, the three brothers of Duke Leszko III met repeatedly at a well along the Olza River. The year was 810 A.D. To this day, the ancient well still exists just on the Poland side of the Olza River, the dividing line between the sister cities. The well is known appropriately as "The Well of the Three Brothers." The river and the well gave life to the region, and eventually a castle was built on a hill on the Poland side of the river. The structure stands to this day on Castle Hill; a square stone tower with a parapet at the top. The Piast Tower, as it is called, has a commanding view of the region.

Piast Tower became the seat of power of the government of Poland in the 10th century. In time the unified town of Tesin spread out on both sides of the Olza. During the first World War, the region of Cieszyn was the home of the Austrian High Command. Then in July 1920, after a territorial dispute, Cieszyn was divided. The rightbank of the Olza, the historic side was ceded to Poland. The left bank, the suburbs, were ceded to Czech Republic.

Errol Bader

When the Nazis arrived in 1938, they forced unification on the two cities again, and only the language of German was permitted to be spoken. Almost the entire Jewish population was slaughtered by the Third Reich. Their synagogues were destroyed; however, the region suffered little war damage from the Allied bombings across Europe.

The footbridge connecting the two cities was still in existence. On the Czech side, one block from the approach to the bridge and within view of the river crossing is where Dieter Manheim did business. Dieter was a bootlegger, a bootlegger in the literal sense. The term "bootlegger" comes from a time when horsemen wore high boots and hid either weapons or contraband in them. This modern-day bootlegger supplied large quantities of liquor to a robust smuggling business.

Every week he or his assistant drove an enclosed van full of legally purchased bottles of liquor from Prague east to the Czech side of Tesin. There, by the side of the pedestrian bridge, in full view, he opened the back doors of the van. As if on cue, a host of locals appeared at the rear of the van. The bootlegger's apprentices came in all sizes and shapes: matronly women, young men, even teenagers. Dieter handed the bottles to his partners in crime as though they were loaves of bread being distributed to the needy. They raised their dresses or trousers and taped the bottles to their legs. Some of the more ambitious workers taped two bottles to each leg. Often the bootlegger cadre arrived with empty beer coolers. They filled the coolers with liquor bottles. Two men usually carried the big containers, one on each side, on their way to eager consumers waiting on the other side of the bridge in Poland.

Alcoholism was a raging beast on the Poland side of the Olza. Demand was high. Authorities in Poland tried to limit the availability of liquor to stem the problem. A rule forbade a person from transporting more than one bottle of liquor across the footbridge into Poland per day. In reality, these bottle-laden people made numerous trips back and forth across the bridge

Geocache

every day. They waddled by the border guards. Seldom were they or the beer coolers checked by the guards. Once on the Polish side of the bridge and just beyond the guard post, the exchange of money for liquor was accomplished. A bazaar with little flea market booths provided the setting for the daylong transactions. Upon their return across the bridge, the smugglers revisited the van and delivered the earnings to Dieter.

Each Friday Dieter delivered one third of the illicit profit for the week to his cohorts at the foot of the bridge. Every one was happy, except the relatives of the addicts who fuelled the demand that enriched Dieter Manheim. Fridays were paydays in Český Těšín. They say there is honour among thieves, but only because it is a necessity to continue in business. Dieter always delivered the cash that kept his workers loyal. He was a popular guy because he fed a lot of mouths. He was driving the van back to the old hotel, where he was a regular guest when he received a call on his cell phone.

"Hallo," Dieter answered.

"Hallo, Dieter. This is Henryk. How was your day?" It was Henryk Kinsky, Dieter's operations manager. Henryk was responsible for the purchasing and stocking of their product. Henryk's Prague activities were legal if not above board. He could buy as much liquor at wholesale prices as his boss desired, and pay tax on everything he bought.

"Dieter, I went by to collect your mail for the week. There was a special delivery notice on your front door. Someone sent you a package that requires written acceptance."

"Okay. Henryk, give me the tracking number. I'll call the post office and ask them to deliver the package to our office in Prague. You can sign for it. When you have the parcel, give it to Oscar, along with my other mail. He's driving this way with another shipment."

"You still talking to your ex-brother-in-law?" laughed Henryk.

"Why not, he's a good worker," chuckled Dieter, then

wheezed. "Besides, I don't mind him making some money on the side. Better it goes to him than his sister." He laughed but the wheeze developed into a full blown coughing fit.

"Did you order something, Dieter?" Henryk's tone became serious.

"No," Dieter frowned, beginning to compose himself once more, then his thick eyebrows rose "Probably a promotion for detergent. I get too much junk mail." Another coughing fit got the better of him.

"You coping okay, Dieter?" inquired Henryk. Dieter, like so many people spending a lot of time in the old city, had developed a respiratory problem. The region was an industrial area. Little had been done to filter the smoke spewing from factory smokestacks in the region. The air quality was amongst the worst in Europe.

"No. I need a vacation from this place" Dieter responded. "If only the Municipals would pull there finger out and enforce the clean environment programme, this city would be fabulous. It's going to take a generation to make this place comfortable again, but it's a living, Henryk, isn't it?"

"Can't complain, we could still be oppressed by the Russians, eh. Least we have our freedom," Henryk chirped.

"Yes, but at what price?" muttered Deiter. "Its getting tougher with the Euro forcing prices sky high."

"That's why we do what we do to make things cheaper," responded Henryk. "We can deliver at the right price and the people want a good stiff drink every now and then, and we deliver. Talk to you later, Dieter. I'll get your parcel and have Oscar bring it to you. Don't worry."

Henryk liked to rationalise away any responsibility for assisting addicts in ruining their lives and others around them. Besides, what he was doing for the enterprise was legal. It was Dieter who took all the risk, not him. Henryk felt like he had a pretty good deal. Dieter even rented the little warehouse and office he worked in.

Geocache

A few blocks from the hotel, Dieter stopped at a traffic light. The car was built with its steering wheel on the right side. He glanced up and to his right and looked at the familiar artwork on the wall of the building next to him. It was a giant faded painting of a Russian peasant — rigid, angular, and standing tall in the traditional heroic communist pose. The peasant's sleeves were rolled up with a raised, strong, right arm holding a farm implement as though it were a weapon. The painting covered the wall from sidewalk to rooftop.

The fresco was a remnant of Soviet rule. He looked at the painting with contempt. Dieter may have been a criminal, but he was also a capitalist. True enough, in some places around the world, these terms were thought to be interchangeable. Communism, in Dieter's opinion, had been a cancer on Europe. Things were much better now, at least in his beautiful Prague, even with the higher prices. But this old city on the Olza River was still struggling with high unemployment. The problem existed on both sides of the river, but it is worse on Poland's side. The light turned green, and after another two blocks, he arrived outside his hotel. Once out of the van, he began walking toward the hotel entrance. He looked up at the grey sky — with its heavy concentration of pollutants in the air. He walked on an old cobblestone street lined with apartment buildings from the turn of the last century. The communists had adorned the tops of these buildings with pre-cast concrete structures, rows of cement bowls with masonry fruit over-flowing from the tops of the urns. The sculptures were a communist symbol — a promise of plentiful fruit for the obedient masses. Dieter had one thought, *Never worked for me.*

Entering the hotel lobby, he passed a door to a little cabaret on his right. Beyond the cabaret entrance was an unoccupied front desk. Light bulbs in the ceiling were connected to exposed wires stapled to the walls and ceiling. Walking by the desk, he climbed a set of stairs that turned at a landing halfway to the second floor. At the landing there was a stained glass window with a hole through it the size of a grapefruit. The damage was done years before, and the landing showed the wear and tear of many a drenching rain. No one cared enough to fix the glass or even to put a plank over it to keep the weather out. This is what decades of socialism had achieved, and this was one of the better hotels in town. *These people here have been ruined*, Dieter thought. He spoke out loud to himself, *"I have to quit this business soon; I want to go back to Prague where they know how to wire light fixtures."*

CHAPTER THIRTY

A MISSING PILOT

"Good morning, Austro Control," the Austro Control switchboard operator answered.

"Good morning. Can you connect me with search and rescue? Danka."

"Yes, one moment, please."

"Search and rescue, Franz speaking."

"Hallo, Franz, this is Paul Freidan. I work for the Diamond Aircraft Flying Club at Wiener Neustadt Airport. I was wondering if you have had any reports of an accident involving a Diamond Twin Star in the last three or four days. We have a club plane overdue."

Peter Leisel was overdue returning the Diamond Twin Star to Wiener Neustadt. When Paul Friedan, the airport lineman, had reported for work he was certain he would have seen the plane registered OE72JP parked back on line. When he saw the aircraft was missing, he was concerned. He had then called Austro Control in Vienna, the Austrian equivalent to the Federal Aviation Administration (FAA) in the United States.

"No, Paul, no accidents at all anywhere in Austria or Germany," reported Franz Zimmer, at Austro Control Search and Rescue. "What was the pilot's destination?"

"I'm sure he told me he was heading for Innsbruck," answered the lineman. "I remember the weather was not so good in the mountains when he left. I'm concerned he may have gone down scud-running in the Alps."

"Why don't you give me the pilot's name and the Oscar Echo number? I'll call up to Innsbruck and see what they have to say. Give me your phone number and I'll call you right back."

Errol Bader

Franz was a dedicated search and rescue professional. He never took calls like Paul's lightly. Franz wasted no time before dialing Innsbruck Airport.

"Good morning, Innsbruck Administration," answered the airport administration office receptionist. "Daniella speaking."

"Good morning, Daniella. This is Franz Zimmer at Austro Control Search and Rescue. I'm checking on the location of a Diamond Twin Star DA42, OE72JP. Is this aircraft on the field?"

"Yes, Mr. Zimmer. The aircraft is still here. We expected the pilot, Mr. Leisel, to have paid his tie-down and landing fee; and have departed by now. When he landed, he told us he would be leaving the next day. That was two days ago."

"I see. Well, at least we know the aircraft is safely on the ground. The aircraft belongs to the Diamond Aircraft Flying Club. I'll give them a call and let them know their aircraft is all right. Thanks, Daniella."

"That's all right. Oh, by the way, Mr. Zimmer, according to the landing fee form Mr. Leisel filled out, he was staying at the Vornehmes Hotel in Innsbruck."

"Thank you, Daniella. I think I'll call the hotel and check on Mr. Leisel."

Technically, Franz's responsibility stopped when he discovered Twin Star OE72JP was safe. He could easily have declared the search over, but he always went the extra mile, never wanting to overlook something that might cost someone their life.

It took Franz a few minutes to look up the number to the Vornehmes Hotel.

"Good morning. Vornehmes. Jade speaking."

"Good morning, Jade. My name is Franz Zimmer. I'm with Austro Control. I'm looking for a Mr. Peter Leisel. Can you tell me if he is at your hotel?"

"Let me take a look at the register. Oh sure, now I remember. Mr. Leisel arrived on the 1st of December. I saw him go out the next morning. He reserved the room until December 3rd. I remember he said he would be back for the night, but I'm not sure he ever did. We cleaned the room on the 3rd and billed Mr. Leisel's credit card. Why? Has something happened to Mr. Leisel?" asked Jade.

"I'm not sure. Did he say where he was going?"

"Only that he was going for a hike," she answered.

"All right, Jade. Thank you. You've been very helpful. All the best."

Franz felt uneasy. This was 5th of December; Leisel had left the hotel on December 2nd. His hotel room was only reserved until the 3rd. Franz had learnt over the years that pilots were, as a group, a fairly responsible lot. He felt that if Leisel had decided to stay in the mountains an extra few days, he would have called the flying club and told them of his plans. Other pilots may have reserved the club aircraft and made plans to fly on business or pleasure. Few flying club members would keep an aircraft beyond its scheduled return without at least placing a call to the club dispatcher. Obviously, Leisel had not made that call or the lineman would not have called search and rescue looking for him. Franz had promised to call Paul at the flying club and let him know what he had discovered.

"Hallo. Diamond Flying Club. This is Paul"

"Paul, this is Franz from Austro Control. I located your aircraft tied down at the Innsbruck Airport. Your customer checked out of his hotel either on the 2nd or 3rd. It's uncertain which day. He has not been heard from since. Mr. Leisel told the receptionist at the hotel that he was going for a hike. Is Mr. Leisel the kind of fellow who would ignore his deadline to return the aircraft?" Franz was hoping to hear that Leisel was a character likely to forget such things.

"No, Peter Leisel would never keep an airplane beyond its scheduled return without calling," answered the lineman.

"Something must be wrong. Maybe he fell and injured himself hiking somewhere in the mountains."

"Paul," he replied, "I think we need to err on the cautionary side. I'm going to call our *search and rescue* supervisor up at

Innsbruck and ask him to do some investigating. Hopefully, Mr. Leisel is sitting in a hostel having a cup of hot chocolate. I'll let you know what we discover. If you hear from Mr. Leisel, please call me right away."

CHAPTER THIRTY ONE

AN INVITATION TO ST. JOHN

Marie fixed Jan a good breakfast. She wanted him to know she could cook a good Czech meal. The evening together had proved Jan was a good lover. She was determined to reel him in. And judging from the way he wolfed down the eggs and sausage, she felt the hook was well set. They liked each other and would plan to attend more concerts together. They had talked most of the night about Prague, about the friends they had in common, and about their individual interests.

Jan was impressed by Marie's love of life and her desire to help others. He knew people who talked about doing work to help others. However, Marie wasn't just talking about making a difference in people's lives, she was working at it. Jan had joined the Prague Blood Donor Registry staff for the same purpose. Neither Jan nor Marie were motivated by material things. They found plenty of rewards in their life-saving work.

It was time for Jan to leave. The two walked to the apartment door, and Jan kissed Marie good bye. As he brushed by her, she smiled and watched him walk down the cobblestone street. She turned toward the little kitchen, intending to wash the breakfast dishes, when she saw the parcel sitting on the side table. The dishes took priority over the package so oblivious was she to material things. Finally, the dishes put away, Marie turned her attention to the parcel. She discarded the brown paper wrapping on the floor. The cardboard box was opened revealing a laptop computer with an envelope on top. Marie lifted up the single envelope and a ten thousand dollar check with her name on it fell to the floor in front of her. She sat on her couch, her gaze transfixed on the check. Who would send her a ten thousand dollar check? She picked up the check and read the name on the upper left-hand corner. "The Jack and Elizabeth Gielgood Foundation" was imprinted on it. The background of the check was covered with numerous images of a family crest printed in grey halftone. There was a small slip of paper with a user name and password taped to the cover of the laptop.

Marie opened the laptop, turned it on, and typed in "*GEO*" and then "*CACHE*." She sat quietly reading the killer's skillfully written letter. As Marie read and absorbed the document's message, she began to plan how best the registry could put three million dollars to use – the whole three million dollars. It never crossed her mind that she should keep any of the money for herself.

The author of the letter had used the kind of guile that the snake in the Garden of Eden would have admired. The killer had found a victim who would not have responded to the greedy prospect of easily-found wealth. This time the philanthropic appeal of the foundation's proposition had found its mark. Marie's innocence and care for the well-being of others would send her packing for a trip to a warm place, her destination, St. John, a small sparsely-populated tropical island in the U.S. Virgin Islands. She had read about the Virgin Islands but never dreamed she would actually go there.

Marie wanted to reach for the phone and call her friend Elli. She was bursting with joy at the prospect of giving all that money to her good cause. But telling anyone about her trip might ruin everything. No, she would just tell Elli she had decided to take a short leave of absence from the registry. She would tell both Elli and Jan that she was going on a trip to Budapest to take black and white photos for an upcoming photographic contest. It's something she had talked about doing before. The ancient castle, gothic cathedrals and historical facades of Budapest were such intriguing subjects for black and white photography. Yes, that is what she would tell them. It would be a little white lie but for a very great cause.

Geocache

She was certain they would forgive her upon her return. The furthest thing from her mind was the possibility she was being stalked by a cold-blooded killer who planned that she never returned. The siren's song of riches, whether for good purposes or bad, was summoning Marie to a tropical island in the Caribbean Sea. It has been said by visitors to that island paradise that the island of St. John is so beautiful that it is "To die for."

CHAPTER THIRTY TWO

INTERRUPTING INTERPOL

45° 46'55.88" N   4° 50'54.15" E

The drive from Paris to Lyon had given Victoria an opportunity to learn about Sean Mason's life and times. At dinner the night before, they had agreed they would work together to keep anymore of the European donors from meeting a violent and premature death. The new Interpol I-24/7 Global Communications System, housed in Lyon, tied cooperating police agencies around the world into one homogenous database. This is where Sean would look for fugitives, missing persons, or persons of interest.

The I-24/7 search engine was powerful, capable of surfacing names of individuals being sought by networked global law enforcement agencies.

Sean and Victoria entered the main river-front entrance to Interpol's headquarters building. Not that it was necessary, but out of habit, Sean clipped his ID badge on his jacket pocket.

"Hallo, Inspector Mason, welcome back." The guard greeted them as they approached the front desk.

"Hallo, Francois. Good to be back. This is Victoria Kavanagh, my guest. She is ex-secret service".

"Pleased to make your acquaintance, Ms. Kavanagh. Please sign the register and pin this guest ID on. Welcome to Interpol."

Behind the guard's desk, the locks on the bulletproof glass double doors clicked to the open position allowing access to the ground floor elevators. Sean pressed the seventh floor button; and the doors opened revealing three young men and a young woman. The woman exited the elevator, but the men stood in place looking at Victoria.

"Well, what will it be? Out, up, or what?" Sean woke the

three out of their trance. They walked past Victoria all the while staring at her. Sean and Victoria stepped inside and the doors closed.

"How does anybody get anything done with you around?" remarked Sean.

"I've heard it all before — even from my boss. It's not my fault. It's aggravating. People are so fixated on the superficial."

The doors opened onto the seventh floor command and coordination centre, a large chamber, a war room with international crime as the enemy. Around the outer walls were circular banks of computers manned by Interpol technicians. Sean led Victoria through the room to his office. She felt a dozen pairs of eyes follow her. The keyboard activity slowed down. As they reached the far side of the room, there were only a few keystrokes heard.

Sean opened the door to his office and ushered Victoria into his home away from home. It was clearly a man's office, nothing sentimental lying around. Three ball caps sat on the credenza.

"What's the story behind the CIA ball cap?" she asked.

"I was an exchange student," he smiled. "The force in Scotland sent me States-side for Special Forces training at Langley, Virginia."

"Ever hear of a D.I. by the name of O'Hara?" asked Victoria.

"O'Hara, O'Hara... Oh, yeah, I heard about him. Some woman trainee kneed him in the balls for making a sexist remark, a piece of folklore I think. If it's a true, she must be a real bitch." Sean smirked, then looked up at Victoria and saw her expression. "No, really? That was you?"

"He called me a piss-ant pinup."

"What happened after you . . . ?"

"He was too embarrassed to file a report. He let it go, but obviously the story won't die. So much for folk lore."

"All righty then; since you stopped the work of Interpol, let's take a tour of I-24/7 and see if we can find out more about your donors," Sean remarked. "Maybe later we can find a dress made of sackcloth, dye your hair purple, and paint some teeth brown. Perhaps that'll make you less of a distraction."

Victoria sneered at him. Sean pulled Doctor Luc's list of donors from his pocket. He typed in his password to log onto the I-24/7 search engine, then Antoine Sandel's into a program text field. A purple Interpol message appeared on screen. Marcus Webber's police report was displayed. No other criminal records were found for Sandel. Next, Sean typed in Peter Leisel's name. A yellow Interpol notice flashed onto the screen.

"What's this?" Sean was surprised to see the yellow warning notice for missing persons. "Victoria, someone's posted a missing persons report on Peter Leisel."

Victoria's pulse quickened.

"Missing?" she quizzed. "Where was the report filed? Who filed it?"

"In Vienna by a Franz Zimmer, replied Sean. "He must be Bundespolizei, Federal Police Department of Vienna. He reported Leisel missing on December 7th. I'll print out two copies."

Sean handed Victoria the first copy and she instantly began to read it. "Look, there's contact information for the Diamond Aircraft Flying Club and Austro Control up at Innsbruck. Franz Zimmer was quick to file the report according to the times and date."

"Victoria, this doesn't look good." stated Sean, his face rippled with worry lines. "Why didn't Leisel call the flying club if he was staying in the mountains? It's been five days since this report was filed, and there is no follow-on reports indicating closure. So, Leisel is still missing unless someone dropped the ball and didn't close the file."

"Why don't we call the flying club and see what they can tell us," suggested Victoria. She suddenly sat upright in the chair.

"You know," she began, a sense of urgency spread across her face. "There's a good chance another donor is dead or on the verge of being so."

Sean picked up the phone and tapped in the Wiener Neustadt's

Geocache

flying club number. "Diamond Flying Club, Jennifer speaking."

"Hallo, Jennifer. My name is Sean Mason. I'm an inspector with Interpol in Lyon. I'm enquiring about a Mr. Peter Leisel. Has he returned your aircraft yet?"

"Oh, let me get the manager for you." Jennifer turned in her seat and saw he was in the club office listening to her conversation. She raised the receiver towards him. He whispered *who is it?* And she replied *Interpol, about the missing pilot*, she whispered back with her hand clasped over the mouthpiece. The manager took the receiver from her.

"Hallo, this is Paul. Can I help you?"

"Paul, this is Inspector Sean Mason of Interpol. We are trying to locate Peter Leisel."

"Yes, I'm glad you called. We have been looking for him also. I called search and rescue in Vienna and told them about Peter's failure to return our Twin Star. He left it up at Innsbruck. We had to send a couple of pilots up to Innsbruck Airport to retrieve the aircraft. Our schedule was getting backed up; it's not like Peter to ignore his responsibility to the other club members. Mr. Zimmer with search and rescue filed a missing persons report on him. I believe that Peter is still up in the mountains. No one has heard from him here in Wiener Neustadt. We're quite worried."

"Paul, was there anything left in the aircraft that could provide us with a clue of where he went?" asked Sean.

"No," Paul answered. "Just the checklist, pilot operating handbook, and the local charts. Nothing else,"

"Have the police started an investigation? Do you know?" asked Sean.

"No. Mr. Zimmer called me to say the police would

not begin looking for Mr. Leisel until two weeks after someone was reported missing." "All right, Paul. Please call me if you hear anything from or about Mr. Leisel." Sean then gave Paul his phone numbers then hung up.

Sean looked at Victoria. "So what's next?"

"I think we should talk to Zimmer," Sean dialed Austro

Control.

"Austro Control, good day. How may I help you?" answered the switchboard operator.

"Inspector Sean Mason of Interpol here. I would like to speak with Franz Zimmer, in search and rescue."

"One moment please."

Sean heard the line click a couple of times, then...

"Franz Zimmer, how can I help you, Inspector Mason?"

"I read your missing person's report on Peter Leisel, and I would like to discuss it."

"I must say I'm surprised to hear Interpol is getting involved," answered Franz. "I thought Leisel's disappearance would stay a local matter?"

"We think there might be a link to one of our own investigations," Sean replied. "I have a colleague in my office. Would you mind if I put you on my speakerphone?"

"Of course. Go ahead."

"Can you hear us okay, Mr. Zimmer?"

"Yes, please call me Franz."

"Very well, Franz, this is Victoria Kavanagh. She has an interest in finding Mr. Leisel also." Victoria and Franz exchanged greetings.

"Franz, do you have any thoughts on Leisel's disappearance?" asked Victoria.

"Well, either he's still in the Alps as a result of an accident or something of a more sinister nature has happened to him," Franz remarked. "Unfortunately, the Vienna police can't mount an investigation until two weeks after his last appearance. I have no jurisdiction because the airplane is safely secured. It's frustrating no serious search has begun."

"Franz, it wasn't mentioned in your report, but do you know where Leisel was staying during his trip to Innsbruck?" Sean asked.

"Yes. He was staying at Hotel Vornehmes. I spoke to the receptionist on the phone. Her name is Jade. She said he left the

Geocache

hotel the morning of the 2nd, but was not sure he came back that evening. He was reserved until the 3rd. He had a hiking backpack with him when he left, and he told Jade that he was going for a hike. It's plausible because it was a beautiful day in the mountains on the 2nd."

"Okay. I think we better catch a plane to Innsbruck," Sean answered. "We need to see if we can trace his steps. Time may be getting away from us."

"That would be good. Please let me know if I can help," offered Franz.

"Thanks, Franz. You sound like the sort of fellow I'd want looking for me if I was in trouble. I'll let you know if — when we find Mr. Leisel," Sean had caught himself. He was not optimistic as he hung up the phone.

"Sean, can we do an I-24/7 search for Dieter Manheim?" requested Victoria. "If he turns up missing, it means real trouble." Victoria feared the worst.

"Sure, we may as well know what we are dealing with."

Sean typed in Dieter Manheim and Prague. The blood donor data base had located him in the Prague Blood Donor Registry.

"Interesting. Seems like Mr. Manheim has a history of trouble with the Prague Police Department. He served two years and three months at Hradcansky Domecek Prison, a small thirty-cell prison in the Hradcansky District of Prague. He was released in 2002." Sean was reading the police report from the I-24/7 system.

"What was he in for?" asked Victoria.

"Transport of illegal firearms. Here is another earlier conviction: embezzlement. He served three years, one month in the same prison. He must have liked it in there. He kept wanting to go back," said Sean.

"Sounds like a real winner. The way my luck's running, we'll find him alive but infected with some autoimmune disease from using bad needles."

CHAPTER THIRTY THREE

MEXICAN DEADLINE

Doctor Levy leant on the nurse's station desk looking over recent scans. The swelling around Maxwell's brain had reduced significantly. Almost a month had past since the accident. It was critical they brought Maxwell out of his coma. Doctor Levy pondered the file and what to prescribe next, when the elevator doors opened and two men exited. The doctor was the only person the men could see dressed in the appropriate garb.

Jorge de la Sierra and Vlad Kornikova had arrived unannounced.

"Where do you have Alex Maxwell? What room, please?" Jorge addressed Doctor Levy with more of a demand than a question. The four other members of the Global Geocache Society had been talking to each other ever since the accident. It was agreed during an early conference call that they would give the American doctors in Denver thirty days and no more to bring about an improvement in their friend's condition. Jorge and Vlad had volunteered to take matters into their own hands if necessary. There were two days left to go before the deadline arrived.

The men had travelled to Denver so they could assess Maxwell's condition and report to Armond and Niko. Vlad's Gulfstream jet had been converted to a hospital room in preparation for taking Maxwell to St. Petersburg, Russia, where some of the best brain-injury specialists were waiting. It was not that they did not trust the American doctors; they had a full background history on the medical team in Denver from the research their security departments had conducted during the preceding twenty eight days. Vlad had a complete file in his hand for both Doctor Levy and Doctor Lomello. However, thirty days was an important benchmark. The doctors in Russia had impressed upon Vlad that if Maxwell was still in a coma after a month, his chance of recovering would drop. They were not going to simply wait for bad news. These men were wired differently than most. They were take-charge types. One way or another they would make certain that Alexander Maxwell would recover if at all humanly possible. Maxwell would not die due to inaction on their part. All four knew that if it were one of them lying in that hospital bed, Alex would have been working overtime to save their lives. Now they were in Denver. They were on deck and God help anyone who got in their way.

"I'm Doctor Levy. I have been handling Mr. Maxwell's case. Can I help you?" answered the doctor.

"Yes. You can wake Mr. Maxwell up so that we can all go home," answered Jorge.

"Excuse me?" the Doctor wasn't expecting a verbal assault.

Vlad was a little more diplomatic.

"Doctor Levy, we know who you are. We know you and Doctor Lomello are very fine doctors, first-class doctors in your fields in fact. We know that this is an excellent hospital with an outstanding staff. We know your head floor nurse, Karin Rollins, is well qualified. Please understand Mr. Maxwell is a very good friend of ours. We have monitored Alex's condition from a distance. We had hoped by now that there would have been an improvement, and so we are concerned."

The doctor was impressed at the special knowledge these fellows had about the hospital and staff, even down to knowing that the floor nurse was Karin Rollins.

"Gentlemen, we are doing everything we can to help Mr. Maxwell. He has our complete attention," answered Doctor Levy, still not aware of who and what he was dealing with.

"Doctor Levy, if Alex is not out of his coma by the 15th of December, we are going to rip him out of this hospital so fast the wind from his gurney will strip you and your nurses naked." de la Sierra stared at the Doctor with eyes as penetrating as lasers.

"I take it you would like to see Mr. Maxwell?" The doctor was composing himself.

"Yes, Doctor. That would be very good," responded Vlad.

Together they walked down the corridor toward Maxwell's private room. As they drew closer, they heard a low voice coming from inside the suite. The doctor stopped at the open door and motioned to the others to be quiet. An almost inaudible whispering was coming from the room. It was a conversation, but at the same time, not a conversation. They strained to hear what was being said. Finally, the doctor led the way into the room. Karin Rollins was sitting at Maxwell's bedside. She and Maxwell were the only ones in the room, her mouth very near Maxwell's right ear. Karin sat upright when she realized she had company.

"Oh, hi, Doctor Levy. I was just . . . "

"I think I know what you were doing, Karin," answered Doctor Levy.

"This is Mr. de la Sierra and Mr. Kornikova. They are close friends of Mr. Maxwell's. They are here to visit Mr. Maxwell and perhaps reduce us to ashes if he doesn't improve soon."

"Gentlemen, why don't you have a seat and visit while I speak with Ms. Rollins for a few minutes. I'll be right back." Karin followed the doctor into the hallway. He walked a few paces down the corridor before stopping to talk.

"Karin, are you up to your old tricks again?"

"Ah, well . . . "

"Karin, you know what the official posture of the hospital administration is toward practicing hypnotism on the patients,"

They heard footsteps coming toward them. It was Doctor Lomello.

"Hey, what are you two whispering about? Gossip? Don't tell me – old Nurse Gerty finally had sex with the 75 year old dance instructor in room 523."

"Well, there are two mad men in the room with Mr. Maxwell, a Mexican and a Russian," Doctor Levy blabbered. "They threatened to strip me and every nurse on the floor of our clothes

Geocache

if Mr. Maxwell doesn't improve by December 15th. Karin here is practicing hypnotism on the patient. Other than that, how was the play, Mrs. Lincoln?"

"Really? They threatened to strip all the nurses?"

"I'm not kidding," Doctor Levy said. "That Mexican has a crazy look in his eyes; reminds me of Captain Hook."

"Okay," Doctor Lomello turned to the nurse. "Karin, are you doing any good? Making any headway?"

"Wait a minute. You're in on this?" Doctor Levy was catching on.

"Listen," Doctor Lomello replied. "I've seen Karin perform wonders with her knowledge of hypnosis. We've tried everything else on this patient. It can't do any harm to let her try. You know as well as I do that if we don't get Mr. Maxwell out of his comatose state soon, we may never see a recovery. There are things about the workings of the brain that we don't completely understand. So, Karin tell me, are you getting any response at all?"

"Yes, I'm certain he can hear," answered the savvy nurse. "Just a few moments ago I actually heard him respond as if he were in a dream sleep. I have been quietly making suggestions to him, talking to him about his childhood. Sometimes a low monotone voice can pierce through the fog of a deep coma. I think if I stay with it, we may see an improvement," She had seen cases like this before. She just needed more time.

"Okay. Now let's talk to the gangsters," said Doctor Lomello. "Keep trying, Karin. Don't worry about the rules; I'll deal with the bureaucracy if it becomes necessary."

The three entered Maxwell's private hospital suite. Jorge and Vlad were standing next to bed talking to each other in low voices.

Doctor Levy did the introductions. "Gentlemen, this is Doctor Lomello. He's the primary physician in charge of Mr. Maxwell's recovery." He was eager to turn them over to Doctor Lomello and quickly excused himself – or perhaps it was the other way around, he was turning Doctor Lomello over to them.

Vlad was the first to speak. "Doctor Lomello, I think we may have been a little rough on your colleague. However, please understand we are here to satisfy ourselves that our friend is improving. If there is not an improvement very soon, we will do what is necessary to intervene. We can obtain whatever authority is necessary to move Mr. Maxwell if we have to. We hope it doesn't come to that, but time is running out."

He was being diplomatic but at the same time firmly informing the doctor of what was coming if results were not imminent. It was what Vlad did best. He was in his element - nice, calm, but results or else.

"I understand your concern. To be honest, I'm also concerned. We know the odds turn against the patient the longer he stays in a coma. I agree we are at a turning point. We will do all that our science allows and some things that are outside the box. I'm afraid I have to leave you now. Let's pray for the best." The doctor left Nurse Karin in the room with them.

Jorge addressed Karin in a more reserved tone. He could be charming when he wanted to be."Karin, how are you doing with him? Are you making any headway?"

"I'm sorry. What do you mean?" she asked.

"You're an expert in hypnotism. We expect you're trying hypnotism to wake up our friend."

"How do you know that?" Karin asked incredulously.

"We know about all of the people who work on this floor. We have the resources to know. You have succeeded in helping brain-injured people recover before. We decided to have Alex remain here until now because Vlad's Russian doctors also use the same hypnotic procedures that you are trained in. But, Karin, time is critical now." stressed Jorge.

"I think I'm close to a breakthrough. Today, for the first time, I saw him mumbling in a dream sleep," she answered. Karin was amazed that these two knew so much about what she was doing.

"Okay, Karin, please keep working with him. We will be back

tomorrow and then again the next day. If Alex is making headway in two days, we will leave him in your care. If not, we will take him to Russia for treatment." Vlad was comfortable with her response. As the two prepared to leave, Jorge placed his hand on Maxwell's shoulder.

"See you soon mi amigo." He turned and handed Karin his business card.

"Karin, if anyone here tries to obstruct your hypnotherapy, call me at this mobile number. I will tie them to a chair and have you turn them into barking dogs."

CHAPTER THIRTY FOUR

GLOBAL EARTH

The commuter plane had just landed at Innsbruck Airport. Sean and Victoria were able to fly out of Lyon and make a connection in Vienna. As soon as they deplaned and entered the small terminal, Victoria placed a call to the hospital to check on Maxwell's condition. Doctor Levy was on the other end of the phone conversation.

"What, you're kidding?" Victoria was alarmed. "They did what? He said what?" She shook her head. Sean gestured to say something but Victoria held her hand up and turned away. This was no time to interfere. Sean stood back.

"No. I can tell you now, Doctor, if they said that is what will happen tomorrow, you can take it to the bank; it'll happen. If you try to stop them, they'll eat you up and spit you out." Victoria was getting an earful from Doctor Levy and shrugged her shoulder to Sean. He in turn mimicked holding an illusionary cup and she mouthed yes just before making her point into the mobile. Sean headed towards a coffee vendor."Doctor, it doesn't matter. If those four people want Alexander Maxwell in a Russian hospital, only Alexander Maxwell can stop them. So you better wake him up, or I'll be visiting him in St. Petersburg." She listened to Doctor Levy's reply.

"De la Sierra said that? The wind from the gurney would . . . Uh-huh. Well, then I suggest you tell the nurses to wear long underwear tomorrow." She looked at Sean, who was making small talk with a beautiful Chinese attendee some 50 metres away. Doctor Levy's voice drew Victoria back to her mobile conversation."Okay." she said "I'll call tomorrow morning. All the best."

Sean returned with two pipping hot coffees and presented one to Victoria. "What was that about?" he asked.

"Two of Mr. Maxwell's friends are in Denver," she answered. "They're threatening to take over the hospital. I knew it was only a question of time before they weighed in. They want to move him to Russia for treatment. Frankly, I expected this to happen sooner. Up until now they must have been satisfied with the care he was getting in Denver, or they would have intervened sooner."

"How can they move him?" asked Sean. "Don't they need someone's permission? Who's your boss's guardian?"

"The closest thing to a guardian would be Jeremy St. Vincent, his attorney. Jeremy isn't strong enough to take on those guys. They would cut through him like a warm knife through butter."

"You don't like him?" Sean commented.

"Does it show that much?"

"I'd say you wouldn't want him in the next foxhole to you."

Victoria smiled, he had got it right

"So, who are these other people anyway?"

"Sean, I don't think you fully appreciate the nature of the membership of the Global Geocache Society," Victoria remarked all serious once more. "These men drive industry and politics in their respective countries. They influence political and legislative agendas, operating out of the limelight — or at least they try to. They cross international borders as though they don't exist. If those four men want my boss in a Russian hospital, that's where he's going and I'll be taking up residence in Russia. Its as simple as that. The doctors in Denver have no idea who's looking over their shoulders."

"So why don't they have ten guys running around Europe looking for a donor for their friend?" Sean was curious. "Surely there's no shortage of ex-cops on the society' staffs?"

"They trust me," stated Victoria. "If they didn't, you would be here with someone else. They don't think they're rolling dice just with me searching for donors. Too many secret service types approaching these donors at one time might spook them. A woman alone stands a better chance of succeeding, at least that's been their logic. They couldn't foresee that a predator would be racing me to the donors."

"Okay, look, our bags should be on the reclaim carousal by now," announced Sean. "I'll go get them, if you call a cab?"

Victoria nodded her approval, as Sean darted away in the direction of baggage reclaim. Ten minutes later, he was back with their luggage. Victoria opened a taxi door. Once in the back seat, Sean asked the driver to take them to the Hotel Vornehmes.

"You know we have to find the killer soon," Sean stressed.

"He knows more than we do. Who the donors are, how and where he wants them to die. We're working to his timetable and if we don't break the code soon, we're going to lose the race."

"What makes you think it's a he?" Victoria asked.

"Why, you think the killer might be a woman?"

"Actually, I haven't the foggiest idea. I've been racking my brain trying to come up with a motive."

"What about Mr. Maxwell's business? Does he have anything in the works that could cause someone to get really pissed off? Oh, look, that must have been where Leisel's plane was tied down." Victoria turned to look at what Sean was pointing at, as they drove by the airport on the way to the city.

Victoria twisted back round to face Sean.

"So, is there anyone?" he asked. "Well, there are things going on in Russia that I think could involve some rough operators. I don't know much about the details."

"What kind of deals?"

"Early last year the Russians nationalised the largest oil company in Russia," answered Victoria. "Putin put the top executives in jail and just took the whole thing over. The government accused them of tax evasion on a grand scale. Maxwell's friend, Vladimir Kornikova, is manoeuvring to keep the same thing from happening to him. I know the two of them have been talking on the phone — I guess strategising on how best to deal with the politics of the situation. It seems that the

Geocache

government is growing concerned that too much wealth and power are concentrated in the hands of just two Russian businessmen. We are talking mega billions and anyone controlling that kind of wealth can influence a lot of things in even the biggest nations. I suppose it's possible that someone in Moscow doesn't like what they are up to, but that's pure speculation on my part."

"Have you discussed this with the Russian?"

"No," she replied, "but I have discussed it with my counterpart, Gregory Savin. Gregory is head of security for Vlad. He told me that when the other Russian oligarch was jailed, it was a big flag. Gregory quietly consulted with some of his former KGB colleagues about the situation. He learned that the tipping point that caused the government to take action against the other Russian was his threatening behaviour toward Putin personally. Putin finally said enough was enough.

"Gregory's KGB contacts told him that Putin believes that Russian oil money is too monopolised. The problem now is that even though Vlad is savvier about not stepping on the wrong toes, he has a spotlight on him. He is the other big oil fish in Russia. Vlad and Maxwell are tightly tied together in business and on a personal level. They helped make each other rich. Vlad still relies on Mr. Maxwell's American engineers. Just how involved Mr. Maxwell is with Vlad's situation I'm not certain."

The cab pulled up to the Hotel Vornehmes entrance. "€15, please." The driver was polite for a change. Quite normal. Sean looked at Victoria and smiled.

"Think we should pay for this ride?" he asked. She nodded her approval. Sean paid the driver, hefted the two bags from the trunk, and the two entered the hotel lobby. It was a busy place, mostly Italian was being spoken. The New Year's Eve revellers were arriving. They had to wait in line at the desk. There were two female receptionists checking the newly arrived guests in at the desk. Sean and Victoria finally reached the front of the line and were greeted by the desk clerk. Victoria saw the name badge on one of the girls' blouse. It was Jade, the American from Florida who had spoken with Peter Leisel during his stay.

"Hello, Jade. My name is Victoria Kavanagh and this is Sean Mason. We have two non-smoking rooms reserved for tonight."

"Welcome to the Hotel Vornehmes," Jade greeted them. "I hope you enjoy your stay?"

"Thank you," smiled Victoria. "Jade, we are also looking for a man who recently stayed here. Perhaps you could help? His name was Peter Leisel."

"Oh, yes! I know who you are talking about," Jade acknowledged. "I received a call from a man from Austro Control search and rescue who was also trying to find Mr. Leisel. Are the two of you relatives trying to locate him? He hasn't turned up yet?"

Sean responded. "No, Jade. I'm from Interpol, and I'm helping Ms. Kavanagh locate Mr. Leisel. His whereabouts are important to both of us. I know you're busy right now, but we would like to talk with you about Mr. Leisel's stay at the hotel."

"I have a break coming in five minutes. If you can make yourselves comfortable by the fire over there, I'll come over shortly."

Jade pointed to a cozy grouping of leather chairs facing a large stone fireplace.

"Save me a seat," she requested. "It's pretty busy here this time of year. I'll bring your room keys over with me."

They were lucky; the seating was just being vacated. There was a large picture window to the left of the fireplace. The sky was clear when they landed, but since then grey layers of cloud had overtaken Innsbruck. They could see snow flurries beginning to fall. By Christmas, Innsbruck would be covered with a blanket of snow. Next to the fireplace there was a table covered by a white tablecloth. The hotel had placed two beverage dispensers on top, one containing hot chocolate and the other hot cider.

"Care for something hot to drink, Victoria?" Sean asked.

"Sure. Do I have to get it?" she answered.

"Depends — feel like being equal today?" He smiled.

Victoria got up and walked to the table, picked up two Styrofoam cups, and half turned towards Sean.

"Pick your poison." Victoria wanted to know if he wanted hot chocolate or cider.

"Ah . . . see, I knew it. You're into poisons. Make it Mostviertel please."

"What's that?" quizzed Victoria.

"It's what the Austrian's call cider, the alcoholic variety," explained Sean. "They call it Most around here.

"It's not just apple juice?"

"Nope, its 7.5% proof."

"Let's not drink on duty, shall we. We have business to conduct," stated Victoria dryly. Victoria was wearing a black turtleneck sweater and long beige pants. She had taken off her jacket and left it on the chair back. She was standing at the table filling the two cups with hot chocolate. Sean looked around the lobby knowing in advance what he would see. He wasn't disappointed. In every corner of the busy lobby, men and women alike were looking in her direction. They were trying not to be obvious, glancing in her direction every now and then. But some of the men couldn't take their eyes off her.

He was impressed with the way she handled the uninvited attention. When she turned away from the table to return to her chair, she surveyed the scene. She half smiled in the direction of the room full of people. It was as if she knew she was the object of their attention. Her response was a pleasant hello, how are you, have a nice day, all silently communicated to the onlookers with a slight smile and a nod of her head.

She sat down and handed Sean his cup.

"Here, and watch it. That stuff is hot."

Sean replied, "You think the chocolate's hot? You turned up the temperature in this lobby when you took your jacket off. Good thing you're a black belt. I'm telling you, we'll have to do something to make you look more like a regular human being.

Maybe it's your makeup. Why don't you lighten up on your makeup?"

"I told you I don't wear makeup, you ignoramus. Beside you can't talk. You think I don't notice women eyeing you up and down," she smirked.

"Really? You think I have a nice butt, do you?" He raised one eyebrow.

"Well, let's put it this way, it must get a lot of exercise because that's where you do most of your thinking." Victoria raised her cup of hot chocolate as if toasting him.

"You know, Victoria, you have a strange sense of humour."

"Where have I heard that before," she answered.

The banter was fun. She couldn't help but be attracted to him. He was handsome, strong, and didn't take himself seriously. The more time she spent with him the more she was intrigued by him, he was hard to figure out. Her beauty didn't seem to faze him. Like her boss, Maxwell, he was more aggravated by its distraction than captivated by it.

Jade arrived and joined them by the fire.

"Looks like a storm is rolling in," Jade said as she sat down in one of the leather chairs.

"Yes. The skiers will be happy," Victoria answered.

"Jade, what can you tell us about Mr. Leisel," Sean asked.

"Well, not very much I'm afraid. He didn't say a lot. Just that he was going out for a hike. It was a nice day for hiking as I recall. He had a backpack with him. A friendly type, asked me where I was from. We talked about the Italians and New Years Eve in Innsbruck. He was apparently a frequent visitor here — had flown a small plane in from near Vienna. That's why search and rescue called; I guess they thought he had crashed in the mountains."

"Did he say whether he was renting a car while he was here?" asked Victoria.

"Yes, he wanted directions for a car rental office. I gave him directions to the one on Main Street. It's just below the clock

Geocache

tower."

"So he arrived by cab?" asked Sean.

"Well I assume so." Jade looked uncertain.

"Is there anything else he said or did that you can remember" asked Victoria. Jade sat quietly thinking. She began shaking her head.

"Did he ask to use the hotel's computer to access the internet?" Sean had learnt this lesson from Marcus.

"You know he did, I had forgotten about that."

Victoria interjected, "Jade, can we see it."

"Okay. Follow me."

Jade took them down a hallway and into the small business office where she had taken Peter Leisel. Sean sat down at the computer and logged onto the internet while the two women looked over his shoulder. He opened the history column of the address bar. There it was, about twenty addresses down the list of websites recently visited: *www.petersgeocachesite.com*.

Sean opened up that website and watched as it slowly began to build. "Latitude: blank- longitude: blank." The killer had not repeated the earlier mistake of leaving the coordinates on Antoine's site. But Sean found it interesting that the site had not been taken down altogether. He reasoned that the killer took the coordinates off the site as a precaution but was unaware that the coordinates for Antoine's site had been discovered. The killer was still confident that the first murder was as yet undetected. He or she was comfortable letting the site remain up. This was a good sign. The killer was smart but overconfident.

Sean tapped the return arrow to go back to the previous page on the screen, the history of website visitations page. He was about to close out of the internet program altogether when he stopped and just stared at the screen.

"What are you looking at, Sean?" asked Victoria.

"Global Earth," he answered.

"Global Earth?" she repeated.

"The next website that was visited on this computer after the

Geocache website was Global Earth," Sean said.

"Isn't that the free software program where you can look at satellite photos of any place on the earth?" asked Jade.

"That's right, anyplace on earth, especially if you have the latitude and longitude of the place you're looking for," answered Sean.

He opened up the site, and they watched as the earth was depicted on the screen revolving until it came to a stop over Europe. Sean's eyes scanned to the left of the screen where there was a window listing specific places that had been marked on the map by a digital thumbtack on the place of interest. It was possible for a visitor to put a place mark at their place of interest and attach a name label to that spot. There it was, a label entitled "*petersgeocachesite*". Sean placed the curser over the label and double clicked the mouse. The digital earth, on screen, began to turn and then zoom in to a site not far from Innsbruck.

The latitude and longitude of "*petersgeocachesite*" were displayed on the bottom left hand corner.

Left-hand corner of the screen. 47° 21' 42.49" North — 11° 11' 59.50" East. Sean looked over his shoulder at Victoria and smiled.

"Hmm, you're smarter than you look," she quipped. There was a pad of paper and a pen on the desk. Sean copied down the coordinates and then returned to the landscape he could see on the screen. The site was at the top of a mountain next to the village of Leutasch.

"How far do you think that is from here, Jade?" Sean asked.

"Not far, maybe an hour's drive up the valley and into the mountains. It's really spectacular up there. You will enjoy the scenery if you go," Jade answered.

"Yes, we will probably enjoy it until we get to these coordinates. Then I suspect it will not be a pretty sight," Sean answered.

"Victoria, did you pack for a hike up a mountain?" he asked.

"Yes, I'm prepared for this."

Geocache

"Okay. It's too late to go today. The weather is closing everything down. Let's reserve a rental car and prepare to go in the morning. Agreed?"

"Agreed," she answered. They both understood there was no hurry now. They knew Leisel was already dead. It was not necessary to say it out loud. There was nothing they could do about it. Leisel had walked in Antoine's footsteps. He was taking direction from the same predator that took Sandel's life in the Black Forest. This time the killer chose a remote mountain peak.

They continued to look at the screen. Global Earth allowed the viewer to tilt the view almost to the horizontal and then rotate 360° around the location. The mountaintop was high enough above the surrounding terrain that a horizontal view was possible. Sean rotated the view around the top of the mountain as though the three of them were in a helicopter flying around the tops of the ridges.

"Think there are bears on that mountain?" Victoria asked. "Except for one clearing at the top, it looks like dense forest up there."

"If there are any bears on that mountaintop they may be dead along with the bunnies."

Errol Bader

CHAPTER THIRTY FIVE

THE WAKE-UP CALL

Nurse Karin was speaking in a low, soft monotone voice. She had closed the door to Maxwell's private hospital suite knowing today was the deadline set by the Mexican and Russian. If he did not improve they insisted on changing the venue. She was determined to succeed, but time had ran out. It was now or never.

"All right, Alexander. You have been dreaming and taking things easy." Karin whispered in to his ear. "But that's not a good thing and it's now time to take action, Alexander. You are a Captain of Industry and your Lieutenants are floundering. They need you to take command and steer them on the right course. Without you your corporation will be dashed across the rocks. They need your light to pilot them to safety. Alexander, it's time to take charge, time to wake up. You can't sleep anymore. You're being lazy. It's time to take charge so your company is not left to fail."

Karin understood Alexander's personality - a driver, ambitious, hardest on himself, an over-achiever taking responsibility for all his actions. She had to jolt him from the subconscious into consciousness. She had to make him angry, to disturb him, agitate him, suggest his pet project was about to be bludgeoned beyond recognition by incompetency. Something he would find intolerable.

"It's now or never, Alexander," Karin repeated several times.

"Now or never! They're going to wreck everything you worked so hard for, Alexander. You need to stop them, take command before it's too late."

Maxwell began to mumble and his right arm jerked.

"They're going off course, Alexander. They're going to sink you. The rocks are straight ahead. All your hard work will be wrecked. You need to take control, now." Karin was speaking in a louder tone now.

"Wake up Alexander. The rocks. Wake up *NOW!*" She shouted so loud it could be heard down the corridor. Jorge de la Sierra and Vlad Kornikova were stunned by the sound as the hospital elevator door opened. The two looked at each other.

"What the hell was that? It sounded like someone yelling in one of the rooms," said Jorge.

"It sounded like Alex's nurse," answered Vlad. "And it came from his room," They stormed passed the nurse's station, leaving the nurse bewildered. Jorge burst open the door to Maxwell's room then froze. Vlad fumbled in beside him and was equally stunned.

"Maxwell?"

He was sitting up in bed, looking confused, but definitely awake, if not alert. They approached Maxwell's bedside as he looked at them with a dazed look.

"What's going on?," demanded Alexander. "Where am I? Is this a hospital?"

"Hey, Alexander Maxwell, you're back in the conscious world," expressed Jorge as he threw his arms around his friend.

Karin smiled to herself knowing her unorthodox therapy had brought this man back from the brink of oblivion.

"Alexander, how are you feeling?" asked Vlad.

"Feeling?" Alexander said gruffly. "Like a truck ran over me. How do you think I feel?"

"Mr. Maxwell, do you know who these gentlemen are?" Karin asked.

He looked at Jorge and Vlad for a few seconds and nodded in the negative. He was still processing his surroundings, trying to get his bearings. Things were foggy.

"Why am I here, Nurse?" he asked looking up at Karin. Before she could answer, he spoke again.

"Those idiots," snapped Maxwell. "I'm not ready to drill any new wells. Besides the rock is too thick, it'll damage everything."

Jorge and Vlad looked at one another.

"Anyway, there's plenty of production left in the ones we have now." He was agitated.

"It's okay, Mr. Maxwell," Karin spoke soothingly. "Everything will be okay now, and you need to get some rest."

"But I have to take charge!"

"You did," Karin remarked, smiling at Jorge and Vlad as they stared at her confused. "The danger has gone. You can rest now."

She motioned for the two visitors to follow her out of the room. Once outside in the corridor, she stopped to give the surprised men her assessment of his situation.

"Well, as you can see Mr. Maxwell is back with us. He woke up just before you arrived — no, actually, as you arrived. So you witnessed his first words since the accident. He doesn't remember much right now. It will take a while to bring him back all the way. His long-term memory will take the longest to restore. In fact, there may be some memory loss that never fully returns. So we have a long way to go, but Mr. Maxwell will be all right. I'm not supposed to say these things to you; I'm not a doctor as you know. But I know how much he means to you. Mr. Maxwell is a fortunate man to have friends like you."

The elevator opened just twenty steps away. Six men dressed in hospital whites and another three dressed in business suits exited the elevator. Two of the men pushed a rolling gurney along toward Maxwell's room. Vlad put his hand up and they stopped

"It's Okay, Vlad addressed the two business men. "Mr. Maxwell will not be moving from this hospital. He is where he belongs. However, I want the two of you to guard his room. This good lady," Vlad pointed at Karin, "will familiarise you with who should enter I will tell Gregory to arrange relief for you."

"Is that necessary?" demanded Karin.

"Our contact in Europe has informed us of several incidents which are quite disturbing to us," remarked Vlad coldly.

"What? Do you mean Ms. Kavanagh?"

"Karin," Jorge's smile was far warmer. He took her to the side and spoke softly. "We believe that someone wants Mr. Maxwell to never leave this hospital alive. Please assist these men; they are here for his protection."

"If there is a problem with any of your superiors," Vlad continued, "have them call Jorge. He has a way of explaining how things have to be, as you know." Vlad smiled at her. She was uncertain how to take his last comment but when she looked back at Jorge, his expression told it all. Karin felt a cold chill ripple down her spine.

"Thank you, Karin," said Vlad as he extended his hand. Nervously, she shook it, realising he must be one of the wealthiest and most powerful men in the world.

"Don't be scared, Karin," smiled Jorge as he grabbed her in a bear hug, lifting her off the floor. "We appreciate what you have done for our friend and are most grateful. You have nothing to fear from us." His voice boomed through out the entire floor. His boisterous conduct would have made his Louisiana pirate ancestor proud.

"You are my most favourite nurse in the whole world. I'll love you forever!"

CHAPTER THIRTY SIX

FAMILY CRESTS

The snow was still falling in Innsbruck when Sean and Victoria left the hotel for Main Street. Sean had reserved a rental car from the same facility that Leisel had used. He carried a printout of the satellite photo they had discovered on Global Earth the day before. They knew exactly where they were going. Even the roads were depicted on the satellite photo. They took a cab to Main Street, directing the driver to take them to the clock tower. Sean and Victoria entered the car rental office door. A door bell chimed.

Inside there was a fire burning in a potbellied stove in the corner. Hans, the clerk, emerged through a door leading to the back of the building where he kept the cars parked. His cheeks were pink from the cold.

"Hallo my friends. I am Hans," he smiled. "I'm sorry, I was just parking a car in the back. How can I help you? Have you been waiting long?"

"No, not long Hans. We're fine. We have a car reserved under my name, Sean Mason."

"Ja, ja, of course. I just filled your car with benzene. Here is the paperwork."

Sean signed for the vehicle and took the keys from the pleasant old man.

"Your car is in the back of the building, a four-wheel drive. You have it until tomorrow, according to your reservation."

"Thank you, Hans. Tell us, do you remember renting a car to a Mr. Peter Leisel on December 2nd?" asked Sean.

"Oh, ja! How do you know this man? He never returned our car," Hans was concerned. "We filed a police report and in another week we will have to report the car stolen. This has never happened before."

"I work for Interpol, Hans; we are searching for Mr. Leisel. That's why we are here. Ms. Kavanagh and I believe we know where your car is. We'll let you know later in the day or tomorrow."

"Do you think Mr. Leisel is a thief?" Hans asked.

"No, Hans," Victoria answered. "He had every intention of returning your car. Something happened that was beyond his control." Hans walked the two through the corridor leading to the back parking lot. He gave them verbal directions to the highway leading west down the Valley Inn.

"Hans, what does the car look like that's missing?" Sean asked.

"It is a blue two-door Jeep."

"Thanks."

Within a few minutes, they were on there way, driving by the airport and the village of Vols to the south side of the valley, then passed Kematen in Tirol. After Kematen in Tirol, the road curved over to the southern most side of the wide valley. To the right of the highway was the market town of Zirl. They knew from looking at the satellite photo printout that it was time to start looking for a road that would leave the valley and enter the mountains to the north. Continuing west they arrived at Sagl and found the switchback road leading up into higher country. As they climbed up along the north edge of the valley, the views of the Inn River snaking its way through the region were spectacular. Victoria thought to herself that few places could match this grandeur. "Beautiful, isn't it?" Sean asked as they climbed higher.

"Yes," she answered. "I would guess there are dozens of geocache sites in these mountains. Wouldn't it be nice to come here in the summer and search these regions? The fresh mountain air, the scenery. Did you see the pictures in the hotel lobby of the fields of wild flowers they have up here in the summer?"

"Absolutely. I can see the travelogue description now - Geocaching in the Alps, bring your GPS unit and gun."

"No. Really," enthused Victoria. "This is the kind of place the Global Geocache Society members would pick to hide their geocaches. June is their month of the year. They can get away from the pressures of business and really disconnect. At first I thought it was a childish game practiced by rich men with nothing better to do, but I've seen how relaxed my boss is when he finishes his month long travels. They reserve a complete month, going to exotic places. They have institutionalised their downtime and the rest of the world has to plan around their absence."

Sean wasn't listening. They had turned a corner and Victoria noticed Sean was looking at something. They had just passed a large house, surrounded by a stone wall. The entrance had an arch topped by the owners family shield.

"Knock, knock. Earth to Scotty," quipped Victoria.

"Yeah, I'm here. I was just thinking about something. It was so faint, so subtle you could hardly see it."

"What was hard to see?" she asked. She wasn't his focus and that was refreshing and different.

"The background on the website. The Petersgeocachesite web page had a faint grey halftone background. It was so faint you could hardly see it," he answered as he negotiated another hairpin turn.

"What was it? Could you tell?" she asked. "I don't remember anything but blank spaces next to the words 'latitude and longitude'."

"Family emblem. The same family emblem was repeated all over the background of the screen. It was done so subtly you had to strain to see it." Suddenly the mountain road crowned, and they found themselves on a large plateau. They were in Seefeld-in-Tirol, a picturesque Tyrolean village high in the Alps.

"Family emblem? Any names? Was it recognizable? You know, could you identify it?" she asked.

Geocache

"What do you think — I'm into heraldry? How would I know whose family crest it was," he answered.

"You're from Scotland, aren't you? Your people invented those things. It's a Scottish tradition; surely you have a family crest?"

"I don't even have a middle name."

"No middle name? Seriously you have no middle name?" she asked.

"Seriously, no middle name," he answered.

"Why?"

"My parents were so poor they couldn't afford one." Victoria turned her face away from Sean. She didn't want him to see the broad smile on it. His rapier wit was just a bit too quick even for her.

"Okay. So what do think about the purpose of the crests?" she asked.

"I've been thinking about that all night, and I have a theory." Sean had been pondering the question. He was certain that the website had one, and only one, purpose; that was to lure the victims to an out-of-the-way place so their screams would not be heard. Somehow the killer had created an enticement, a powerful enticement.

"Victoria, do you watch much American football?" he asked.

"Yes, I like a good ballgame every now and then. I'm a Broncos fan," she answered, wondering where he was going with this.

"You know when the quarterback fakes and then does the unexpected. He's selling the fake. If the defence buys the fake, the play succeeds."

"Yes, I understand, go on."

"The killer is selling something, but it's a fake. The website and its subtle shade of halftones are designed to look official, legitimate, credible, but it's a fake just the same. The crest is just a fabrication and a clever one at that. Whatever the killer is selling, these people are buying it."

They continued west through Seefeld-in-Tirol until they reached Leutasch, a quaint mountain village. There were skiers walking with their skis over their shoulders, a few in-the-know tourists and then the locals enjoying the winter sports. There were snowmobiles parked everywhere. Leutasch was a wonderland in winter and a fairytale place in summer.

They came to the west end of the village. Then followed the road north towards Weidach, along Leutascher Str. About two kilometres further the sat-nav indicated they should turn right at Neuleutasch. Continuing on for another two kilometres, they came across a dirt track leading south into the mountain. At the summit, some 1490 metres above sea level was the coordinates Leisel had been given. They were at the base of the mountain. Sean opened the trunk and took out additional layers of clothing, passing a sheep-skin coat to Victoria, to protect themselves from the cold of the higher elevation.

Properly bundled up, they left the car and headed towards a track, lined by evergreens, leading to the mountain. Victoria stopped at the edge of the treeline. Sean was a few steps behind her and looking down as he walked. He bumped into her.

"Hey, sorry," he said. Then he realized why she had stopped.

"What's that over there between the trees?" quizzed Victoria. Sean ran under the folliage and began to brush away the thick snow. Beneath was a blue two-door Jeep. Clearly it had not been moved for some time. Sean went to the front of the car and brushed the snow off the front bumper. The frame around the license plate had the name of the car rental company. They had found the missing rental car. Victoria looked up at the mountain top in front of her.

"Hope there aren't too many bunnies in these parts." Sean tried to lift her spirits, but it didn't help.

"You ready for this, hot stuff?"

"Yeah, let's go," Victoria's mission was failing and she knew it. "Let's get it over with. Maybe the bastard made a mistake up there and left a clue behind."

Geocache

She was making a transition. This was no longer a search for blood donors, they were hunting a predator. Her donors were the prey. Now she would become the huntress. She was angry and behind in the race. The killer was one step ahead and it was only a matter of time before all the donors were dead. Sean looked into her beautiful eyes and recognised the burning rage.

"Don't worry. We're getting closer. We have an advantage," Sean reassured her. "The killer doesn't know we are on to him. He'll make a mistake."

"There you go again. You think it's a man we are looking for."

"I'm hoping it's a man. If it is, I'm going to kick the shit out of him before I arrest him. He deserves special treatment for making me climb this mountain in the middle of winter."

They were negotiating six inch deep powder along the way. Both were in good physical condition, nevertheless they were still exerting a lot of energy. About half a kilometre up the path they came to a clearing. They could see the ridge ahead through another batch of trees.

"Let's go down the tree line and see if we can find another trail," Sean suggested. Walking south-east they continued on through the forest before picking up a snow covered bike trail which exited the trees to the east. Almost to the top they both began to tire. Sean was in the lead. They were breathing hard and sweating. When they spoke, their hot breath turned to steam. Something crunched under Sean's foot. A branch. The sound echoed through the trees.

Suddenly, three large birds launched into the air, startled by the unexpected visitors.

"They're vultures aren't they?" Victoria asked.

"Yeah, Bearded Vultures,"

"Not just any kind of vultures. Bearded Vultures?" Victoria asked.

"Misunderstood buzzards, the last Austrian Bearded Vulture was killed off in the 1900s – unjustifiably."

"You're an expert on buzzards?"

"Unfortunately, they arrive at crime scenes before we do. Buzzards are occupational hazards."

"So they were exterminated but now they are back?" she asked.

"People in the Austrian Alps thought the vultures were killing their lambs," Sean answered. "The predator was really a wolf. The Austrians reintroduced the Bearded Vulture to the Alps in 1986 to make amends."

"So do you think these rare birds were feasting on Leisel down there?"

"Maybe, but I wouldn't expect his body to be this far down the mountain. The coordinates are at the top." They walked the short distance to where the scavengers had collected. Sean stopped in the middle of the trail.

"What is it?" she asked. He pointed to a tree a few meters off the trail. There's something behind that tree. Victoria remained on the trail while Sean approached the tree. As he walked around behind the tree, he winced and backed away a few feet.

"Is it Leisel's body?" she asked.

"Not unless the full moon turned him into a werewolf, it's a dead wolf. Must have found Leisel's body and thought he had died and gone to heaven. Hmm, you think wolves go to heaven?" Sean asked.

"No, Sean. Only dogs and cats go to heaven. Any more deep questions?"

"He's probably full of Aconite, poor fella. Probably some little wolf's dad laying there," answered Sean. "This doesn't bode well for the Bearded Vultures." They continued climbing until passing the last switchback before the crest. They were breathing hard and needed a rest.

"Okay. Let's take a breather here for a second," Sean reached under his jacket and pulled out his service revolver from a holster under his armpit.

"You think we need that?" she asked.

"When was the last time you approached a crime scene without a gun at the ready?" he answered. "I would expect the killer to be long gone, unless that is, you're his next target. It wouldn't be the first time the hunted hid in the weeds waiting for his hunter to make a mistake. You want to die up here today?" He looked out across the valley. They could see Seefeld-in-Tirol in the distance.

"Wouldn't be a bad place to go, however. Look at that view down there." Sean had been a cop for a long time. He had learnt not to take things for granted, not to get sloppy, especially when trailing a predator. They had a way of surprising you, turning the hunter into a victim. They reached the top of the trail which transitioned into a clearing, a small mountain meadow on the crest of the mountain. They stood in the middle of the field while Sean held the satellite picture in alignment with the ridge. The mountain they were standing on formed the juncture of three valleys. They could see the region in all directions. They were both thinking the same thing. Leisel must have enjoyed this view before he died. If the climb didn't take his breath away, the view would have.

"The coordinates are east of this clearing over there," Sean pointed to the tree line to the east. They began to walk toward the edge of the meadow and through a thin line of trees when they spotted a piece of clothing. It was bloody and torn. (47° 21' 41.09" N 11° 11' 57.66" E)

"There goes the neighbourhood," Sean said quietly as they walked forward. They both scanned the area for any sign of the killer. Suddenly the quiet of the meadow was broken by a loud noise. It was the flapping wings of an eagle launching into the sky from a nearby tree.

"Sean, there! Over there!" Victoria pointed to a large tree. There, next to the tree, was Leisel's lifeless body. An animal had mauled the left leg of the body. They stood still, contemplating the grisly find. There were no signs of a struggle such as knife slashes or gunshot wounds. If it were just a hunter who found his body, the authorities might not have suspected any wrongdoing. Perhaps a hiker attacked by a wolf or bears bled to death. The police might not have conducted an autopsy. Not too many people are found poisoned on the top of a mountain.

"Well, that's that. Only one donor left." Victoria was thinking ahead, thinking about where Dieter Manheim might be; or for that matter, if he might already be dead.

"Not so fast. I'm still working with this one." Sean was leaning over the body. "There's something under him." Leisel's body was laying face down. He slowly rolled the body over, and suddenly the red flag attached to the thin plastic pole snapped up from beneath Leisel's body knocking Sean backwards to the ground. Leisel had fallen on the pole, hiding it with his body. Victoria stood over Sean, looking down and smiling.

"Sean, what are you doing down there?" she asked.

"Conducting an investigation, you have to look at things from all angles, you know." He winked at her. She gave him a hand and pulled him to his feet.

"So the red flag marks the spot," she remarked.

"Yeah," he agreed. "What else was left behind?"

They looked closer around the body. There was an imprint in the snow at the base of the tree and not far from the flag. It was rectangular, about the size of a suitcase. The snow had been raked with something to remove footprints, but there was still an imprint.

"There was something here, Victoria, a box or container of some kind. Leisel came here for what was in that container." The backpack was on the ground next to his body.

"I would guess that Leisel believed the contents of the container could be carried down the mountain in this sack." He picked up the backpack and hefted it.

"So it had to be something that could conform to this sack — like drugs, jewels, or maybe cash." Sean postulated about what Leisel's expectations were in travelling to this remote place. Two murder victims had worked hard to reach cold and remote places in search of something important. Both had died in the process. He wondered if they had anything in common apart from their killer.

"Victoria, we need to get some DNA from this fellow. The flag has his blood on it which should give the lab what they need. We already know that Leisel has the same rare blood type that Antoine Sandel had. It would be interesting to find out if they were related to each other."

"Related. You think they could be ... you know, Sean, you just might make it as a cop after all."

A few snowflakes began to fall through the treetops. They processed the crime scene, making certain no clues were missed. The beautiful view took a back seat to the professional task at hand. Their missions were merging. They had to find Dieter Manheim, not just to save his life, but to capture or kill a very clever criminal. And they had to do it soon. Victoria walked back into the meadow with Sean a few steps behind. She looked up at the overcast sky.

"You know, Sean, the winds up here are unusual. They come straight down from the sky instead of across the valleys and ridges, almost like a constant microburst. "

"It's the Furn winds. They come across the Alps from Italy, and drop vertically straight down into the Inn Valley. This time of year our pilots won't fly into Innsbruck — too dangerous for their liking."

"So Leisel shouldn't have been flying up here in a light plane?"

"No, I suppose not, now that you bring it up. He risked his life to get to this place. Bad judgment on his part I'd say," Sean remarked.

"Uh-huh, bad judgment or maybe just plain greed," she turned towards Sean. "Greed can lead to bad judgment."

"It's time to go to Prague. If we are lucky, Dieter Manheim will be sitting in a Prague jail where the killer can't get at him."

"No such luck, unless he was locked up today. I've had Teddy

Errol Bader

Johansen, my assistant at Interpol, trying to locate Manheim for a week."

"Why didn't you tell me?" Victoria couldn't believe what she was hearing.

"He's the last one; I didn't want to worry you."

"If you ever withhold important information from me again, I'll break both your knees"

"Really?"

"Really," she answered.

"Well, okay then. There is one more thing that you might think is important." He raised an eyebrow and looked at her.

"What's that?" she asked.

"You know that eagle that took off when we arrived here at the top? When it flew overhead it relieved itself all over the back of your jacket. That fella is a real ace I'll tell you."

"Seriously?" She began to remove her jacket.

Sean answered her, raising his hands up, palms facing her.

"Okay, okay. I admit I'm attracted to you. Every man is. But you're moving a little fast for me. Keep your clothes on. I mean, don't you think it's a bit cold up here for this sort of thing."

"Sean, stop. Did the bird really . . . "

"No, just kidding. Put your coat back on before you catch pneumonia."

As he had done before, he was using humour to soften the bad news. He knew Teddy Johansen had no success at locating Manheim. The odds were shifting against them with the passage of time. Victoria was right, perhaps the answer was in Prague. Prague was the thread that connected all three donors. Doctor Luc had given Antoine Sandel's address to be in Prague. Sean's researcher had learnt of prior addresses for Peter Leisel were also at Prague. They were still researching Manheim's whereabouts.

"Yes. I think you are right, Victoria. Prague is our next stop," he agreed.

As they descended along the switchback, Victoria stopped abruptly, turned and stood in the path looking at him.

Geocache

"What?" quizzed Sean uncertain what to expect. There was a slight smile on her face. He waited for her to say something, a Mexican standoff of sorts.

"First one speaks loses," he quipped. Without a word she turned and continued down the trail. One thing that sets human beings apart from the rest of the animal kingdom is the ability to experience more than one emotion at once. Victoria's brain was crunching a mix of anger, concern, and a growing fondness for the man behind her all at the same time. When she first arrived in Paris, there was only one man whose survival was important to her — Maxwell's. Now there were two.

Errol Bader

CHAPTER THIRTY SEVEN

A FOURTH DONOR

The flight from Innsbruck to Prague only took a few hours. Sean and Victoria found their luggage and rented a car at the airport. Their destination – The Prague Blood Donor Registry. Doctor Luc had found all three donors listed at the registry attached to the Czech Ministry of Health.

"Here's the address." Sean pulled a slip of paper from his pocket and handed it to Victoria. She read it and replied.

"Videnska 2087/8, 179 22 Prague 4. It's in the old part of the city. Make a right at the next corner."

"You know your way around Prague, do you?" he asked.

"The President made a number of trips here. I had to do a lot of groundwork in Prague."

"Ever been to Scotland?" he asked.

"You know, that's one trip I never got to make," she answered.

"Well, this case won't take us to Scotland," he said.

"Why not" she asked.

"Scottish blood is all the same – no exceptions"

"Well, my father was Irish," she said, folding her arms across her chest and raising her head high.

"That's the reason I'm putting up with you; you come from good Celtic stock," he answered. The street was narrow and there were few places to park. Sean pulled up to the steps of the health ministry.

"Why don't you go in?" Sean said. "I'll find a place to park and catch up."

The ministry building was large, and it required a visit to the building index to locate the registry. A short walk down the first

Geocache

floor corridor and Victoria entered the registry lobby. The receptionist was finishing a phone call. She placed the receiver on its cradle and looked up with a smile.

"Hallo, I'm Nicole, may I help you?"

"Yes, Nicole, my name is Victoria Kavanagh. I'm searching for a specific individual with a very rare blood type. They are listed with the Prague registry. It's very important I find this person. Is there someone on staff who can help me ?"

"Yes, I'll see if our Director can meet you. Her name is Katrina."

Nicole spoke briefly to the director on the phone and hung up.

"She is happy to see you; her office is down the hall, last door on the left."

"Thank you, Nicole. I'm expecting a gentleman to join us shortly; he's parking our car."

"Certainly, how will I know him?"

"He's very good looking and he has a quirky demeanour."

Katrina Talmen's office was very organised. As Victoria entered, she noticed the director kept track of documents and files on her desk and credenza by step laddering, so that each file could be easily identified and pulled, rather than stacked one on top of another.

"Hallo, I'm Katrina. I understand you are trying to locate someone in our registry?"

"Yes, my name is Victoria Kavanagh. I work for a gentleman in the United States who is very sick. We are looking for potential blood donors. I have spoken to Doctor Luc in Paris, and he has been very helpful."

"Oh, yes, I remember this," answered Katrina. "Doctor Luc called me about your situation. We sent him three names I think.".

"Yes, that's right. Unfortunately two of the men on your list have died, and so locating the third has become critical."

"Two are dead! I didn't think these men were old at all."

"No, they didn't die of natural causes, I'm afraid," Victoria replied. "They were both murdered."

"What a horrible coincidence," her voice was sympathetic.

"I don't think it's a coincidence at all, Katrina. That's why it's so important we find the third donor before he becomes a victim."

"I see. What can I do to help?"

"We are hoping you have an updated address for Dieter Manheim. Here is the last address we have." Victoria handed her the slip of paper with his blood type and address on it. Katrina turned to her computer and began typing.

"Here he is. Oh, I see now. Mr. Manheim was entered into the system in the old days, before anyone was asked permission. That is how his blood type and name were entered into our database. I have just this same address listed."

"In the old days?" Victoria asked.

"When the communists were in power they kept track of such things without the knowledge or permission of the people. Only recently have we been accessing these old data bases." Katrina continued to look at the paper that Victoria had handed her, she was studying it closely.

"What is it?" Victoria asked.

"Well, it's this blood type." She was looking at the paper.

"Yes, I know it's very rare," Victoria said.

"Yes, I know. But believe it or not, we have a new employee who has this same blood type," answered Katrina. "We were all amazed when we took her sample to add to the registry. I questioned the results and am having the test done again because I didn't believe they could be correct. She's not on the registry yet because I wanted to confirm she had this type. The second test results came back yesterday, and indeed, it confirmed this is her blood type."

"So this person's name would not have been transmitted to Doctor Luc?" Victoria asked.

"No. Marie is not in the data bank as of yet."

"Whatever you do, Katrina, do not put her name in any data bank. To do so would be as good as signing her death warrant.

Tell me about this person, please?"

"Her name is Maria Tereskova, a sweet girl. She is single and likes to do volunteer work. We have been so impressed with her we recently hired her full time."

"Is she here today? Can we speak with her?" Victoria's heart was beating faster. She was close to finding a donor who was still breathing."

"Well, no. She took a leave of absence. She did not have enough time to accumulate vacation yet. She said it was very important that she go away for a week."

"Did she say where she was going?" Victoria asked.

"Actually it was a little strange. Marie was very excited about the trip. She said the registry would benefit in some way, but she would not elaborate. The only thing she would tell us is that she was going to take black and white pictures of cathedrals in Budapest."

"Katrina, please, I need all the information you can give me about Marie. Her life is in grave danger and we need to find her now."

At first Katrina was reluctant. It was a breach of confidentiality. However, there was something about Victoria's demeanour that made her credible. She decided to take a chance and wrote Marie's name, phone number, and address on a slip of paper and gave it to Victoria. Katrina then called the number and there was no answer.

"What about any relatives or close friends?" Victoria asked.

"Yes, hold on a moment." She pressed an intercom button on her phone.

"Hallo, Elli speaking."

"Elli, come to my office right away, please." A moment later Maria's good friend Elli entered the office.

"Yes, what do you need?" Elli inquired.

"Elli, this is Victoria Kavanagh. She needs to speak with Marie right away. Do you know where she is?"

"She left this morning on her trip; I dropped her off at the airport myself."

"Elli, do you know where she was going?" Victoria asked. Elli was standing next to a chair and sat down without answering the question.

"Elli?" Katrina was waiting for an answer from her employee, still no answer. Elli looked down at the floor and squirmed in her seat.

"Elli, Budapest is a short drive from here. Why was she getting on a plane?" asked Victoria.

"Marie made me swear I would not tell a soul. She said she was instructed not to tell anyone where she was going."

"Instructed by whom?" Victoria demanded.

"I don't know the details, but she said she had been selected to participate in some event and that it would mean a great deal of money coming to the registry."

"Listen to me very carefully, Elli. Marie's life is in danger. We must know where she went. If you care about your friend, you must tell us what you know." Victoria would beat it out of her if she didn't. Elli looked at Katrina. Katrina nodded her head in affirmation.

"St. John, in the Virgin Islands. It's a small island in the Virgins. She didn't tell me until I was taking her to the airport. At first she told me she was going to Budapest to take black and white pictures, but she couldn't lie about it in the end. Her conscience was bothering her. What's wrong? What's happening?" she asked.

"Katrina will explain. I have to go. There is no time to lose. Thank you for your help."

"Please let us know how she is," requested Katrina.. "Please get Marie to call me as soon as you find her."

"I will." Victoria hoped she would be in time. As she was leaving, she met Sean as he entered the lobby.

"Where have you been, Sean? On tour of Prague Castle?"

"No. I've been on the cell phone with my office. Teddy called to tell me they located a Prague business address for Dieter

Manheim."

"Let's go there. I'll tell you about my meeting on the way. You're not going to believe what I just heard in there." She told him what she had just learnt as he drove across town.

"A fourth blood donor?" he blurted. "You must be kidding."

"No, it's true," Victoria brushed her hair away from her eyes.

"I'm beginning to think everybody in Europe has your boss's blood type. We should have just kidnapped Pierre, the cab driver, and taken him to Denver and be done with it."

They arrived at an industrial park and found Manheim's warehouse and office. There was no problem with parking, and so they only walked a few paces to the unlocked glass door. They entered and a bell rang. The office was empty but noises could be heard in the back warehouse. There were cases of liquor stacked along the walls. The door to the warehouse opened, and Henryk Kinsky entered to see who had arrived. Henryk was not accustomed to visitors.

"Looking for directions?" he asked.

"My name is Sean Mason and this is Victoria Kavanagh. I'm with Interpol, and we are looking for Dieter Manheim."

All Henryk had to hear was Interpol. He defaulted to an assumption that Interpol was there to arrest Dieter and any of his associates.

"Hey, I have done nothing wrong. It's Dieter you want. I do not break the Polish contraband laws; I am innocent, completely innocent. It's Dieter who runs the liquor across the border, not me!" Henryk would give up his own mother to save his skin. Sean and Victoria understood immediately what was happening and they both knew Henryk would tell them everything he knew since birth.

"Then if you know what's good for you, tell us where he is," Victoria said in a stern voice.

"He is in Český Těšín, about a three-hour drive from here."

"Where is he exactly in Český Těšín," she asked.

"During the day he will be in his van, a blue van. He is

always parked by the footbridge to the Polish side of the Olza River. If he is not there, he will be at the old hotel in town," Henryk answered.

"All right. What is your name?" Sean asked.

"Henryk, Henryk Kinsky."

"I want you to go home, Henryk," Sean ordered. "Do not call Mr. Manheim. If you do, I will make sure you are charged as an accessory. Do you understand my meaning?"

"Yes, of course, of course. You were never here. I understand."

Sean and Victoria had a difficult decision to make, which direction to go in first, which donor to try to intercept. It was now early afternoon in Prague, eight hours ahead of Denver. Sean contacted his Interpol travel agent and booked a flight from Prague to Vienna. A connection there would get them to St. Thomas, the nearest airport to St. John.

"We have a few hours left to find Manheim; the only way this is going to work is if we fly a small plane to Český Těšín," suggested Sean. "There isn't enough time to drive. I'm going to call Kyle Insdorf, my counterpart in Prague. Maybe he can arrange a flight over there."

Sean was fortunate, Kyle Insdorf answered on the first ring.

"Okay. We're in luck. Kyle is going to meet us at the airport. He will have a plane ready to take us to Český Těšín in thirty minutes. We can sleep on the plane from Vienna to St. Thomas tonight."

They knew the race was close to over, the outcome anything but certain.

CHAPTER THIRTY EIGHT

THE AMERICAN TREE

It was close to 4 p.m. when the little single-engine plane touched down at Český Těšín Airport. Kyle had called ahead and arranged for a rental car. Sean and Victoria discussed going first to the old hotel. However, they decided not too. Manheim was a frequent visitor there and the staff could not be trusted. The desk manager might call and tip Manheim off someone was looking for him. They did not want to have him spooked before explaining the danger he was in. The directions were good and easy to follow on the Český Těšín street map.

Sean drove towards the footbridge straddling the Czech Republic and Poland. They turned into a street that ran towards the Olza River and could see the footbridge ahead. The entrance to the bridge was formed by the intersection of three streets. On one corner of the intersection, there was a public museum with a window looking out at the intersection and the approach to the bridge.

"No blue van anywhere in sight," said Sean.

"We could go on to the old hotel and see if the van is there," Victoria answered.

"Let's wait near the bridge. We could go into that old museum at the corner."

"You want to visit a museum? Don't you think we have more pressing things to do?" Victoria said.

"I'm a very cultured guy, bet there's some neat stuff in there."

"Maybe you can come back on your next holiday," she answered, glaring at Sean.

"Actually, I was thinking that we could wait inside by that window and see if he shows up."

"Okay — as long as you pay the entrance fee," she quipped.

They entered the old brick building and found themselves in a hallway lined with fading black and white photos of Český Těšín. The museum was free, only donations kept the place open. As they walked down the hallway, they could see the images they were looking at were before and after. They entered a large room with a window that most interested Sean. There were photographs of the grand little city before the communists took over. The after pictures were a sad reflection of the damage done by uncaring rulers ignorant of the value of the ornate Baroque architecture of the old city.

In the corner of the room opposite the window, there was a centuries old music box covered by clear Plexiglas. A rotating brass barrel with its small protrusions was visible and quite large, at least three feet long and eighteen inches in circumference. Sean posted himself by the window while Victoria paused to contemplate the old musical instrument. She was thinking about the countless generations of Europeans who were entertained by the old mechanism.

"Hallo, welcome to our museum." a petite woman entered the room and addressed Victoria. "I am Desiree, the museum's curator. I see you have discovered our music cylinder."

"Oh, yes, Desiree. My name is Victoria and this is Sean," motioning toward the window.

Sean responded politely but kept his gaze on the street intersection.

"Would you like to hear it play?" the curator asked.

"Really? After all these years it still works?" remarked Victoria. "You don't mind?"

"Yes. Of course. We do not receive guests very often. It just sits here waiting to be heard. It's only happy when it's listened to."

Desiree and Victoria lifted the clear lid off of the brass drum. Desiree turned the hand crank and the room filled with music formed by the pinging metal tabs as they clicked over the little

Geocache

metal protrusions on the drum. The three were listening to Green Sleeves, the haunting ancient melodic tune written by an unknown composer. Unlike a recording, they were hearing virtually the same sounds vibrating off their ear drums as did the long dead aristocrats of centuries ago.

"Sean, come over here and look at this," Victoria said.

"I'm busy." Sean continued to stand watch by the window.

"C'mon, just look at this for a minute; you may never see one of these again actually working."

Sean left the window and stood by the old brass drum, watching it turn and listening to its lilting sounds.

"Isn't it magnificent? It's the original sound you're listening to," remarked Victoria.

"It's great," Sean said impatiently.

"You're a Neanderthal, Sean" Victoria commented.

"It's putting me to sleep; they must have been bored to death in the old days. When they cranked that thing up, the guys must have wanted to go out for a beer." Sean said returning to his post at the window.

"Ah, Victoria, our blue van is here." Sean watched as Dieter parked the van on the far side of the street. Victoria approached the window to see for herself. Dieter opened the back doors of the van. As if on queue, bootleggers began to collect at the back of the van. Deiter's cell phone rang, and he opened the flip phone as he stood by one of the open van doors. He put his head down and shook it from side to side. He began scanning the area nervously. As he turned in the direction of the museum, he saw Sean and Victoria framed in the museum window. They made eye contact.

"Okay, Henryk. I see them. Thanks. I'll talk soon."

Dieter slammed the van doors shut and jumped into the driver's seat. Seeing his intention to run, Sean and Victoria headed for the museum exit. On the way past the exit door Sean reached in his pocket and pulled out a ten dollar bill, stuffing it in the museum donation box.

"Even Neanderthals can be philanthropic," he said, glancing back at Victoria as they ran from the building.

To their surprise, the van had not moved. They were crossing the street when Manheim leaped from the vehicle and ran on foot toward the bridge. The old van had a dead battery. He had a head start, but was carrying a computer case over his shoulder, and it slowed him somewhat. Regardless, he was determined not to be caught and sent to jail.

Once across the footbridge, Manheim passed into Poland. Sean had his Interpol credentials out, and Victoria was prepared with her passport. The guards respected Sean's credentials and passed them through quickly. Dieter was bumping into people in the tent bazaar, and the computer bag was cumbersome. Victoria spotted him.

"He's there, heading toward the castle," she yelled.

They were in better physical condition than Dieter, and so the distance between them was closing. To Sean's amazement, Victoria was pulling ahead of him. The cobblestone streets were narrow and not made for foot races. A driver negotiating the narrow streets would never expect to meet a pedestrian running at full clip through these streets. The truck driver never saw Dieter as he turned his vehicle from a side street into Dieter's path. The impact threw him twenty yards through the air. Dieter's body crashed against a tree and fell to the ground.

Victoria reached Dieter before Sean. The gravely injured man was gasping for breath. She could see the extent of his injuries, blood running out of his ears. There was no saving him. Sean leant over Dieter to check his vital signs as he breathed his last.

"He's gone. I don't know what his problem was, but he was determined not to talk to us." Victoria stood up and saw a plaque affixed at eye level to the tree that had stopped Manheim's body from its flight through the air. The plaque was in English, "The American Tree" brought from America and planted on this spot in 1778.

"Well, that's ironic," she said. Sean picked up the computer

Geocache

bag and looked inside to find a laptop.

"C'mon, Victoria. We can't help this fellow, and we don't have time to talk to the policia. We have a plane to catch."

The pair walked briskly back through the tent bazaar and across the Olza River footbridge. There was a long line of people waiting to be cleared into the Czech Republic at the customs and immigration checkpoint on the Czech side of the river. However, the line was moving swiftly. The Czech border guard waved the travellers through without checking their papers.

"Good. The line is moving fast," observed Victoria.

She was next in line. The border guard behind the open window raised his hand to stop Victoria and Sean from following the others through the gate. He motioned for them to hand him their passports. The guard held Victoria's U.S. passport up at eye level and slowly turned each page, closely examining them one by one. He repeated the same slow process with Sean's passport. The line of people behind them grew longer as the guard delayed their passage. Then he made his way over to a couple of colleagues a few paces away.

"What's the problem?" whispered Victoria to Sean.

"Look at the guys name tag," Sean whispered back.

Victoria surreptitiously scanned the guards name tag above his left breast pocket. It read Husak.

"Does the name ring a bell?"

"Not really," answered Victoria under her breath.

"Gustav Husak was made first secretary of Czechoslovakia after the Warsaw Pact invasion in '68," Sean whispered. "This must be his grandson or some relation. Husak was like a mini Stalin in the late '70s in his attempts to suppress dissenters such as Charter 77."

"Hey, you, Amerikan. Be quiet," ordered Husak's grandson.

Finally, after what seemed like hours, the guard threw the passports down on the counter in front of Victoria as if in disgust. He waved them through without another word spoken.

"Nice fellow, don't you think?" Sean remarked as they

departed the checkpoint on their way to the rental car.

"I can't believe it, Sean. We were so close. Now Manheim has to go and get himself killed."

"Yeah, one look at you and he ran for his life," Sean quipped. "And if that tree hadn't been a sapling in America and brought all the way to Poland and transplanted on that very spot, he might still be alive. You ought to buy a lottery ticket. Odds don't seem to matter much where you're concerned."

Their small plane lifted off from the runway at Cesky Airport just as the sun set. Victoria was buckled in to the back of the four-seat aircraft. A few minutes after takeoff she reached over and picked up the laptop case. She pulled the computer out and saw the slip of paper with the password and username still taped to the front cover. She turned the laptop on. It was dark now in the cabin and the glow from the computer screen illuminated her face. She typed in *"GEO"* and *"CACHE,"* and began to read the skillfully-crafted letter which had doomed its recipients. The computer gave up the killer's secrets as she read. On closer study, she became more aware of the genius that went into the diabolical plan to kill Maxwell's donors. It was the kind of genius that crossed the razor-thin line into insanity. She tapped Sean on the back. He turned round as she handed the opened laptop to him. He took it from her and sat forward. After a few minutes he just looked up, straight ahead into the night sky. They both had the same thought; Marie Tereskova may not have much time left on earth.

As soon as they landed, Kyle Insdorf was waiting for them. He drove them to the terminal side of the airport just in time to make the flight to Vienna. As they were waiting to board the plane, Sean checked his voice mail. Victoria could tell there was something he was listening to that had his complete attention.

"What is it?" she asked.

"That was Teddy, my researcher. The results of the DNA tests we ran on Leisel and Sandel are ready."

"And?" she asked.

Geocache

"They are definitely related," Sean answered.

"Well, aren't we all?" she answered sarcastically.

"Yeah, but most of us can have sex and still produce normal babies," Sean replied.

"You mean the DNA shows them to be closely related?" she asked.

"Yeah, but they couldn't have babies because they were both men," he answered.

"That is very cogent thinking, Sean."

"On the other hand, had they been brother and sister, they would have spawned some really ugly and probably stupid kids," he added, smiling.

The aircraft began the boarding process for their international flight, and there was extra security screening in force. Some passengers were randomly selected for special treatment. A folding table was just by the door to the flight entrance. Victoria watched as an older woman handed the security agent her handbag. He removed a clear plastic tube containing white baby powder from the bag.

"Okay. You can carry this on board, Madam; we are looking for liquids, not powders," the agent told her. She shrugged and proceeded to board the aircraft. Sean and Victoria made their way to their seats. The airline assigned them to a small commuter jet for the short flight to Vienna. They had window and aisle seats with no seat in between. Victoria took the window. There were a number of passengers still to board, and so they had a few moments to get settled. She kept thinking about the woman's baby powder — that white powder.

"Sean, how did you say Aconite poison is made?" Victoria asked.

"It's from Monkshood, a plant," he replied.

"But how does the plant become a poison? Do I remember you saying it was ground into a white powder?" she asked.

"Yeah, then it's mixed with alcohol, Why?"

"What profession would provide the necessary knowledge

and equipment to turn a plant into a white powder?" she asked.

"You think the killer's a witch?" he asked.

"No, seriously, who has the skill to produce Aconite?"

"Okay, okay. A chemical engineer?" he replied.

"No"

"A Navy SEAL?" he asked.

"No"

"MacGyver?" he asked.

"No"

"A pharmacist? A — What?" He could see her wheels turning.

"I've been racking my brain, trying to find a clue as to who the killer might be. It has to be someone close to Maxwell, someone who knows about geocache and someone who has the skill, equipment, and knowledge to turn a plant into a poison. I have someone in mind. I don't know what the motive could be, but the proximity to Alexander and the skill is there."

"Who are you thinking about? Tell me quick before they button up the door," Sean demanded.

"I remember in the emergency room after the helicopter accident," Marsha Thompson's son arrived just before she died, his name is Chandler Benson. He was listening to his mother's final words and looking over at Maxwell. Benson is a pharmacist. It's a long, shot but he meets those two requirements." Sean reached for his cell phone and began to tap out a text message to his assistant, Teddy, at Interpol. He had just enough time to complete the message before the flight attendant closed the door and ordered all electronic devices turned off.

"When we land in Vienna, we will know whether Chandler Benson travelled to Innsbruck under his own name. If he bought a ticket to St. Thomas we will know that as well. Let's hope, if you are right, that he doesn't know we are on to him. If he gets careless and thinks he is performing perfect crimes, he might not bother to use an alias."

"So we know Marie is on St. John by now," said Victoria.

Geocache

"The killer is either there or on the way there. How do we find Marie when we get there? There isn't much on that island."

"We don't have to find her; we have to find her geocache site. Everyone will converge on that site. Marie, you, me, and the killer. It'll be a party."

"And how do you know where that will be?" she asked.

"Teddy has been logged onto *www.mariesgeocachesite.com* since this afternoon. The site is up, but the coordinates were still not posted when we boarded this airplane. The second the coordinates are posted, Teddy will text them to me. The fact that they have not been posted yet means Marie is still alive. When we land, we will be boarding an Army National Guard helicopter for St. John. Teddy has it arranged; there isn't time to take the ferry between St Thomas and St John. It's a forty-minute boat ride"

"You amaze me; I didn't realise Neanderthals were capable of such deep thought," she smiled.

"Hey, you want to hear some dumb blond jokes?" he responded.

"No. Wake me when we land."

CHAPTER THIRTY NINE

CAPTAIN DRAKE'S SEAT

Marie leaned against the teak railing on the fantail of the high speed ferryboat. The island of St. Thomas was receding from view. Both the direct sunlight and the glare from the shimmering turquoise sea, scorched her face. She had to squint, even with sunglasses on and a large brimmed straw hat shielding her eyes, to keep them from watering. The catamaran headed south through the busy harbour of Charlotte Amalie. Three cruise ships were docked in a row at the mouth of the Caribbean's deepest natural harbour. Marie could see passengers and crew members walking briskly on the main decks in preparation for departure. Horn blasts from one of the vessels reminded passengers they should return to the ship or be left behind.

The ferryboat captain throttled up the craft's two Cummins diesel engines as Frenchman's Reef passed by on the left, signalling the exit from the navigable channel. He turned the bow east, keeping the St. Thomas shoreline to the north. Marie was pleased that the trip from the airport to the neighbouring island was going so quickly. She walked to the bow and could see St. John, the smallest of the Virgin Islands looming in the distance. Attached to the bow rail was a large bronze plaque with a line drawing of the elevation of St. John. Below the drawing there was a brief history of the island. In the 17th century the island and its neighbouring islands of St. Thomas and Tortola were divided into the British Virgin Islands and the Danish West Indies. During the 18th and 19th centuries, sugarcane plantations thrived throughout the archipelago, dependent largely on black slaves to perform hard labour.

In November of 1733, the slaves at Coral Bay on the southern shores of St. John rebelled against their owners. The uprising quickly spread across the island, leaving the plantations burning and in ruins. A year later the Danish quelled the rebellion with the help of the French.

In 1917 the United States purchased the island chain from the Danish government and subsequently sold St. John to the Rockefeller family. They eventually donated the subtropical paradise to the territorial government with the requirement that two thirds of the island remain undeveloped.

The catamaran was halfway across Pillsbury Sound, when Marie saw Cruz Bay Harbour come into view. Her pulse quickened as thoughts of finding the treasure-laden cache on the beautiful island flashed in her mind. She was a day early and eager to explore the island. She wanted to gain some sense of familiarity with the landscape. She even thought about possible photographic opportunities St. Johns long abandoned sugarcane plantations might provide. And she wanted to experience the islands palm tree-lined white beaches and crystal clear waters.

The catamaran eased alongside the concrete seawall at the Cruz Bay Wharf. The town's shops and several rental car agencies were just a few yards away. Marie had reserved a four-wheel drive Jeep just to be safe. She had no idea where on the island she would find the cache. She would not know the coordinates until morning, when she expected to find them posted on *www.mariesgeocachesite.com*. She entered the small office of Anegada Passage Car Rental and was greeted by a young man shuffling a half dozen car keys in his hands.

"Hello. Are you Ms. Tereskova?" asked the Caucasian attendant.

"Yes. My boat just docked. Your place is very convenient to the wharf."

"Yeah, this is the best location. All tourists arrive by ferry."

"This is my first visit to St. John. Can you suggest where I should drive to see the sites and take some pictures?"

"Sure, here's a map of the island," offered the attendant. "See, there are two paved roads that run almost the length of the island from the town all the way to East End. The roads are separated by mountain ridges. About ten miles from Cruz Bay you run out of paved road just at the beginning of East End. You can see on the map that East End is almost an island, but it has a land bridge so I guess it's a peninsula. If you drive that far, you may have to use the four-wheel drive in some places. But it's worth it. From there, you can see Captain Drake's Passage and Tortola on the other side of the passage. The North Shore Road is on the north side of the island and Route 10 is on the south side."

"What is out there at East End? The map doesn't show any settlements?" asked Marie"Well, I go out there for the best garlic chicken on the island," he answered.

"There is a restaurant at the end of the island?"

"No. Actually, just a roadside wooden shed with a couple of tables," said the attendant. "There is a black lady who sits by the roadside and serves food to the few tourists who make it that far. If you go there, its great barbecue."

"Okay. I should check in to the hotel first. I'm staying at the Casteel Bay Resort. Which route shall I take?"

"Take the North Shore Road to the hotel. When you leave the hotel, continue east on North Shore until it intersects with Route 10. Go east on ten until the pavement runs out; then follow the dirt road and you will see the little shack on the roadside."

Marie checked in to the hotel, took a bottle of water from the room, and departed for the East End. She turned left out of the hotel parking lot and drove east along the winding coastal road. In some places the road came within yards of the water's edge. She was enchanted by the lush green vegetation, palm trees, bleached white sand, and turquoise waters. This place was everything she had always imagined a deserted Caribbean island would look like, balmy breezes swaying tall palm trees in quiet hammocks.

It would be an easy place to live, she thought.

Marie drove east along the coast until seeing a sign for

Geocache

Cinnamon Bay. She noticed a few cars parked near the entrance to what looked like a swimming area. She pulled to the side to look things over and was surprised to see some old ruins. They were by the beach and partially hidden by a canopy of trees. She left the car and approached the stone foundation. The structure was so close to the ocean, waves were lapping against it. She could hear digging and scraping noises beyond the old stone wall. Looking over the wall and down into the foundation, she saw a man and two women sifting through the dirt. They looked up and smiled; the nearest woman lifted her arm and waved at Marie.

"Hello. Welcome to Cinnamon Bay Plantation or what there is left of it. I'm Toni," said the young woman.

"Oh, this is an archeological dig! Neat. My name is Marie."

"Hi, Marie," answered Toni. "This is Doctor Lance Dixon and Nancy Powers from the University of Tennessee. Nancy is our expert on slavery."

"Slavery expert?"

"Slaves lived here. This building has a special place in Caribbean history. The inhabitants pre-dated the big sugarcane plantations. They were from a time before slaves thought they were slaves. There are real treasures to be found in this dig."

"One more hurricane and the sea will claim this place like it never existed," commented Dr. Dixon. "We're trying to recover what we can while there is still time," Marie aimed her camera at the three historians and their surrounding artefacts.

Seems like this island has treasures of all kinds, she thought.

"Okay. Smile," Marie requested. Click. "So what happened here that was so important?"

"There was a slave rebellion on the island in 1733," Dr. Dixon explained. "Each slave on every plantation on the island joined the revolt — except for the three slaves that lived in this building,"

"Really!" Marie replied.

"The slaves at Cinnamon Bay Plantation defended the owners, Johannes and Lievan Jansen. They fought alongside them. Apparently they viewed themselves more as family than slaves. They and the Jansens were forced to retreat to Cinnamon Cay — that little island over there." He pointed to a small cay a few hundred yards off the beach.

"Together they watched the rebels burn this and the other larger buildings nearby. The oldest of the three Cinnamon Bay slaves was a man called Joshua Gundi. He saved the Jansens' five-year-old daughter from a rebel attack. The Jansen family, Gundi, and one other slave survived on the Cay until the rebellion was put down a year later."

Marie wished them well in their endeavour. She wanted to reach East End and get back to her hotel before dark. She found the intersection of the two routes and drove east until the pavement ended as predicted. After driving two miles over the single-lane dirt road, she came to the wooden shack. There she was, as predicted, an attractive black woman in her early fifties sitting on a folding chair looking out at the sea. She was smiling and holding a paperback novel in her lap. Marie parked the car and walked toward the woman.

"I understand you make the best garlic chicken in the Caribbean," Marie announced.

"If you want the best barbecue in the Caribbean, you've come to the right place. My name is Miriam."

"My name is Marie. What is that you're reading, Miriam?"

Marie took a seat while Miriam pulled some chicken from a cooler and placed it on an open fire pit.

"Exodus, a book by Leon Uris. Where do you live, Marie?" Miriam asked.

"Prague."

"Oh, yes. A beautiful city, from the Hapsburg Dynasty. I have been there."

"Do you travel a lot, Miriam?"

"Yes. There are only a few continents I have yet to visit."

Marie was intrigued by this articulate black woman sitting by the side of a dirt road at the end of a remote island paradise.

Geocache

Miriam was reading about the early struggles of the newly created nation of Israel in 1948. Here was a world traveller serving barbecue to tourists on the side of a dirt road overlooking the sea.

"Have you lived on this island all your life?"

"Yes, all my life. My ancestors can be traced back to the days of slavery on this island."

"Do you live in Cruz Bay and drive out here every day?"

"No, Marie. My house is just over those sand bluffs, on Black Rock Hill. We have a wonderful view of Drake's Passage. In fact, Captain Drake's Seat is on our property."

"Drake's Seat?" Marie asked.

"Legend has it that the old concrete and stone bench which looks out at the passage was built for Sir Francis Drake. He sat there contemplating the passage and Tortola, listening to the sounds of the ocean. The story has been passed down through the generations of my family."

"You own a home here, overlooking the sea?"

"Actually, my family owns the entire East End peninsula. We inherited it. The land has been in our family dating back to when this was the Danish West Indies."

"Miriam, this land must be worth millions of dollars!"

"Oh, I think tens of millions of dollars, Marie."

"Well, I don't want to pry, but ahh, well, ahh . . . ."

"I know. What am I doing sitting by this dirt road cooking for the occasional tourist. That is what you're thinking. Yes. I have visited so many places, but I'm always happiest right here. There is no more beautiful, more peaceful place on earth than this island. This spot. The sound of the surf and the view of the eastern sunrise carry me to places that cannot be visited on this earth. The East End is the most spiritual place I have ever experienced, and I am lucky to live here, thanks to my ancestors. And nice people like you come searching for me. Mostly nice people."

"Mostly nice people, but not always?" Marie asked.

Errol Bader

"Every now and then I am disappointed by some visitors. Just this morning there was a man that drove by me without stopping. He headed for the sand bluffs in such a hurry, he covered me with dust. It takes all kinds to make a world, doesn't it, Marie?"

"Miriam, what is your last name?"

"Gundi. My last name is Gundi."

CHAPTER FORTY

PREDATORS

The wheels had just kissed the runway at St. Thomas when Sean turned his cell phone on. He sat reading and making notes as Victoria was shaking off a deep sleep.

"Morning," Sean said.

"Good morning. What country are we in? What planet is this?"

"You awake enough to understand anything yet?"

"Yeah, okay. What is Teddy telling us?"

"Chandler Benson arrived in Innsbruck a day before Peter Leisel. He arrived on St. Thomas yesterday. We have the coordinates of the geocache but not the exact time. But you can bet it's today. So collect yourself, cause we are about to go down to the wire with this bastard. I'm just glad it's a man." Sean wanted to meet Chandler Benson personally.

"Wow, that Teddy never sleeps, does he?"

"We have a lot of dedicated people in Lyon. They work harder than they are given credit for. I'd be lost without Teddy. By the way, Teddy is a she not a he."

The St. Thomas police chief met them at the gate. He drove them to the waiting National Guard helicopter at the general aviation end of the airfield. Teddy had done her job well.

They boarded the helicopter, put on the headsets that were lying on the seats, and introduced themselves to the aircraft commander. Sean pulled out his hand-held GPS, loaded the coordinates he received from Teddy, and handed the colour moving map unit to the first officer. The pilots had all they needed to find the location. They lifted off from the airport and climbed up and over the mountainous ridges of St. Thomas. As soon as they cleared the highest ridge, they could see St. John in the distance.

The helicopter crossed the thirty miles of Pillsbury Passage in ten minutes. Victoria was looking over the first officer's shoulder and could see the crosshairs of the coordinates on the GPS unit. The site was on the windward coast of the island, at the East End. She looked ahead through the windscreen and could see lush green tropical growth running down to the sandy beach. They headed for the sand bluffs at the end of the East End peninsula.

Sean pointed to a small figure walking among the windswept sand dunes and sea oats near to the ocean. The aircraft commander found a flat place to set the helicopter down a hundred yards short of the tiny figure. He could not get closer without risking hitting the rotor blades on the hilly sand dunes.

Victoria and Sean jumped from the aircraft even before it had settled on its skids and began running toward the small figure. It was Marie. She had a suitcase under her arm, and she was running from them. They knew from having read the killer's instructions that she probably thought they were paparazzi. Marie had found the suitcase but was startled by the helicopter before she could open it. She had not yet been exposed to its lethal contents.

Reaching the edge of the sand bluffs, Marie stopped. She was out of breath and could run no further. She sat down in the sand and began to open the case. From thirty yards away, Victoria pulled her PKK Walther hand gun from her waistband and dropped to the ground supporting her right gun hand with her left hand. She was determined to shoot the case away from Marie's hands. Sean shouted at Marie and sprinted toward her. They were downwind from Marie, and the surf was loud as it came ashore. Marie could not hear what Sean was shouting at her.

Damn you, Sean. You're in the way, Victoria thought to herself.

She took careful aim and sucked in a deep breath. Sean was bobbing in and out of her line of fire. She had to time her shot with the rhythm of his cadence. She was concerned she might hit him, but she had no choice. Victoria slowly squeezed off one round. Sean winced as the bullet grazed his left tricep on the way to its target. Marie's hand reached for the open lid of the case just as the bullet crashed into its hinges, forcing it shut. She fell backwards screaming and crawling away from the case.

"I've got you, Marie. I've got you. Everything's okay." Sean held her as she trembled from the shock of the noise and the impact of the bullet. As Victoria caught up to them, Marie recoiled at seeing the person she thought just tried to shoot her.

"Marie, that suitcase is loaded with poison," Sean explained. "This lady just saved your life."

"Sean," Victoria said grabbing his arm. "You're bleeding."

"Oh, yeah, and Marie, the lady's a lousy shot."

Victoria caught something moving in, her peripheral vision, along the dunes. It was Benson. He was wearing a wet suit and had been watching the scene unfold. He bolted for the beach. Victoria stood up to take chase, but Sean grabbed her arm.

"No. He belongs to me; I've been waiting for this," he said.

They could see an open cockpit skiff anchored just offshore, Benson's escape route. Benson dove into the surf and swam towards the little boat. Sean ran into the surf, shedding his shoes, and following Benson into the turquoise waters of the Caribbean. Benson was ahead by just a few yards, but Sean was a stronger swimmer. They were almost to the boat when Sean grabbed Benson by his ankle. Benson reached out and grasped the boat's boarding ladder. He kicked his foot free from Sean's grasp, climbed on to the stern, and jumped to the deck. The boat had a centre console which permitted easy access to the bow. The killer had left a cocked spear gun leaning against the console's steering wheel. Sean pulled himself on to the stern, saw Benson had grabbed the spear gun and was turning to fire at Sean. Sean launched his body through the air and slammed into Benson's upper body before he had a chance to aim the weapon. The impact stunned Benson and knocked the weapon to the deck. The two fought until they reached the bow pulpit. Benson had Sean bent backward over the stainless steel railing, his hands around Sean's throat. Sean was still losing blood and feeling light headed. A wave rocked the boat and caused both of them to lose their balance. Sean was falling and grasped Benson's arm, causing them both to fall overboard.

They fought in the shallow water just below the surface. Sean took in a deep breath and pulled Benson under. Then he saw it. The blood from his flesh wound had attracted a hungry tiger shark. The shark lunged for Sean's arm. He twisted and pulled Benson in between them. The shark's powerful jaws clamped down on Benson's head. It was Benson's blood that satiated the big shark, as it shook Benson's body apart. Sean swam toward the beach as the shark finished his meal. Victoria and Marie met Sean, exhausted, in the surf and pulled him ashore.

"Hey, how you doin', Scotty?" Victoria asked as she held his head in her lap.

"Okay. Better than the pharmacist. I introduced him to a predator higher up in the food chain."

CHAPTER FORTY ONE

REWARDS

They had rested for three days in Denver. On the third morning Sean, Victoria, and Marie boarded a cab for University Hospital. Marie's donation of bone marrow had saved her previously unknown grandfather. Maxwell had known he had illegitimate children in Europe. He instructed his executive assistant, Marsha Thompson to send plenty of financial support to the children anonymously. That included support for Chandler Benson, the son he and Marsha unintentionally brought into the world. Maxwell never wanted to be a father, but he did have a conscience. All of the children received the best educations and never went wanting.

Marsha had diligently followed Maxwell's directions and kept their secret, even from her own son, but she never told Maxwell about Marie. She did not want him to know he had a granddaughter. She knew the bond between a man and his granddaughter could be even stronger than that of his own children. She was a jealous caretaker. On her death bed, she told Benson who his father was. She told him about his sibling relatives Maxwell had fathered after the war, and where to find their European addresses at her home office. Then she gave him his lethal mission. She wanted her son to be the sole heir to Maxwell's fortune. Marsha had raised him strictly, producing a brilliant but empty shell. Benson was an extension of his mother, under her control even in death. She released a homicidal maniac on Europe.

"Here we are, Marie. Ready to meet your grandfather?" Victoria asked, as they pulled up to University Hospital.

"Yes, I'm so excited."

Nurse Karin stood beside Maxwell when the three entered his

private suite. The old man sat next to the bed in a chair. He smiled broadly when he recognised Victoria. She gave him a hug.

"Mr. Maxwell, this is Sean Mason. He is the Interpol agent who helped me in Europe",

Maxwell winked at Sean.

"And this," Victoria continued, "is your granddaughter, Marie Tereskova."

The two stared at one another, fearful to move. Maxwell managed to find the initiative and gave a slight nod, enough of a signal to have Marie race across the room. He embraced Marie with tears in his eyes.

"My dear Marie, I can't tell you how happy I am to meet you. And thank you for saving my life."

Marie was too choked up to speak, but her tears were of joy.

"There's so much I need to find out about you," Maxwell whispered to her as he gently stroked away some fallen strands of hair from her face.

"We should go," suggested Victoria to Sean. "Oh, before you go, Sean," summoned Maxwell, "I have a favourite sport I would like you and Victoria to experience with me when I'm up and around. Let me tell you about it, it's called geocache. Ever heard of it?"

"Geocache, geocache . . . You know, I think I have," Sean answered.

Both he and Victoria smiled at each other as they left the room. Nurse Karin went to follow.

"Karin, its a bit stuffy in here," Maxwell observed. "Would you mind opening a window?"

Karin smiled and walked over to the window, turned its crank handle and felt fresh cold air flow passed her cheeks. She looked out at the foothills west of Denver.

In the distance, beyond her view, a full grown grey wolf stood on a snow covered ridge above the city. His thick fur rippled in the breeze. He looked eastward toward the city; it was breakfast time in the Rockies.

Geocache

Errol Bader

Another novel from
GULLION MEDIA LIMITED

The Fall (Paperback Book - Horror)

Michael witnesses the brutal killing of his bride, Melissa's, by supernatural forces. Falsely accused of her murder, he spends years in a psychiatric hospital and comes to believe what he saw was all in his mind.

But as he rebuilds his life the nightmare returns when demonic powers target Mara, a young heavymetaller.

Michael races against time to save her before a Nephilim child is conceived, a biblical giant born from the union of a fallen angel and a daughter of Eve. Torn between his own past and a sceptic world will anyone believe him?

About the author of 'The Fall':

George J. Kingsnorth began his career in television. Since 1984 he has worked on over 200 productions. His journey led him through an Open University degree, a Masters Degree in Media Studies and a Postgraduate Diploma in Further & Higher Education. During the mid-1990s, he was the technical editor for Regional Film & Television newspaper and later co-authored four training manuals for Friends of Ed. During 2004 to 2006, he co-wrote, produced and directed the digital feature film, Fiddler's Walk. He has lectured in Media Production. In 2008 he set up Gullion Media Limited.

For more information visit
www.gullionmedia.co.uk